The Airship

by

Cassandra Leuthold

The Airship
Copyright © 2016 Cassandra Leuthold
All rights reserved.

Published by Green Hill Press
South Bend, IN

ISBN-10: 0-9911319-7-5
ISBN-13: 978-0-9911319-7-6

Cover design by Deranged Doctor Design

for my great-grandmother, Ethel Ciani,
who traveled by herself from Budapest, Hungary,
to join her husband in the United States

The Airship

1901

Albany, New York

Chapter One

In the wind's fingers, Amelia's finer hairs tickled her neck beneath her hat and twisted updo. Blooming flowers scented the air like a velvet-soft bouquet as she rubbed her thumb back and forth across the reticule in her hand. Standing in the field's green grass at the back of the crowd, she stepped aside to watch the activity at the front of it. A procession of men in crisp, decorated hats and tailored suits left the station on her right, carrying cases of luggage. They swept across the asphalt walkway to a hair-pin staircase and ascended it to a wooden platform. With quick, steady steps, they disappeared through the open portal in the airship. Its gleaming aluminum side hovered behind the platform's metal supports, extending high above its restraining ropes. Amelia ran her eyes the length of it, the *Duchess*, thirteen stories tall and wider than a major-city block. The bulk of it formed a near-perfect capsule except for an open deck cutting into the top thirty feet of its bow.

Elated sighs and chipper applause rang out from the people waiting nearest the platform. Another crewman squeezed onto the airship burdened by baggage as Captain Silas Barrett emerged from the hull.

The morning sun sparkled in his silver beard, and his smile rivaled it. Deep-set eyes shone under the brim of his jet-black and stark-white captain's cap. He raised his hand to the crowd. Amelia's exhale released some of her jittery apprehension as she stepped closer to hear him better.

"Dear friends." Captain Barrett's baritone resonated through the field. The applause quieted, and he lowered his hand. "Nothing in life has given me more pleasure than to stand here before you today. Except, of course, marrying my sweet Caroline and welcoming our three glorious children into the world."

The women around Amelia relaxed in small movements. A petite, wide-waisted woman pinned adoring light brown eyes on the man beside her. A willowy, statuesque brunette offered a wisp of contentment to her companion.

"You don't know how much work..." Captain Barrett waved a finger at the *Duchess*. "...how much labor, how many *years* my good friend, Samuel Pierpont Langley, poured into this machine."

Captain Barrett extended a flat hand down toward the audience closest to him, barred by a waist-high, black iron fence. An array of flowers lined both sides of it, tall irises intermixed with short geraniums. Butter-colored daffodils created sprays between beds of golden, dark-topped black-eyed Susans. A white-haired man with a trimmed beard waved from just behind the iron partition. The people applauded him, shrill whistles piercing the warm spring air.

The captain pursed his lips, rocking his fist as he raised it. "Did the newspapers capture the failure and frustration crushing him when he traveled all the way to Indianapolis to see the celebrated Steampunk Carnival?" The captain scrunched his face up, swatting his hand through the air. "Of course not!" He pointed to the crowds. "If we could go back in time, I'd show you a man I hardly recognized. Disheartened. Overworked. Depressed. About to give up when he took a train to see how Mr. Brady Kelly was running those rides and contraptions. But you know something?"

Captain Barrett leaned over the rail of the platform and motioned the crowd closer. The people swayed toward him, and he sprang up, shouting to the clouds. "Samuel came back with the brightest ideas this world has ever seen! Gone were the days of worrying and researching only how birds flew through the air. Samuel learned to question everything, examine every detail. He obsessed over the way boats cut through water. He spent many a sleepless night reading about wind turbines, steam engines, and submarines. Ladies and gentlemen." Captain Barrett chuckled. "I'd like to tell you the entire story start to finish. I really would, but we're on a schedule, and I'm guessing you've seen where the story ends. Right here with this beauty, the *Duchess*, bigger than anything man has ever put in the sky. More luxurious than the first-class section of any ocean liner, and faster, too. Here she floats on her maiden voyage to France!"

The crowd burst into passionate applause. Amelia joined them with a little more restraint.

Captain Barrett turned to the packed section of the crowd accompanying Samuel Langley on the other side of the fence. Cameras and pencils set to paper rose out of the sea of bowlers, fedoras, and trilbies.

The captain rested his forearms on the railing. "I won't tell you how to do your job if you won't advise me on mine," he joked with a wink. "I've been a captain of boats at sea for nineteen and three-quarter years. But there are two men on the cusp of flight who haven't succeeded yet and aren't here today. Everyone else is here, all the principal players. Myself. My crew. My esteemed friend and colleague, Samuel Langley, among others. But just in case you've forgotten their names, I brought along a little reminder."

Captain Barrett straightened up, pulling a rolled newspaper out of his suit jacket. He unfurled it and swept the front page high above his head. "You probably can't read this, whether you're waiting to board or just bidding us farewell."

Amelia took in the thousands of onlookers beyond the fence. Their clothes ranged from shredded rags to fine bowlers. Some devoured every detail of the scene with interest, and others licked their lips in fear.

Captain Barrett pointed to the headline, underlining it with his finger. "It's an interview with Orville and Wilbur Wright, those two brothers from Ohio experimenting with gliders in the North Carolinian winds. Orville's quoted right here as saying..." Captain Barrett sank the newspaper where he could read it. "No flying machine will ever fly from New York to Paris because no known motor can run at the requisite speed for four days without stopping."

The intended passengers snickered with triumph, and the spectators whooped with sarcasm. Amelia allowed herself a grin of smug amusement, her anticipation still wavering between the rising heat of impatience and the cold sweat of dread.

"Well, thank God he was wrong!" Captain Barrett threw his hands in the air, the newspaper doubling over in his grasp. "He was wrong, and the *Duchess* has made numerous successful, sustained flights since its completion. But let's not be sore winners." The captain lowered the paper and poked his finger against it. "It was Samuel Langley's explorations in the field of flight that first encouraged the brothers to write to him at the Smithsonian requesting further information. Samuel obliged. Perhaps if the brothers had waited, Samuel would've had something much more fascinating to write to them about besides birds and winged flying machines. Perhaps if the *Duchess* had taken an extra year or two to construct, the Wrights would've succeeded in beating her to the clouds. But that's not the way we know the world today."

Photographers snapped their cameras, and Captain Barrett posed for them with one hand hooked on the front of his uniform jacket.

He cleared his throat, adopting a more solemn tone. "Today, we leave New York on a journey across the Atlantic to arrive in Bordeaux, France, on the twenty-seventh of May six days from now. It's the first time she'll ever hold both passengers and crew. Seventy-three passengers and forty crew, including myself."

A man in the pool of reporters cupped his hand around his mouth, magnifying his call. "Is there anything you don't know, Captain Barrett?"

The crowd laughed, and Amelia joined them in subtle enjoyment.

"I know..." The captain adjusted his white-and-black hat on his head. "...that's one hundred and thirteen lives counting on me, plus all our families, employers, and employees. That's thousands of people trusting in me to keep the *Duchess* steady when we try to fly under the westerlies sweeping over the coast of Spain. That's a lot of people hoping and praying I'll ferry their loved ones overseas to Europe and back without loss of the engines or running into a storm. I know the eyes of the nation are fixed on me and her–" Captain Barrett tossed his head sideways at the *Duchess*. "–wondering if we're really going to pull off what we set out to. If it ends in disaster, do the Wright boys ever try to get a glider off the ground again at Kitty Hawk? I don't want to think about that."

Captain Barrett observed the rapt passengers. All of their luggage waited on board, leaving them with the appearance they were not traveling at all. Amelia, like the other women, had retained her reticule, which she held against the thick wool of her brown tweed skirt.

The captain's eyes seemed to find hers, and he grounded his intensity as if he were speaking to her directly. "I promise you, all of you, I will do my best as your trained captain and fellow passenger on the airship *Duchess*. There will be no vodka or gin for me. No shirking my sleep or my duties. I'll remain alert, eat only the most healthful meals, and pay only the highest awareness to all mechanisms and maps before me. But you–"

Captain Barrett wagged his outstretched finger at the travelers. "For you, I prescribe only the richest foods, the loudest music, the fastest waltzes, and the finest experience any of God's people ever had on his green earth. Pardon me," he corrected himself, pointing upward. "In the clouded blue sky."

The passengers and onlookers roared with applause. Amelia raised her head higher, waiting for more.

Captain Barrett inspected his gold pocket watch. "Only a few minutes late, despite my elaborations. Now, if you're ready to board, please approach the stairs and ascend to the platform. It's only fifteen feet high, and I assure you, ladies, quite sturdy." Captain Barrett pulled and pushed on the rail, which remained solid and secure. "I must see to the final preparations in the control room. The stewards will help you if you have need."

Captain Barrett faced the opening in the hull as photographers flashed more pictures. He swung back around, his wooly eyebrows hunched low. "I have every intent, as does Samuel, of making this not just the first voyage of the *Duchess*, but the first flight of all the airships we might build in this country. Never again might the homelands of our fathers or ourselves loom at the end of a long, treacherous journey across the waters. We're making history, ladies and gentlemen, for good or ill. You pray for good, and I'll do the rest."

With a nod, Captain Barrett strode away through the airship's entrance. The passengers rustled to life, adjusting hats, tightening jackets, and stepping forward.

Amelia slipped a small white paper out of her reticule. The clerk in the station had noted down every case the stewards carried away along with her room number. Amelia secured it in her pocket, listening in on the others around her.

A stocky man in a steel-grey herringbone suit spoke with a thick, condensed Polish accent. "I suppose it's time." His dark hair curled beneath the brim of his bowler. The short woman's hand rested in the crook of his arm, her emerald-green jacket the same bold shade as her dress. He patted her fingers as he guided her toward the platform.

A tall gentleman in a dark coat and striped pants regarded the fine-boned woman beside him. His nose extended in a long, tapering tip above his thin lips. *"T'es prête?"* The woman murmured a reply, swathed in a lavender dress hemmed in loose ruffles. They drifted forward with slow, even steps.

Amelia trailed behind them at a snail's pace. Some of the passengers hurried over to the iron fence separating them from the fascinated crowd. The travelers stretched over the strip of garden and its fence to embrace their friends and families.

Three children capped in varying shades of blond crowded up against the partition.

"Are you scared, Mama?" the tallest boy chirruped, a Boston accent pinching his words.

A woman with rich dark hair wrapped her gloved hands around the iron spikes decorating the top of the fence. "Not really." But her crystal-blue eyes reflected like glass as her focus loosened on their faces.

"Can I go with you next time?" the shortest boy piped up.

"Maybe. This trip is for adults. The tickets were quite expensive. It'd be a shame if you didn't like it."

"I would!" The boy pouted and stomped his foot. "I would like it."

The woman stroked his golden-strawberry hair. "We'll be home before you know it."

The others moseyed toward the platform. A brimmed hat topped every head, women carrying their reticules and the occasional parasol. Most people huddled in pairs or small groups. Very few of them moved alone as Amelia did. Huge gasps and short shrieks split the air at the front of the crowd.

Amelia's arms tensed, clutching her reticule closer. Her eyes jerked to the apex of the zigzagging line. Two figures cut off the rest, darting up the stairs to the platform.

"There's Elizabeth Cole, the murderess!" A man speared his finger up at them.

Women screamed, some gawking while others scuttled away. The photographers clicked picture after picture.

Amelia relaxed her muscles and squinted at the racing couple. Their details eluded her, a blur in a green silk dress pulling a brown-suited young man behind her.

"Mrs. Cole!" A reporter pushed closer, shouldering the suited men around him. "May we have a word with you, please?" He lifted his foot to the highest horizontal bar in the iron fence. A security guard on the other side marched up to him, shaking his head until the reporter backed away. The journalist followed the pair with his eyes. "Mrs. Cole!"

The couple whisked across the platform. The woman shielded her profile with her hand, yielding nothing as she led her companion onto the ship.

"Did you see her?" a woman cried from the crowd. "Did you see?"

"Good riddance," a man spat. "France can have her."

Another man bucked his head up, standing on the other side of the fence. "Seven years in prison wasn't long enough for that selfish bitch. They should've let her rot."

Amelia sank back on her heels. She let the rest of the passengers collect themselves and resume their walk in front of her before she joined them in wandering toward the platform.

She returned her eyes to the broad, starboard side of the *Duchess*. The late-morning sun blasted the full height of its arcing metal, illuminating three low rows of windows. The crowd's reactions jockeyed between cowering, shrugging, and seething as they scrambled in place, held together by the fence and each other. Soon, their animosity and dogged curiosity would remain on the ground. Elizabeth Cole would leave them behind, caged in with Amelia and over one hundred others. Amelia sized up the buzz and jostling, physical metaphors for her thoughts and concerns. She resigned herself to the obvious truth. *It's not going to be a quiet, uneventful journey overseas.*

Chapter Two

Amelia followed a fair-haired steward into the ship, a teenaged boy with a mature and serious air. A wallpapered entry hall welcomed her, more like a mansion than a traveling craft. Glass panels in the French doors on her right framed cloth-covered tables and mahogany chairs filling a long room. Centered against the wall behind them, a map stretched from floor to ceiling, rotating in slow increments inside a glass case. She glanced left in time to catch a small office marked *purser* on the overhead door frame. Just past it, two plush sofas and an oval coffee table provided an open parlor.

"This way, miss," the steward instructed, his voice fluid with youth but confident in purpose.

Amelia peeked down a hallway of doors on her right where passengers mingled and entered their rooms. A square wooden stairwell with carved railings stood on her left, one side ascending to the upper decks and the other dropping down to a lower floor.

A woman's mature soprano piped up, muffled by the space between them. "Would you mind moving my trunks for me?"

Men's deeper registers rumbled through the common area as well. "I guess this is our room."

The steward veered right, leading Amelia down a second hallway of doors. Two of them offered signs marking the men's and women's lavatories. Amelia noted their location in her mind, but the steward stopped two rooms away at the end of the hall. He swung open the door marked with a golden 20 embossed on a square brass plaque.

"Your room, miss." The steward reached for something on the wall, and with a quiet click, the gas chandelier flicked to life, revealing a double bed beneath it. "Are you familiar with Mr. Tesla's lighting system?"

Amelia nodded. She had seen it more and more since her return to the States. She had read about Nikola Tesla's rocketing to popularity while she was still abroad.

Thomas Edison's failed electrical experiments might have plunged Mr. Tesla into complete ruin with him if Mr. Tesla had not already broken ties between them. George Westinghouse's brilliant mind rose up to rival his by the next World's Fair, and its committee accepted his exploratory exhibit over Mr. Tesla's, jilting him at a crucial point in his career. Instead of straining for precarious and unbelievable heights, Mr. Tesla changed his approach. He set the American people as his audience and reimagined the gas lamps already in use. In the cramped space granted to Mr. Tesla at the Chicago Fair, he demonstrated his clever additions. Rotating a small, cylindrical switch triggered a sparking mechanism to strike at the head of the attached lamp's gas piping. As he twisted the switch farther, the flames fanned higher, and by spinning it counterclockwise, he doused the flames until the apertures closed, shutting the room in darkness.

At the end of the fair's seven-month season, Mr. Tesla's exhibit attracted far more visitors and press than Mr. Westinghouse's flashy dabbles in electric currents. Everyone who witnessed Mr. Tesla's improvement wanted it, and he spent the next few years setting up the company needed to distribute it. He fielded all interview questions with deprecating wit and the insistence he had used minimal brain power to invent it. His offbeat charm did little to detract from his fame or that of his new, efficient contraption.

Some labeled him proud or eccentric, but Amelia saw no shortcomings in knowing one's full capabilities. She embraced Mr. Tesla's dimmer switches with complete faith. Whichever facilities installed them meant no more fumbling in the dark for matches or guessing at the placement of a candelabra. The *Duchess* had been fully planned and assembled indeed.

Past the right-hand corner of the bed, Amelia's luggage sat against the wall. A forty-inch steamer trunk, cobalt blue with brown leather reinforcements, dwarfed the other pieces. A smaller flat-top trunk echoed its rectangular shape, and a brown leather bag hunched beside them, its handle resting on top of its dome.

The steward adjusted his copper-colored spectacles over his thin nose. "Is this everything? Do you have your receipt from when you signed in?"

Amelia fished the paper out of her pocket and handed it over.

The steward scanned it and checked the paper tag strung around each luggage piece's handle. "Will there be anything else?"

She shook her head.

"We'll be taking off soon from the landing. Here's a pamphlet of everything available to you on board." The steward plucked it from a dark wooden dresser beside the door. "If there's anything else you need, staff will be around the ship to assist you, or you may inquire with the purser by the door we came in."

Amelia perused the brochure in her gloved hands. *Welcome aboard the airship* Duchess, *completely furnished to delight and pamper, fulfill and accommodate! Our highly trained staff stands at the ready, night and day, to answer your beck and call.* Amelia trailed her fingertip past sections detailing the dining room, lounges, ballroom, and open deck atop the vessel. She barely heard the steward's retreating footsteps.

His inquiry interrupted her reading. "Miss?"

Amelia found the steward inclining through the doorway from the hall.

His mouth bent in a sheepish curve. "I forgot to mention lunch will be served at one in the dining hall. We passed it just now on the way in."

Amelia bobbed her head in remembrance.

"Enjoy your trip."

The steward strode away, and Amelia closed the door. She stood alone, soaking in every part of her surroundings. Although the walls of her room buffered the conversations from the hall, she could hear their hums and undertones. The fresh, clean carpet cushioned her feet, and the wallpaper repeated around her in a lovely pattern of royal-indigo irises on soothing sage green. Amelia laid the pamphlet on the dresser. She stepped over to a matching stand offering a topaz-blue wash bowl with a gilt rim. In place of a pitcher, a curved faucet emerged from the wall above it. Amelia tested one of its knobs, crystalline water flowing into the bowl and out through a small metal drain. The only other pieces of furniture were two small bedside tables and two chairs flanking the whole ensemble.

The padded arms, backs, and seats called to Amelia from a pattern of cream-on-purple scallops. Although she wanted little more than to drop into a chair and rest her feet, the excited chatter in the hallway reeled her toward it. She left her reticule in a dresser drawer and slipped her room key out of her pocket. She ambled into the hallway, locking the door behind her.

Several people lingered in the corridor.

A man pointed to the papered wall. "Sturdiest construction ever designed. I read every newspaper article they printed before I bought tickets."

A woman's nasal enthusiasm broke through the conversations further down the hall. "Where should we go first?"

Eager to learn more about the ship's layout, Amelia peeked around the corner from her room. A slightly narrower corridor ran across the front of the ship, offering an alternative route to the main open space she had already traversed. On the other side of French doors, several armchairs sat in small groups accented by tables with silver lamps. *One of the lounges*, Amelia assumed. She started back the way the steward had guided her and paused by the staircase. Several couples ascended it, chattering.

"Do you think the top deck's really that high up?"

"Why wouldn't it be?"

"They could've exaggerated it. None of us would know."

Hands clapped together behind Amelia. "Well," a woman sighed, partly exasperated and partly self-congratulating. "It's exactly as I thought."

Amelia softened her investigative demeanor. Behind her, she discovered a short woman outfitted in a spring-green dress and jacket. Her white gloves stood out as she raised them to adjust the lie of her hat atop her slate-and-charcoal hair.

Amelia cocked her head in response and gestured to the interior of the ship around them.

"No, Elwood." The woman flicked her grey eyes up the stairs, down the hallway behind her, and past Amelia's shoulder to the parlor. She threw her hands up. "My son. We've been on board less than fifteen minutes, and he's already run off with his wife without me. I told him I'd only be a minute."

Heeled shoes tapped on the staircase, and the woman raised her hopeful expression to the couple descending. The Frenchman and his wife stepped down onto the patterned, crimson carpet. The woman's face fell. They moved away to the nearest doors and passed into the lounge.

"I told him it would be like this." The woman poked her fingertip into her opposite palm. "I said, 'Elwood, remember the day we took the paddleboat up the North River and you promised you'd stay right next to me? You sat there for five minutes and spent the rest of the ride at the back of the boat with Dorothy, prattling about the big wheel's wake.'"

The woman held her arms out from her sides. "He told me he wouldn't leave me for a second, and here I am, alone on another voyage between land and land. At least there's a bar upstairs to take the edge off." She flicked her frown into the slightest upturn of pleasantness. "Are you traveling with someone, or are you alone, dear?"

For the first time since entrusting her luggage to the clerk at the station, a question forced Amelia to answer with words. "I'm alone."

Her deep, rough timbre widened the woman's eyes. She rested her hand on her chest, swallowing with a gulp. She blinked in a flutter. "I beg your pardon. How dreadful of me to act this way. You just seemed like such a young thing. I wasn't expecting any gruffness from you. Forgive me for saying so."

Amelia's spine stiffened. "It's all right."

The woman closed her eyes for a moment. "Good for you, booking this flight by yourself. " Her sincerity betrayed a hint of resentment. "You might as well come alone if that's how you'll spend all your time."

"You mentioned a Dorothy?"

"My daughter-in-law." She lifted her chest, adorned with a heart-shaped locket. "I'm not like a lot of mothers, going around complaining she stole my precious little boy away from me. He was bound to grow up and get married sometime. I'm happy for him. But they do like to run off together, seeing the sights, jabbering on about this and that. Inventors and parties and the Eiffel Tower. Are you married, dear?"

"No. Amelia Harlow. How do you do?"

Sarcasm ridged her words. "Claudia Molt. Fine, thank you. I only have six days to fill on my own, hundreds of feet above the ground. Knowing nobody with nothing to occupy my lonely hours."

Amelia mellowed into warm hospitality. "You won't be alone. I'll be around if you want to talk to me. And there are dozens of other passengers."

Claudia's mouth drew in, deepening the fine lines along the top of it into grooves. "I know." She surveyed the open area around them and stepped closer to Amelia. The color drained from her face, and she quieted in confidence. "Are you nervous about Elizabeth Cole flying with us?"

Amelia gestured past the open parlor toward the airship's entrance in a display of ignorance. "The woman the reporters hounded? I saw her come in, but I don't know her beyond the name."

Claudia raised her dark eyebrows. "Don't you read the papers?"

"I've been traveling. Perhaps I've gotten behind with current events."

Claudia's eyes shimmered, and she tapped her index finger in Amelia's direction. "You were young when she did what she did and hit the papers. Off courting or learning the piano, were you?"

"Possibly."

Claudia brightened, humming with dreamy nostalgia. Her eyes darkened. "Elizabeth Cole murdered her husband eight years ago. Sensational trial. It dragged on for months before the jury sent her away. She served time for it until she was paroled some weeks ago. I saw she'd bought a ticket – the newspapers report every step she takes."

"But you came on board anyway?"

Claudia squared her shoulders. "It's my best chance to see France before I get too old for adventures like this. It beats the steamer ships any day. Who am I to judge whether Mrs. Cole should be released back into society? The board declared her fit, so maybe she is. She only killed one man, so I'm sure I'm not in any danger. But my Elwood..." Claudia spied at the surrounding rooms and passages. Her fingers fumbled with a gold-and-pearl flower brooch pinned to her lapel. "I didn't anticipate Mrs. Cole staying in the room right next to his."

Amelia wrapped a languid hand around her opposite wrist. "I'm sure he's fine. The airship office wouldn't have sold her a ticket if they thought she'd pose a threat to our safety."

Claudia pulled back. "I don't know about that. My late husband would've accused them of selling tickets to anybody to fill these cabins and make their money. God rest his soul. A lot of the passengers are uneasy being in the air with Mrs. Cole."

"How do you know? We've only been on the grounds for an hour or two. The ship hasn't even taken off yet."

Claudia stroked her hair where it flowed in smooth contours to the back of her head. "I know everyone and everything, given the time to talk to people. I've spent the last ten minutes roaming the ship searching for Elwood and Dorothy. They're probably on the top deck already, trying out their new spyglass. Most of the passengers are gossiping about Elizabeth Cole. Only a few of them are distracted by what might be on the menu for lunch."

Claudia's fingers fidgeted together. "That's why I'm alone now, I suppose. Elwood's embarrassed of me. Probably thinks I'm a nosy busybody running around collecting everybody's private business. I'm talking. That's all. Just being friendly. My husband died and left me alone. Am I doing something so terrible?"

Amelia laid her hand on Claudia's arm. "I don't find you nosy at all. It's been a pleasure to meet you, Mrs. Molt, and I hope to chat with you again."

"Please." Claudia winced. She took Amelia's hand and held it between hers. "It's a name I've shared with my mother-in-law for fifty years. A stern woman. Never did learn to take a joke. Bless her soul. Dorothy's much the same way. There's no resemblance between us, so I always ask my friends to leave the title to them. Call me Claudia. Will you be in the dining room at lunch time?"

"Yes."

"I might have something for you. A little treasure to fill in your memory about Mrs. Cole."

Amelia was about to thank her when a metallic clang sounded from the ship's entryway. Claudia jumped and spun toward it. A uniformed man approached the women, tipping his hat before disappearing down the stairs.

Claudia's breath eluded her. "Did they close the door?"

Amelia sidestepped so she could see down the short hall to the entrance. Instead of the rectangular portal open and streaming daylight, it rested shut. "We'll be taking off soon."

"Mercy me. Back in my day, we didn't have contraptions like this, Amelia. I'm much more comfortable with boats, trains, and bicycles."

"It's just an air submarine," Amelia explained to soothe her. "Like they use for pearl diving and explorations."

"I don't trust those, either."

"They're simply underwater boats."

A rustling hum rose from the floor, and subtle vibrations trembled through Amelia's feet.

Claudia clutched Amelia's hand. "Have you been in a submarine?"

"No, only a lot of boats and trains."

"You're not scared?"

Amelia tilted her head to one side. "Of what?"

Claudia's face flushed around her bulging eyes. "Of what?"

Amelia's stomach lifted like it never had before, accompanied by a pressure in her ears. Claudia's fingers tightened their grasp around Amelia's. Several passengers scurried from their cabins into the lounge beyond the stairs and the dining room by the entrance, where they peered through the windows slanted toward the ground.

Amelia stayed where she stood, averse to witnessing any remaining onlookers in the field shrink to the size of ants on a celery stick.

A woman cried out in astonishment from the dining room. "I can see them waving!"

An older woman's grump cut through the excitement. "I wish I'd remembered my glasses. Of all the things to leave behind. I can barely see anything down there."

A man announced with smug certainty. "We've cleared the platform, and we're still aloft. We'll be headed east between Boston and Portland, if my calculations are correct."

Several passengers cheered, and applause erupted from various places on the ship. Amelia hoped the new sensations would fade as quickly as they arose.

A proclamation thrummed, reverberating against metal. "This is your captain, Silas J. Barrett, speaking to you from our extensive, modern address system. We're in the air, and I invite you to relax as I steer us toward France. *Bon voyage* to us all!"

Amelia traced his speech to a round metal grate about six inches wide in the parlor wall across from her.

Claudia bounced Amelia's hand up and down. "Scared of what, indeed? It's only death. Is that your rule for living? It's quite different than mine, which is to stay alive as long as possible and experience as much as I can." Claudia patted Amelia's arm. "Never mind that. It's no great difference to me. I've lived a full life already. I think we're going to share many wonderful experiences and conversations on board the *Duchess*, Amelia."

Amelia squeezed Claudia's hand, counting on bringing that plan to fruition. "I think so, too."

Chapter Three

The *Duchess'* dining room hummed with motion and overlapping conversations. Several servers attended the buffet just inside the doors and to the right, helping passengers choose their lunches and fill their plates. Chandeliers dangled numerous tear-shaped crystals, reflecting the ample flame light in all directions. A clean, white cloth draped over every round table. Six chairs, their backs carved into elegant shields, sat at each one, mauve and gold swirling across the upholstered cushions. Cranberry carpeting stretched the full size of the room.

A tanned woman, her wheat-blonde hair twisted high on the back of her head, settled in at a table catty-corner to Amelia's. "A buffet. How chic!"

Her sterling-haired friend jerked her nose up even as she raised a piece of caviar on toast to her mouth. "I've seen better."

Seated alone, Amelia's own plate awed her. Oysters slathered in red cocktail sauce and topped with rectangles of crispy bacon. Sautéed crabmeat with sliced mushrooms. Steamed carrots oozing golden butter. A bowl of onion soup topped with browned cheese, and a piece of chocolate cake filling a tiny dessert plate. Unlike the line to board the airship, Amelia had not waited to be the last person to arrive in the dining room. More passengers wandered in, murmuring in wonder and approval at the food spread out before them.

Elizabeth walked in, surprising Amelia to see her, clutching the arm of the young man beside her as if she depended on him for support. She could not have aged past forty-five, but silver hairs glinted among the raven locks braided about her head. Although she held herself stiffly, almost regally upright, the contours of her cheeks and the sallow hue of her skin proved Claudia right. Elizabeth had suffered terrible things beyond the imagination, let alone the experience, of the others on board the ship. They hampered her and fatigued her even now that prison had released her and she was leaving the country.

Discomfort needled Amelia's stomach. She continued eating her sweet-and-savory soup to avoid scrutinizing Elizabeth for too long. The next time Amelia raised her eyes, Elizabeth strode toward her, headed for the far end of the room. Beneath a pale-blue jacket, Elizabeth's white dress featured extraordinary crisscrosses of cream-colored lace. Black piping trimmed every hem of her jacket and dress. Impressive sapphires rounded in diamonds hung from her earlobes. Whatever Elizabeth had been forced or allowed to wear in prison, Amelia could not picture her wearing this finery during that time. Elizabeth ignored Amelia as she passed her, fixated only on the deepest wall in the room. Amelia cast a glimpse at the back tables near the continuous, revolving map and found them all empty. At the front of the room, Elizabeth's companion stood at the buffet, holding two plates while the servers topped them for him.

Claudia emerged into Amelia's view, prompting an easy smile. Claudia held up a newspaper in front of her. *Murderess Flees Prison, Then Country!* shouted the headline. Claudia rested the paper on the table. "Here's that little gem I promised you. I didn't get to finish reading all the newspapers I bought in the last week or so. I was too busy packing and writing letters to my family about the flight. I brought the papers with me to finish up with them, but you can have this one. It's only the jokes left, and I seldom care for them. What good are the ads now, either? I can't patronize a store from here."

Amelia traced a fingertip across the sleek front page, delighted with Claudia's offering. "You're very kind. Did you find Elwood and Dorothy?"

"Oh, yes. I was right. They took their spyglass up to the top deck to watch the State Capital Building disappear below us. Typical." Claudia clucked her tongue but fortified her stance. "That's behind us, I suppose. They've agreed to eat lunch with me, and they've actually showed up to the dining room."

"I'm glad to hear it."

Claudia considered the five empty chairs encircling Amelia's table. "Would you join us? You don't need to sit over here all alone. I could introduce you, then you'd know two additional people on the ship."

Most of the tables around Amelia had full seats. The close proximity and constant conversation made Amelia grateful no one else had joined her table. "It's a lovely offer, but I'm all right. The excitement of the day has left me quite unfit to hold any valuable conversation."

"Perhaps another time."

Amelia dipped her head.

"You have your soup and your cake and your paper." Claudia licked her lips at Amelia's plate. "I better join the line before they run out of oyster thermidor. Not every lunch item has white wine cooked into it. I'll see you later, Amelia."

Claudia set off toward the buffet.

Amelia sobered as she pulled the paper into her lap, angling it against the table's lip. A photograph captured Elizabeth and the young man midstep. They blurred as they raced for the arched entrance of a house, flanked by the up-close bars of the tall, iron fence surrounding it. Amelia speared a bite of crab and mushroom onto her fork. She enjoyed its salt and butter as she delved into the article elongated beneath the image.

Three weeks ago, the parole board of the State Prison for Women at Auburn agreed to release convicted murderess Elizabeth Hunting Cole. One could scarcely walk out one's front door without hearing some shred of public outcry. "How could a murderer be hailed as a model prisoner?" some bellowed. "I don't want her within miles of my children!" mothers decreed.

Even so, word has tipped off the press that Mrs. Cole plans to run much further from Auburn than her mansion-like home in Ithaca. Does Mrs. Cole intend to return to the boroughs of New York City to attempt anonymity amongst the crowds who once invested in her late husband's banks? Is another state, California, perhaps, her latest destination?

No, esteemed readers! Think farther out. For Mrs. Cole intends to do her country a great service and catch the upcoming maiden airship flight all the way to France. Whether she balks at the conditions of her parole to remain under New York's supervision or does us a favor by dismissing herself from our fair state's vigilance may become a new topic for debate.

For those of you who've forgotten what sent Mrs. Cole to the Prison for Women, I'll gladly refresh your cobwebbed memories. Eight years past, Arthur Cole lived as a happy and successful man. Until, that is, the night his servants found him murdered in the doorway of his study. He lay bloodied from the butt of a flintlock rifle, one of his collection of artifacts given to him by a team of African explorers. The killing force was not blunt, however, but sustained by the rope found around his neck.

And where was Mrs. Cole at the time of the murder? "Out," she claims. Out where, she could hardly say, but I'd be shocked if anyone forgets exactly when she was out. She left her lover's illicit embrace at eight thirty, arriving conveniently at home after her husband's death. Several witnesses testified to the whereabouts of said lover, Lewis Blakely, at the time of the murder, but no such witnesses came forward to save Mrs. Cole from her dark fate. She herself offered little aid to her cause, choosing silence and compliance when her flimsy alibi failed to fool us. The jury wisely found her guilty of the heinous crime, and she languished in prison until the committee agreed to repay her repentant attitude with relative freedom.

What of her young lover, Mr. Blakely? He's traveling with her, of course, as loyal today as he was all those years ago. The lad who once acted as her proxy in selling Mr. Cole's establishments and artifacts is the one and same reported to have bought them both a one-way ticket overseas.

I think we can all agree no matter what Mrs. Cole chooses to do with her life abroad, we can say "Bon voyage!" *to the complex chapter she wrote while living here in the United States. I'll raise a glass of Champagne in a generous hope Mrs. Cole decides to stay out of those harsh, inescapable, rat-infested French prisons.*

Amelia hit the end of the article and tossed the paper on the table. She helped herself to another spoonful of onion soup, deciding lukewarm was better than cold.

The Polish couple drifted past her seat. "Should we eat back here by the windows, Yetta?" Without his hat, the husband's spirals of hair exposed a bald patch of pale scalp.

"Yes. The sun is beautiful today." Yetta's expressive enthusiasm changed, and she bristled. "No. Let's go back to the other half of the room."

Rudolf canvassed the tables from beneath his bushy eyebrows. "There's not many chairs left."

Yetta spied Amelia's table with popping eyes and dove toward it.

Amelia forced a few coughs into the crook of her elbow. She repeated the same lie that had kept everyone else who tried from sitting with her. "I'm sorry. I'm just getting over something contagious. You probably want to sit somewhere else." Her gruff timbre gave her the added impression of truth, and for once, she heard it with gratitude.

Yetta gave a startled exhale. Rudolf led her two tables behind Amelia, where they sat down one party over from Elizabeth.

A woman's easy, Southern accent slipped out. "You're welcome to sit with us. Don't be shy."

Yetta spoke up. "Will the sun come in like this every day?"

The man who had broadcasted the ship's takeoff an hour before answered her. "It should. It's the south-facing wall of the ship if we maintain our course."

Amelia peeked over her shoulder. Elizabeth's table, centered near the back wall, sat empty except for her and Lewis. The map shifted in its infinite loop behind them, and the tables around them had only filled halfway.

"I brought you lemon meringue." Lewis arranged the plates in front of them on the table. "They have chocolate cake and lady fingers, too."

Elizabeth's olivine eyes glimmered in a strange mix of pride and fear as she pulled a plate toward her. "I'd prefer lady fingers if they still have any."

"Of course." Lewis sprang out of his chair. Elizabeth snatched his arm, her eyes boring into him as her knuckles blanched. Lewis rubbed her anchoring hand with patience. "I'll only be a second."

Amelia faced her plate by the time Lewis swept past her table. He positioned himself near the people waiting in line at the buffet. A steward on the other side of the courses noticed him, and Lewis pointed to what he wanted. Amelia could not hear what he said to the server, but the uniformed man promptly picked up a set of shiny silver tongs. He arranged four lady fingers on a small plate and handed it to Lewis.

Amelia delved back into her lunch so Lewis would not catch her careful observances. But an upward glance seemed only natural, and Amelia learned what she could in the few moments her eyes pinpointed Lewis. As the newspaper called him, he might have been a lad when he first met Elizabeth. His pale features still marked him as young but certainly a boy no longer. Subtle lines creased his forehead beneath short, straight brown hair. He moved with a sense of purpose even more authentic than the professionalism shown by the teenaged stewards. Like Elizabeth before him, Lewis hurried past Amelia, concerned only with slicing across the room in record time.

Amelia scooped the oysters from their half shells but kept her ears perked up for the couple behind her.

"Here you go," Lewis said with encouragement.

"Thank you." Elizabeth's reply was mostly constructed of trembling breath, fortressed by dogged strength and the grace of her station.

"Let me know if you need anything else."

Bitterness added traction to Elizabeth's speech. "No one will even look at me. Seven years I spent in there, and they're all imagining I'm not here."

"Don't worry about them." Enthusiasm gave Lewis' advice uplift instead of growl. "You'll have only the finest for the next few days. Then we'll land in France, and we can live wherever you want."

"I'm not a ghost, Lewis," Elizabeth insisted, almost seething. "I served my time. I lived, and I'm out. And now–"

Elizabeth cut off without warning.

The French couple wafted past Amelia.

The husband tilted his head forward in a tranquil gesture. *"Asseyons-nous ici."*

His wife addressed the room with cheeriness. *"Bonjour."*

After a long pause, Elizabeth eked out a rigid response. "Hello."

Lewis joined in with casual formality. "How do you do?"

The Southern woman piped up. "You can join us."

Amelia peeked over her shoulder. The gilded blonde waved the French couple toward her. They settled in next to Rudolf, Yetta, and the other couple. Amelia carved away her first forkful of chocolate cake, listening to the buzz of other tables' conversations.

Confusion warped a young man's Scottish brogue at the table beside her, missing some letters and roughly pronouncing others. "I don't understand why you'd spend so much on a pendulum. Especially if you can't use it for anything else."

A woman's clear, mature diction fielded his remarks. "Everything has its purpose. It doesn't need to accomplish anything else."

"How much did you spend on yours?"

"Nothing–"

"Ha!" He pointed at her. "So you're on my side."

The woman stiffened. "I'm not. What I use is personal to me. It's my mother's wedding band strung on my grandmother's necklace. They cost someone a pretty penny. It just wasn't me."

Amelia finished her rich, sweet cake. She pushed her plates away, and an aproned steward appeared from nowhere to carry them away. Amelia almost reclaimed the newspaper to occupy her time with when Lewis' dark blue suit passed her by.

Lewis dodged around the steward, headed straight to the front of the dining room. He breezed out the open French doors and around the corner to his right. Amelia disciplined herself not to peek behind her to see if Elizabeth remained at their table. After a minute, Elizabeth's blue jacket and white skirt paraded past.

Amelia licked her lips. She waited several seconds before she stood up and followed six feet behind her. Claudia had mentioned Elizabeth's room being next to Elwood and Dorothy's, but Amelia wanted its precise location for herself.

Elizabeth swished past the parlor and headed down the first corridor of cabins. Amelia hustled on tiptoes to reach the hallway. At the opposite end, a man in a black suit and bowler stepped into view, approaching them. The woman took a few quick steps but squared her shoulders and returned to walking.

The man lifted his lips in an enigmatic crook and tipped his hat to her. "Good afternoon, Mrs. Cole."

Amelia watched for a sign of recognition from Elizabeth, but if she greeted him, she did so without moving her head. Elizabeth ducked into an open door and shoved it closed behind her, revealing the glinting number 5.

As Amelia neared him, she took in every detail of his appearance. Full, angled eyebrows shaded his mottled-grey eyes. A few days' growth of beard traced his squared jaw to his dented chin. A smolder constricted Amelia's chest. She braced herself against it and strengthened her momentum. He eyed Elizabeth's door and retraced the way he came. He produced a key from his pocket and stopped in front of room 8. His cool, ashen-blond hair glinted in the chandelier light glowing beneath his bowler.

Amelia raised her hand to her mouth. She cleared her throat in a few soft rasps as she passed the lavatories between Elizabeth's room and his.

Rotating the key in the lock, the man's gaze met Amelia's over his arm. She offered him a coy, flirtatious grin. She swung her hips a little wider as she passed behind him, pausing at the intersecting hallway.

The man flicked his attention over Amelia, his lips parting in a shallow motion. He raised his eyes to hers for a moment, their chests lifting with quickened breaths at the same time. He lowered his head and stepped into his room.

Amelia turned left into the next corridor to arrive at her cabin, her mouth curving with satisfaction. She had gotten exactly what she wanted.

1,500 Feet

Above the Atlantic

Chapter Four

In the diffused morning light of the ship's port side, Amelia sipped sweet, sugary iced tea. One of the first-floor lounge's wide, deep-cushioned armchairs cradled her in luxury. The wooden frame was carved into a scalloped apron beneath the seat, and the legs ended in tight scrolls above the floor in elaborate Louis XV style. Despite the almost-familiar surroundings of furniture, wallpaper, and lamps, Amelia could not mistake the airship's elevation. Behind her, clouds that should have been glimpsed from below floated at eye level beyond the slanted windows. The looming scene had gripped her stomach in unease before she sat down.

Amelia hunched her shoulders away from the clear panes, which could also show her the view below the airship. The other passengers had exclaimed during breakfast it now passed entirely over the deep blue waves of the Atlantic. She did not need to see the ocean to believe it rolled far beneath them.

The snooty woman with white, wrinkled skin from the dining room the day before sat in another grouping of armchairs. She scrunched her eyes up. "My ears are still stuffed." She raised her gloved fingers to massage the hinges of her jaws beneath her long, jeweled lobes.

The pressure had persisted in Amelia's ears, too, something Captain Barrett had apologized for over the speakers. It seemed an unavoidable side effect of rising to their ideal elevation, and Amelia was glad her discomfort had subsided by the time she went to bed.

The old woman's blonde friend piped up, her large azure eyes giving her an appearance of perpetual innocence. "Mine returned to normal after dinner."

An oversized man with a wide moustache twirled the ends of it, keeping its fashionable curls tight and upright. "Mine did, too. Thank God." He wound one moustache tip into a finer strand. "I studied music at the Peabody Institute in Baltimore. Not being able to hear the musicians properly would sink me straight to the depths of hell."

The bejeweled woman gasped, bunching her forehead in folds.

Her friend only deepened her pleasant mood. "I saw you tapping your foot during last night's performance."

The man broke into an all-encompassing gleam. He plucked his monocle from his face and shined it in quick swipes of his handkerchief. "How observant of you. I can name any song I hear, be it played by chamber group, pianist, orchestra, or band."

She batted her darkened eyelashes. "That's quite impressive."

"Only the best from Peabody." He replaced the monocle with a practiced ritual, setting the bottom against his fleshy cheek and securing the top beneath his thick eyebrow.

Amelia took a longer drink, the late-morning tea refreshing her fast-paced nerves. She swung her sleuthing to the back half of the lounge, where three mahogany writing desks sat against the wall. Each one offered two tiers of drawers atop its surface and one more underneath. A man in a black, straight-legged suit hunched over a woman in cream tweed perched at one of the desks, the same fragile figure who had bid goodbye to the pouting boy at the iron fence.

The man's dark blond hair tapered into a widow's peak above his short forehead. His close-set eyes pierced the woman while he badgered her in a harsh version of her own nasal accent. "What do you need to write to the children for? We've only been gone for a day."

She sat back and lifted the pen from the page. Sections of her hair interwove in a tight, meticulous pattern above her porcelain neck. "Everything's been lovely. They'll be pleased to know that."

"We can't even mail the letter until we've landed."

She poised the pen nib above the paper. "If I wait to write it all down, I might forget something."

He grimaced. "Pity."

The Polish couple ambled in through the doors, lighting up at the sight of the duo at the desk.

"Ah," the Polish man said. "I haven't found the chance yet to make your acquaintance. I'm Rudolf Greisman, and this is my wife, Yetta."

The blond man offered a stiff, cursory handshake. "Spencer Burgess. My wife, Cora." His hands flexed at his sides. "Our oldest son, Alvin, is hiding around here somewhere."

Rudolf plunked a hand in his pocket, his hazel eyes bright and jovial. "On the open deck, I suppose."

"Perhaps," Spencer allowed in clipped syllables.

"What's your business, sir?"

"Clothing. Cotton goods. I have a factory and a store based in Fall River. That's Massachusetts."

Rudolf swung his arm down in disappointment in front of him. "We're in the food business. Polish sausages in Buffalo. Not much of a reason for us to do business together, eh, Mr. Burgess?"

"I'm afraid not."

Rudolf bent toward him. "Unless you're willing to go into linen napkins or cotton aprons?"

Spencer gritted his teeth. "No."

"Sausages can get a little messy, not that ours are greasy, mind you. We've had no complaints."

Amelia swallowed the last of her iced tea and left the glass on a silver tray beside her.

The pale, wrinkled woman rubbed the flaps of her ears in vigorous motions. "These darn ears."

"These darn beds," the large man countered with rueful pleasure. He covered a stifled yawn with his hand. "So comfortable, I can't seem to wait to return to mine. It'll ruin me for my own bed and any hotel's accommodations in Europe."

"Don't yawn where I can see it. Soon enough, I'll do it, too." The woman's gaping jaws parted her lips. She raised her gloved hand to her mouth, blinking in surprise. "That cleared my ears."

From a card table behind the trio swung four pairs of excited eyes. "Yawning helped you?" the Southern belle asked in a gliding drawl.

The stodgy man often at her side spoke up across from her. "Let's all try it, then."

Before Amelia knew it, half the room faked yawns, stretching their chins down to their chests. She got up from her chair and drifted past Rudolf and Spencer.

The Pole snapped his fingers, eyebrows rising. "Perhaps we have golfing in common?"

Spencer's flat enunciation made his words almost unrecognizable. "No. We don't."

Amelia slowed down in the open area around the staircase. Beyond it in the parlor, a set of four she recognized from the dining room huddled close together on one hunter-green sofa.

The young woman on the left end smoothed the skirt of her dress. Fine lace outlined the blue-and-white plaid, her figure exaggerated into a wasp waist and generous curves. Her hair blazed red in a high pouf above her forehead, the length of it falling into loose ringlets about her neck. "I channeled a spirit three days before I left for Albany." Fluid British vowels tinged her speech. "Pages and pages of her life story. Her marriages and her children. The deaths of her parents. Her older brother's travels." She rubbed her fingers around one delicate wrist. "My hand cramped for hours."

The older woman spoke up from her side. Her neat brown hair and snow-white dress made her much less conspicuous. "Did her brother want to fly in an airship?"

"No, he was a traveling salesman for Colgate toothpaste."

The brunette clasped her hands in her lap. "Luther, did you ever buy the new pendulum you wanted? We talked about Lorena's."

The man beside her fished into his jacket pocket. "Better. Feast your eyes on this beauty." He lifted out a silver-and-gold pocket watch nestled in his wide palm.

"It's gorgeous," breathed the redhead. "I've never seen anything like it."

The brunette touched it with her fingertips. "It shows the moon, stars, sun, everything. Well chosen. You have excellent taste. Have you tried it yet?"

"Certainly." Luther tucked the timepiece away in his pocket. "I've learned some interesting things about our voyage overseas."

"Can you tell us?"

Luther's eyes wandered over her rectangular face before he answered. "It wove a tale of adventure, of freedom, and of love."

The brunette ducked her chin, her ears reddening.

The titian woman giggled. "But will we dock in France safely, Luther?"

"Assuredly. It would take something bigger than exists to bring this ship down."

The fourth member of their party, a young man with slick reddish-brown hair, rolled his eyes. "Gravity, some would say." His throaty words danced under his Scottish influence.

Luther raised his index finger. "I believe in Captain Barrett, Harold. He'll see us there safely. He has thus far."

Harold baited Luther with a smirk. "It hasn't even been in the air a full day yet." He wiggled further down into his seat. "Indisputable logic."

The others groaned and threw their hands up.

The redhead leaned forward to address Harold past the others. "*Logic* is Luther's least favorite word besides *impossible.*"

Luther cupped his hands over his knees. "I see you still have some doubts, young man, but we'll convince you. You came to the spiritualists' convention. You stayed for the trance lecturer's symposium, and you agreed to meet us in Albany to board this ship. Although, maybe in the end, it'll only be Lorena who convinces you."

The redhead's mouth dropped open, but she laughed as she wagged her finger at Luther. "Don't open any doors you can't close. Or perhaps you wouldn't mind being behind a closed door with Cee."

The brunette's cheeks caught fire. Her dark eyes threw daggers at her teasing friend.

Learning little of value from the idle chatter of the public rooms, Amelia wandered back toward her cabin. The dapper man from the day before loitered at the entrance to the corridor that held his room. His bowler shaded his eyes as they followed Amelia. She slowed her pace. He raised his hand and beckoned to her.

Conceited enjoyment twinged Amelia's lips. She hid it behind carefully constructed poise as she crossed the floor to him.

"Darius Shank." He lifted his bowler. "I believe we met too briefly yesterday to exchange names."

She met him with demure pleasantness. "Amelia Harlow. Pleasure."

"How are you adapting to our strange new surroundings?"

"Well enough."

"Have you forayed up to the open deck yet?"

Amelia stiffened whether she wanted to or not. "No. I won't until I have reason to."

"That's a curious attitude."

Amelia sorted through her thoughts for how much truth she wanted to share. "I'm on board with the goal of attaining Bordeaux five days from now. I can cross the ocean just fine on the inner decks."

Darius twisted his lips. "You haven't been by the windows, either, have you?" he guessed. "Fear of heights, perhaps?"

"Uneasiness," Amelia corrected. "Not as strong as fear."

"My mistake. Would you walk with me?"

Amelia dipped her head.

Darius started up the hall at an easy pace, and Amelia fell into step beside him.

"You're riding the *Duchess* alone, Miss Harlow?"

She took him in, the unshakable confidence, the humor, the questions. "Yes. Aren't you? I haven't seen you with anyone."

"*Touché.* I'm alone. Can you keep a secret?"

"Yes."

"I wondered if you could do me a favor. It requires a bit of finesse and prudence I'm afraid I'm sorely lacking."

Irony tinged Amelia's response. "A woman's touch."

Darius glowed. "Precisely. You do catch my meaning. I assume by your presence on this airship you're at least a somewhat adventurous person?"

"I think so."

"And you're sure you're not above... being where you shouldn't?"

Amelia overlapped her hands in front of her in a show of propriety. "Perhaps you'd better explain before I get the wrong idea."

"Correct again."

At the end of the hall, Darius signaled Amelia to the right. They approached the French doors at the back of the dining room, and Darius drew one open. Amelia moseyed in, not sure what he had in mind but ready for it.

The door padded closed. He joined her near the back tables and the rotating map, its motor emitting a gentle whir. "I imagine you know Elizabeth Cole's on board and who she is."

Amelia gave a loose gesture toward the table she had occupied at breakfast. Her pitch rose in innocence. "I caught up on her history during my reading yesterday afternoon."

Darius bowed toward her. "Brave of you to walk so close behind her down the hallway yesterday."

"Braver of you to greet her. She killed a man, not a woman."

"Good point. But I have to tell you Mrs. Cole didn't kill her husband the way they said in the papers."

The details popped into Amelia's mind. "With the bludgeoning and the rope?"

"No, that's what happened. But it wasn't Mrs. Cole who did it. It was me."

Amelia stepped back from him, flicking her narrowed eyes to the nearest exit.

"But you have nothing to fear from me." Darius held his upturned palms out. "It was the last thing I wanted to do, honestly, but I needed money. Mrs. Cole hired me to do it. She insisted. I didn't ask many questions, and I failed to realize what it would mean for any of us. I've always been sorry for what I did, and I've left that part of my life far behind me, as you can see. There's just a little matter of the debt."

"Debt." Amelia's echo fell flat, intrigued he would center on money after the brutal extinguishing of a human life and in the midst of his current success.

"Mrs. Cole promised me a certain sum of money for my..." Darius consulted the slowly spinning map. "...services, and she never paid me in full. I tried to contact her lover in charge of her estate, but he wasn't keen on settling, either."

Amelia prodded his story further. "I saw you say hello to her. I couldn't tell whether she knew you or not."

Darius rubbed one set of fingers against the other. "She has every reason to pretend we've never met. Don't you agree?"

Amelia gave a short hum of acquiescence. "I'm surprised the way your luck's improved you'd pursue the rest of the payment. It was for something awful."

"I agree, and I can't take back my actions. But Mrs. Cole made a promise to me, and this gives her a chance to make good on the rest of it. It's about the principle of the situation. I'm sure you believe in making things right when one can."

Amelia assessed her options. "What do you want me to do?"

Darius sidled closer. "After Mrs. Cole's seven-year stint in prison, I'm assuming she doesn't trust anyone but herself with her cash and her belongings. She must be traveling with the money she owes me. In all probability, she'll never set foot in the States again."

"And you want me to settle her debt with you."

Darius held up his vertical palms. "I'm only concerned about what's owed to me. Far less, in fact. Five thousand dollars ought to cover me. It's sure to be somewhere in her room." His lips, the sharp arches the perfect space apart, eased into a charismatic curve. "You've done some sneaking around in your day, haven't you, Miss Harlow? That's why you're still here listening to me. Nicked a few pennies or picked a neighbor's flowers?"

The corner of Amelia's mouth ticked up. "Yes, little things like that."

"You can keep a secret?"

"One or two."

"I'd gladly share part of the pot with you for doing me this good deed. Ten percent will cover much of your traveling expenses for you."

"That's very generous. I can try to get your money for you, Mr. Shank."

"Excellent!" He pulled two keys out of his pocket. He held one up and secured the other. "I even have a copy of Mrs. Cole's key. No lock picking or door forcing involved."

Amelia eyed the cut metal with real interest. "How did you get that?"

Darius shrugged. "I bribed one of the staff during lunch yesterday. Don't worry. This is the only time I'll need to use it."

"A bribe? Like you just did me?"

Darius widened his gleaming smile. "It's called sharing the wealth and showing my gratitude for your assistance."

Amelia closed her hand around the offered key. She scrutinized every inch of his face. The subtle scars fading into the shadows beneath his hat brim. The dark mists of his eyes. The slight crook in his strong nose above the self-assured purse of his lips. If he noticed or objected, he hid it.

Amelia stashed the key in her pocket. "How soon would you like this done?"

"As soon as possible, assuming you can do it without detection."

"How will I get it to you?"

"There's a bench outside my room for those waiting for the lavatory." Darius dug into his pocket and handed Amelia a small silver key. "I'll store an empty suitcase beneath it. Use this to open it and stash the money inside."

"How will you open the case if I have the key?"

"I have a spare one. I can get this one back from you later."

"What if somebody finds the luggage?"

"My name is on the tag, so it'll come right back to me if somebody supplies it to the purser."

Amelia sank the metal into her pocket. It landed against Elizabeth's room key with a gratifying clink. "I'll deliver it to you as soon as I can."

Chapter Five

Most of the passengers gravitated toward the dining room by one o' clock.

Amelia stationed herself on the parlor sofa, abandoned by the spiritualists minutes before in favor of the lunch offerings. Even Darius walked by, meeting Amelia's eyes for a twinkling moment. Shoes and boots thumped down the stairs as the second-deck tenants descended for the midday meal. A lull fell over the wide, open space before Lewis peeked around the corner of the hallway diagonal from Amelia.

"There's nobody–" His eyes widened at her, and he tipped his hat. "How do you do?"

Amelia bowed her head in response.

Elizabeth appeared at his side, squinting with skepticism and displeasure at Amelia's presence.

Lewis stroked her arm. "Just relax."

Elizabeth wrapped her hand around Lewis' arm. With regal silence, they glided past the parlor to the dining room's French doors.

Amelia waited in case Elizabeth changed her mind. With seventy other passengers crowding the buffet and the tables, Elizabeth might retreat and take her chances with their leftovers. No one emerged from the dining room, and Amelia rose from the sofa. With quiet and casual purpose, she strode into the nearby hallway.

The third door on the right bore the number 5, between Elwood's room and the men's lavatory. Amelia checked both ends of the hall for bystanders before producing the pilfered key and using it in the lock. Within seconds, she slipped inside and locked the door behind her. Her fingers found Tesla's switch and rotated the cylinder halfway.

On cursory inspection, Elizabeth and Lewis' cabin matched much of Amelia's. A bed for two flanked by end tables and bookended in chairs. A dresser stood beside the door with a bowl sink on the other side. Several large steamer trunks and smaller, matching cases sat along the wall. The wallpaper flourished in spring greens and golds above dark wood wainscoting with a few framed paintings for diversion.

Such details did not excite Amelia. She limited her focus to the items unique to Elizabeth and Lewis' room: their luggage, their habits, their belongings.

A metal jewelry box adorned the top of the dresser, the flat center radiating grooves from it like a sunburst. Intricately arched and engraved sides sat on fan-shaped feet. Amelia flipped the lid open. Royal-blue velvet nestled a collection that surpassed Amelia's own at its greatest height. Sky-colored opals set in gold rings. Countless strings of white pearls. Oval lockets engraved with leaves and flowers. An aquamarine brooch ringed in three octagons of diamonds. Amelia only dared remove the larger pieces like the brooch that she could easily set back in place. Beneath them, she found older, less expensive designs. Pins, pendants, and earrings set with small paste stones instead of the radiant genuine articles.

Amelia replaced the jewelry from her hands and lowered the lid of the box. Several pairs of gloves decorated the dresser top, ladies' and men's, along with a sterling silver button hook. Amelia slid open each drawer of the dresser, out of curiosity more than anything else. The finery inside echoed the clothes Amelia had already seen Elizabeth wear. White, scalloped lace and interwoven ribbon. Embroidered flowers and decorative braid. Plain silks, few patterns, in majestic purples and whispering ceruleans.

Amelia moved on to the luggage, much less than she would have expected for a couple moving their entire lives abroad.

She cemented in her mind the placement of each bag and box before she disturbed it. Wrapped up amongst more clothes were items that piqued Amelia's interest. A hefty bronze statuette of a woman, each feature realistically cast, every fold of her gown wrinkling in stark relief against her satiny skin. An album of photographs covered in downy velvet brushed Amelia's fingers, patterned with roses accented in gold filigree. A box of letters tied up with pink ribbon. Amelia slid one free and opened it.

My dearest Elizabeth –
I count every hour we're apart.

Embarrassment crawled over Amelia. She skipped over the remaining rows of short, clear script. At the bottom, Lewis had signed his name. She closed the letter and secured it with the rest. She packed up the trunk and surveyed the bed beside her. Lifting up the covers where they hung near the floor, Amelia found the extra luggage she had missed before. She assumed without investigating this was where Elizabeth hid her cash and that these cases remained locked at all times.

Not needing them or any money they contained, Amelia flattened the wrinkles out of the bedcovers and left the room in darkness. The jumble of dining room conversation continued in full swing behind the row of cabins. She stole down the hallway to the end and followed the outer corridor to her room.

Like Elizabeth, Amelia concealed her cash where others would not easily stumble across it. She pulled out the bottom dresser drawer, reaching into the vacant space where her bound bills rested in dollars and francs along the back board. She counted out fifty hundred-dollar bills before storing them on the dresser top.

Amelia fished her box of butterfly-and-peony stationery out of her flat-top trunk. She laid a piece of it on the dresser and wrote a note to Darius in her neatest hand. She creased it twice to fit between the bills near the end of the stack and stuffed it into one of the white envelopes. Amelia packed it into the full length of her pocket and let herself into the hallway.

Laughter bubbled up from further down the corridor where it opened up around the stairs. The spiritualists, perhaps, or the others who were forming fast, temporary friendships for the duration of the flight. Amelia decided to take the thinner, outer hallway rather than risk running into passengers leaving the main doors of the dining room.

Amelia strolled away from her cabin around the nearest corner. By the far doors to the dining room huddled Harold and Lorena, spasming with a shared joke.

Lorena's large, grey-green eyes landed on Amelia, their bright lights dimming. She drew away from Harold and wrangled her mouth into a frown. "You shouldn't say things like that." Her cheeks twitched, and her eyes shimmered.

Amelia continued toward them. Lorena broke into long strides toward the opposite end of the hall, and Harold trailed close behind her. Amelia acknowledged them with the barest of nods and entered the next corridor. The bench Darius had mentioned sat just past his door, the second on the right. Amelia crouched down, thinking it the fastest way to fulfill her obligations. She unlocked the suitcase, dropped the straining envelope inside, and secured it.

A man's hushed insistence sounded down the hall. "Quick! This way."

Amelia stood up, raising her hand to one of her earrings, pretending to replace one she had dropped.

A woman's harsh whisper broke out. "Before she sees us."

The couple rushed to the second door from the end in a frenzy of clothes and limbs. As the man drew himself upright, his body stretched thin and straight as a post. The woman shadowed him, short and buxom in a flowered blue dress.

She whipped her head around. "Won't she look for us here?"

The man fit a key into the lock. "She can knock all she wants. It's the only place on board we have the key for." He opened the door – the one past Elizabeth's room – and in three seconds flat, Elwood and Dorothy Molt disappeared as if they had never occupied the corridor.

Knowing Claudia might arrive close behind them, Amelia retraced her steps to her room. She also believed once Darius retrieved his suitcase and sorted through its contents, she would see him, sooner rather than later.

Chapter Six

Amelia loitered in the dining room, polishing off her dinner of tender spring lamb with cool mint sauce. Earthy asparagus tips grounded her palate. A vibrant mirabeau salad combined toasted nuts, tangy goat cheese, and other splendors under a kick of balsamic vinaigrette. As she suspected, everyone remained in their original seats chosen during their first lunch on board, and the rest of her table stayed empty. She took her time finishing a generous slice of tart green apple pie, listening in on any conversation that pleased her. She was also learning more and more of her fellow passengers' names, which made it easier to keep them all straight.

Edwin Ames, the large man with the high-maintenance moustache, bounced his fist off the table he resided at, catty-corner from Amelia's. His monocle popped out of place, falling to dangle from a cord around his neck. "Yes, I relish a rousing game of tennis." He plucked up his monocle and set it back in place between his cheek and his eyebrow.

Priscilla Banks, the petite blonde seated beside him, lit up like a chandelier hooked up to Tesla's switch. "Me, too. I play every Saturday and Sunday when it's pleasant out. Unless it rains. Sometimes I'll finish a game if it's only a drizzle."

On Priscilla's other side, her friend Iris Coates shook her head in small movements. She finished a bite of lobster and lifted her slim, crooked nose in the air. "I don't care for tennis. Never did."

Edwin inclined towards her. "How about cycling?"

Priscilla's delight flared to full flame, her shoulders rising in their pink sleeves. "I love riding. I even started a club for it back home in Cincinnati."

Iris rolled her dark brown eyes. "In case there weren't enough of them already."

"You know," Edwin boasted, "I like to compare the flow and rhythm of such activities to the various kinds of music."

Almost as bored by Edwin's topics as Iris was, Amelia swiveled toward the table on her right.

Celia raised a brow, motherly concern firming her jaw. "Where were *you* all afternoon?"

Lorena's round cheeks brightened to rouge. "On the top deck, admiring the ocean through the glass."

"You know what's so tricky about the top deck." Celia lilted with warning. "The stairs can wear you down. When you finally get to where you always thought you wanted to go, you suddenly trip, and you're left with nothing."

Luther, who was idolizing his pocket watch in his hands, slipped it into his jacket. "You're not exactly left with nothing. You're still all the way up on the top deck. That's about a ten-story climb from here according to the brochure in my room."

Celia's brown eyes flashed at him. "I'm talking about more than the deck, Luther."

Harold raised his glass of pale-gold iced tea toward Luther. "What do you say, old man? Dancing and drinks after this? Get something a little stronger in our veins?" Harold crinkled his cheeks up when he addressed Celia. "It's only one floor above us, so nobody will get too *worn out.*"

Luther lifted his glass and clinked it against Harold's. "Superb idea, sprout. Give me just one minute to finish off a few more of those lady fingers."

Luther sipped his tea while he stood up from the table. He lowered it from his mouth as a young man slammed into him in the aisle. Tea sloshed out of the glass in a long wave. It arced across the table and slapped straight down Celia's face.

The young man's jaw dropped. Luther stood frozen, the glass in his hand, his wide eyes locked on Celia. She sat motionless, her eyes squeezed shut, hands raised, and mouth agape.

"I'm terribly sorry." The young man's high Boston accent lingered in Amelia's ears. "Is there a napkin?"

Harold snatched up a white linen from the table and handed it to Lorena.

"Hold still, Cee." Lorena dabbed the napkin to her friend's face.

The young man deflated. "So sorry about that." He raised his eyes to Luther's face. "What were you drinking, friend? I'll order you another."

Luther set his glass on the table. "Never mind that. I was three lady fingers away from going upstairs."

"To the ballroom?"

"You, too?"

"Certainly." The pale young man offered his hand. "All this, and we haven't properly met. Alvin Burgess."

Amelia's ears perked up at the same name she had heard that morning in the lounge. She tried to fit him into the same family with his parents, the overbearing clothing mogul and his letter-writing wife. She ate her final sharp, sugary bite of pie and set her fork on the plate with a clink.

"Luther Wallace. I recall meeting your parents yesterday before Captain Barrett's speech on the platform. They seem more interested in the physical world of necessities and money making. They're not too keen on spiritualists, I take it."

Alvin's straw-blond eyebrows ticked. "Not too keen on anything, I'm afraid."

"So they won't be upstairs dancing?"

"Not likely."

Luther clapped Alvin on the arm. "Then give me a moment to fill the top of my stomach, and we'll be off for the ballroom. All of us, together."

Alvin took Luther's arm in a similar pose and rocked it. "Fantastic plan." He grimaced with sympathy down at Celia, who took the wilted napkin from Lorena and finished dotting dew off her forehead. "I apologize again."

Luther patted Alvin's arm and walked away toward the buffet.

The spectacled steward who had shown Amelia to her cabin the morning before arrived to cart her plates away.

He peeked at her as he bent to retrieve them. "Are you having a good time so far?"

"Yes, thank you." Despite the plush comfort of resting in her chair, Amelia rose to her feet. Half the dining room had cleared out already, and Amelia finally forced herself to head back to her cabin.

The parlor couches sat empty as Amelia passed them. Footsteps echoed up the stairs on her left. Straight ahead in the lounge, the French couple sat together toasting flutes of bubbling Champagne. Amelia entered the second hallway near the lounge's doors, taking it all the way to her room. She stepped in as she switched on the chandelier with a click.

In the chair to the right of the bed sat Darius beneath his bowler, blinking in the brightening light. He kept his eyes trained on Amelia as she continued in and closed the door.

"Good evening." She sounded almost casual despite the tension straining her throat. Amelia had expected he might invite himself in, given he already possessed a key to Elizabeth and Lewis' room.

"Who are you?" Darius slid her packed stationery envelope onto the bedside table next to him.

Amelia stayed across the small room, determined to keep her composure. She peeled off her gloves and laid them on the dresser. Digging his suitcase key out of her pocket, she tossed it to him.

He caught it and slapped it down on the corner of the end table.

She braced herself against his temper. "You lied to me." After a beat, when Darius gave no answer, Amelia sank her weight into one hip. "I know you weren't paid to murder Arthur Cole. Nobody was. It was a thief's knee-jerk reaction to being discovered, not something premeditated."

Darius issued his next demand. "How do you know?"

Amelia admitted the truth for the first time. "I was in the house that night."

"Did you kill him?"

"No." Amelia gave Darius a chance to respond, then added, "I went there to steal something, and after I witnessed the brawl leading up to the murder, I left with nothing."

Darius tilted forward, his sharp eyes scrutinizing every feature of her face. "Who are you?"

Amelia waited for him to guess and guess right. "You know who I am, someone who knows you well enough to hide a note near the end of that money, knowing you'd count every single bill."

Darius stared at her, his rising and falling chest his only action. In one motion, he pushed himself up and strode across the room. He took Amelia by the arms and kissed her hard. Amelia felt more for him than she anticipated, meeting his desire more than halfway. He slid his arms around her back, pulling her against him.

When Darius leaned away, he regarded Amelia with a new appreciation, a questioning warmth in his eyes. "I thought you were dead. It's the longest we've gone without seeing each other since we met."

Amelia's heart hardened but harbored the slightest sliver of respect for their relationship. "I wasn't dead, but it took some time to heal. I had to have surgeries, recover, and try to get back on my feet."

Darius held her face in his hands and kissed her cheeks from the supple apples to the rigid bones.

"Why did you ask me to steal Elizabeth's money?" Amelia asked, interrupted by Darius kissing her lips. "You can't possibly need it."

"It was a ploy to get Elizabeth out of her room later when she works with the purser and security to find it. I assumed you'd leave evidence of a break-in before I knew it was you." Darius unbuttoned the front of Amelia's red silk jacket. "I know she has more with her than cash. I just wanted to create the opportunity to steal more than that fake debt was worth." He slipped the jacket off her shoulders. "I apologize for using you so I didn't have to put myself in danger."

The smooth silk rustled against Amelia's dress and skin, calling her back to the familiar patterns of his methods. The give and take she grew used to years ago reassured her, and she appreciated the slow pace to get reacclimated to it now. Amelia slid out of her jacket and laid it on the dresser behind her. Her matching dinner dress opened in a wide, square neckline that bared her collar bones. "I wasn't surprised. I only caught your eye so you'd contact me. I knew you couldn't resist using a pretty face."

Darius propped his fingers under Amelia's chin and lifted her face to the chandelier light. He marveled at one side of it, then the other. "How different you look now." He touched the cinnamon locks gathered on the back of her head. "You're almost unrecognizable, obviously."

Amelia kept her anger light. "What did you expect when you left me in the blaze at the Archduke Stephan hotel in Prague? Did you set the fire?"

"No. Why would I burn down a brand new building?"

Amelia did not doubt he would for the right price but said nothing.

Darius pulled Amelia to him, nestling his face in the crook where her neck met her shoulder. "I was afraid you might've forgotten about me. If you survived, of course."

"Oh, Darius," Amelia sighed, considering her situation. "I remember you every time I open my mouth and speak." She owed her life to Václav Petzel, the obsidian-haired doctor with the tidy moustache. His astute choices and tireless hours of work salvaged what remained of Amelia's face although it altered her appearance into something new. "Dr. Petzel did a good job of patching me up. Makeup can hide the scars, but my gritty voice is likely permanent. I inhaled a lot of smoke, they told me."

"And what about this new name you've chosen for yourself, Kate?" Darius murmured against her neck.

Amelia stiffened at the mention of the name her parents gave her. Her jaw jutted forward at his audacity to speak it. "Amelia Harlow. It's my name as surely as yours is Darius Shank."

"Surely."

Amelia helped Darius take his jacket off with brisk fingers, laying it over hers. She worked through the buttons of his vest, which he tossed to the chair across the room. She unfastened the stiff white shirt beneath his suspenders and pulled the bottom of it loose from his pants. Drawing the material away from Darius' left side, Amelia lifted his silk undershirt, exposing a two-inch scar on his abdomen. Her mouth ticked up with condescending fondness. "Your body still remembers when I stabbed you in Berlin."

Darius' eyes retained their sparkle. "Was it worth it?"

Amelia traced the grooves of his chiseled abs, the muscles tight and distinctive. She ran her fingertip in a dismissive swipe over his scar. "I made a fortune off those rubies."

"And your unwitting accomplice?"

"I left him with nothing. Except," Amelia added, knowing the effect it would have on Darius, "memories of what he gave me."

Jealousy cut through the games in Darius' mood. "Say what you want." He slid his fingers down the bare skin of her chest. "I know I'm the only one who can really satisfy you."

Amelia half agreed with a tilt of her eyebrows. Darius' touch was exact, adept, and charged like lightning. But he was not the only man who had ever made her feel something. "There was a cabana boy in Cuba the summer of ninety-two."

Darius kissed her, and Amelia gave in, letting her words fall away. He flung his hat away and splayed his hands across her back, squeezing her against him. Amelia wrapped her arms around his neck and jumped into his embrace, Darius dropping his hands to support her body. He turned and laid her down on the bed beneath him.

Darius pushed away the layers between them, her dress, her petticoat, and her chemise. Usually, he would have drawn off every last stitch of her clothing before continuing, but even Amelia lacked the patience for that. She unhooked the buttons closing his pants and opened the front of his silk drawers. Darius cradled her cheek, his other hand supporting him above her. Amelia kissed him with all the turmoil of the past seven years: anger, longing, blame, and the merest glimpse of understanding. He inched into her, and as with every bittersweet reunion they had, Amelia found their time apart had not disturbed their chemistry or their rhythm.

Amelia wrapped her legs around him, keeping him against her and unable to pull away. He gave a light, low chuckle, enjoying her attempts at control and revenge. He rocked his pelvis sharper against her until the tension peaked in Amelia's body. Darius kissed her neck, nestling his face in the hollow of her jaw. He only slowed for a moment, picking back up until he left Amelia gasping with him in breathlessness and pleasure.

Amelia's legs released their hold, and Darius dropped himself to sitting beside her. He caressed her calves through their silk stockings, placing a parting kiss on her knee before he climbed off the bed.

"So what brings you on board?" Darius asked. "Are you here because of Elizabeth, too?"

"Of course." Amelia propped herself up on her elbows. "She's likely transporting a great deal of money, but I still want the thing I broke into her house to steal eight years ago. She has to be traveling with it."

Darius straightened up from where he recovered his hat, brushing off the underside of the brim. "You never told me you were there that night. I never read anything about a witness or a second thief."

Amelia's trespassing in Elizabeth's Manhattan mansion made her heart race even now. She had relied on all her willpower to stay committed to finding the map with numerous indigenous artifacts, distracted servants, and sky-high ceilings around her. Amelia knew why she had not confided her dead-end adventure in Darius. Despite her time at the Archduke Stephan ending in her collapse in an upstairs hallway, she preferred to dwell in its happy memories than her time in the Cole house. The hotel's wide, arched doorways between halls, dark wooden bar curving in a half moon in its café, and grand white fireplace gracing its formal dining room. "It was before our tangle in Prague. I saw no need to mention a botched robbery."

Darius set his bowler on the dresser. He fastened his drawers and his pants. "You could've testified, you know. You could've told the court what you knew and saved Elizabeth all that trouble and time in prison."

Amelia sat up the rest of the way. "I doubt they would've believed me. I would've had to admit to my own thieving intentions. And I was out of the country within a few months, anyway."

Darius tucked his undershirt and cotton shirt into his pants. He adjusted his suspenders over them. "You must've been after something special to try for it again after all these years."

Amelia gave her choices a split second of thought. "It's a map detailing part of central Africa. It could prove exceedingly useful for those eager to communicate with native tribes, expand their country's territory, or bring home artifacts for museums."

"In our case," Darius surmised, "useful for offering to European governments to the highest bidder. They'd drain Africa dry of its resources if they could."

"Or for sale to an explorer or a museum directly. Or I could use it and go there myself."

Darius crawled onto the bed and sat down beside Amelia. "You wouldn't. It's too dangerous. You like surer bets than that."

"I spend time with you, don't I?"

Darius kissed her and continued buttoning his clothes. "How did you find out about the map, anyway?"

The party in Manhattan rivaled any Amelia had attended in several countries around the world. She spent an hour casing the large paintings and gilded knickknacks throughout the spacious rooms. Only when she gravitated toward the crowd ringed around a single man did she perk her ears up.

Red hair and long sideburns framed the speaker's coy expression. He gestured to a guest with a long, wide moustache. "I've given Arthur a host of artifacts I've brought back from Africa. Guns, knives, masks. He displays quite the collection now."

His audience's mouths popped open in marvel and interest.

Their murmurs rose and died out in Amelia's ears. "I found out the explorer Mr. Cole invested in gave him gifts from Africa when he returned. None of them intrigued me until I heard about the map."

"How, though? I never read it mentioned in the papers."

Amelia tilted her head, enjoying the upper hand. "I rubbed elbows with a lot of dandies and snobs to get that information. Back when I had the money to pass for upper class." Most of her money since then had disappeared into Dr. Petzel's pockets. She had needed to cheat and steal just to leave Prague, then again to afford her ticket on the *Duchess* and the wardrobe to match.

Darius planted an approving kiss on her cheek. "You could pass for royalty if you had the diamonds. How do you know it's still worth anything?"

From later in the evening, the explorer's quieted bass rang in Amelia's head. "It's not just a map, Arthur. It's a copy of the truth, my real findings in Africa. You wouldn't believe the wealth I've discovered. Fertile soil. Oil, loads of timber, natural gas."

Arthur crinkled his thin eyebrows. "But the articles said…"

The explorer's hand slashed the air. "It was a cover up. I'm going back there as soon as I can, and I don't want anyone else to know how much is there. If they think it's a wasted effort, they won't encroach on my operation."

"Why give it to me?"

"Your investments and support mean the world to me. It'll be a souvenir one day when I've finished my explorations and announced my true findings."

"I wish Elizabeth were here to hear this instead of sick at home with a headache."

The explorer clamped a thick hand on Arthur's shoulder. "Let her rest. I want as few people as possible to know what I'm hiding until I can afford to share it."

Amelia combed her fingertips through Darius' lustrous hair. "The map reveals the locations of valuable resources the explorer never made public. He died with most of his team on their next expedition, and no one has ever capitalized on his research."

Darius kissed Amelia's palm. "Are you sure Elizabeth has the map on the ship?"

"She has to. She might not know its full value, but I can't imagine her mailing it to France. She'd want it where she could keep an eye on it."

"Do you know how her infamous one-way ticket ended up hitting the papers? I'm sure she wasn't happy about that." Darius pressed his lips against Amelia's ear.

"One of the ticket sellers must've leaked it, but I don't know for sure."

"Thank goodness for that. It's what lured me on board." Darius slid his hand up her arm, holding onto her shoulder. His open mouth tasted her neck.

The complicated meanings of their reunion distracted her from his romance. "Me, too."

"There must be plenty to steal from her, even discounting the map." Darius lowered his hand along her side, brushing her breast where her corset pushed both of them forward.

He always reached for the stars any way he could, but he certainly proved more attentive than usual. Perhaps he retained a tiny glowing fragment of his soul, emerging as guilt and repentance. "It's good to see you," she said, feigning nostalgia in place of her complex resentment and longing.

Darius' chest touched her arm, his lips following the trail of her skin from neck to shoulder.

"I wasn't expecting you," she added, the absolute truth.

Darius slipped the short sleeve of her dress off her shoulder, exposing more of her.

"I could share the map with you," she suggested, "as one more of the plots we've hatched together. It would give us a reason to see each other beyond the few days we have left on the *Duchess.*"

Darius stopped feasting on her shoulder and raised his tumultuous eyes. "You don't have to share it with me, but I wouldn't mind playing along with you for old times' sake."

The unknown picked at Amelia and made her more serious. "I don't know where Elizabeth keeps the map yet."

"That's okay. We've got days before we land. That's all we need. Are you up to the challenge?"

"Of course."

"Since you've already had one chance in Elizabeth's room, do you mind keeping an eye on the lovebirds while I dig around?"

Amelia shook her head. "First thing after breakfast?"

"Naturally. We have to take advantage of the time we have left."

Chapter Seven

Darius slipped out of the dining room while most of the passengers were only halfway through their breakfasts. Amelia squirmed to get a second peek in Elizabeth's room, to leave the rest of her eggs Benedict to grow cold while she used the illicit key. But she obeyed their agreement, finishing her hearty meal in the dining room while Darius retreated to the parlor to wait for her. At last, Lewis strode past Amelia's table toward the exit. She ate the final few bites of breakfast, waiting for Elizabeth to dart by any second.

Instead of disappearing, Lewis stopped at the open doors and gestured to someone clear across the dining room. Amelia did not dare seek out whom it was, and within moments, Elizabeth passed her. She linked her hand around Lewis' arm, and Amelia stood up before they could take more than a few steps.

The couple retreated out of view, and Amelia hurried to tail them. Striding through the doorway, she caught them starting up the stairs. Ten feet to her left, Darius rested on one of the parlor couches reading *Treasure Island*. His eyes simmered with sport and impatience. Amelia nodded once, and Darius closed his book. He left it on the coffee table and walked toward Elizabeth's room. Amelia ascended the stairs, listening to the clambering of boot heels above her. When the sounds picked up echoes, Amelia's plotting mind relaxed while her belly constricted. Elizabeth and Lewis must be headed to the open deck, not the lounge or the bar on the next floor.

Amelia had only overheard the facts and opinions about the long climb to the tallest accessible point on the *Duchess*. She arrived at the landing for the second deck, almost identical in layout to the first. She paced herself as she followed the railing around to the next flight of stairs. Nine more stories to go, and Amelia lost the luxury of the open staircase. Walls closed in around her, forming a vertical tunnel lined with nothing but shaded lamps, photographs, and articles chronicling the history of the *Duchess*. Amelia concentrated more on these than her ascent. Pictures captioned with Samuel Langley's name portrayed a fair-haired, bearded man with kind eyes and an easy, confident expression. The Smithsonian Institution where he had served as secretary rose up behind him. Another front page featured dozens of workers scaling the metal skeleton of the airship, welding and hammering. A lustrous Captain Barrett posed in front of the finished *Duchess*. Lastly hung a recent article from the *Albany Evening Journal* boasting *Langley Outs Embezzling Assistant and Retires!* Amelia swayed closer to read a little more. *Trusted friend proves greedy; Airship builder maintains his institution's sterling reputation.*

Amelia achieved the top of the stairs, finding herself in an ample-sized room on the topmost deck. French doors led outside while floor-to-ceiling windows opened up the two adjoining walls. Only the wall behind her stood impregnable. Amelia stepped over to the windows for a moment, white lines marking a shuffleboard court on the wooden floorboards outside the room. A few people played with cues in hand and pucks on the floor. Closer to the bow, people gathered by the rail, peering out at sky and ocean. Elizabeth and Lewis meandered along the railing, their backs to Amelia.

She took a deep, steadying breath and opened a door to fresh air. Halfway along the deck's length, sloping green glass panels rose from the top of the railing, reinforced by metal poles between them. The glass rose steadily upward on both sides until it met over two hundred feet in front of her with a curving metal spear rising from the tip of the *Duchess*. With this architectural feature in place, the ship's brochure had assured Amelia, she could enjoy the open air without fear of bugs, birds, or constant wind.

Half a dozen teak lounge chairs sat arranged in the middle of the deck. Amelia gravitated toward them. She could sit here and follow Elizabeth and Lewis downstairs when they left. But with the great length of the deck, Amelia already could not hear their conversation or if they were having one. She forced herself to walk to the railing, a reinforced wooden wall built to waist height. She kept her eyes at cloud level or higher. Seeing only blue sky and puffs of clouds at her standing height made her lightheaded enough. She wanted to quicken her steps to catch up to Elizabeth and Lewis, but she held her distance. Their body language told her volumes.

They walked close together, only as far apart as their arms hooked around each other. They strolled in perfect rhythm, their bodies swaying with intuitive timing. They bent their heads together, Elizabeth flashing Lewis a smile he returned twice as bright.

Amelia ignored the boredom picking at her brain and used it as a reason to shorten the gap between them.

Elizabeth's chatter rose. "I loved that café." Comfort and happiness warmed her reminiscence. "No one knew me there. We could sit and talk for hours."

"There was the small hotel around the corner," Lewis reminded her. "They barely spoke English. They wouldn't have known who you were if you told them."

"Maybe I should've tried. It would've given us something to joke about."

"They adored you, I remember."

The light dimmed in Elizabeth's eyes. "I wish we could go back. Before everything else happened." She clung to him.

Lewis clasped his free hand over Elizabeth's. "We will. We can do all the same things in France. Whatever part of it we choose."

"Not like it was before." Her eyes stared, blank and distant. "Arthur's dead. I've been without you for seven years except for your visits and your letters."

Elizabeth touched Lewis' face, and Amelia consulted the endless sky rather than watch the woman fall apart on her lover's arm.

"Listen to me." Hope flooded Lewis' plea. "A cottage surrounded by vineyards and countryside. No more big cities for us. Just grapes and cows and goats. There would be nobody to see you unless you wanted them."

Elizabeth sharpened, incredulous and sullen. "Look at me, Lewis. I'm not young anymore. They taught me how to sew and clean houses. The other women had done those things and worse, but not me. You've seen my hands. Locked in that hard, cold fortress with two hundred other women. They gave me no peace by day. The screaming and crying and pleading at night was even worse."

Lewis bowed under the immensity of his empathy. "In the country, it'll just be me."

Amelia braved their vulnerability and snuck a peek at them.

"It'll just be me." Lewis peered deep into Elizabeth's desperate eyes. "The two of us. Grass and vines and animals and time."

"You'll have to work."

"Not much. I can raise animals on the farm. I'd never have to leave you for long."

Elizabeth's frown thawed. "The cottage is a farm now? And you're suddenly a farmer? You grew up in Brooklyn."

"I can learn." Lewis gave her a quick peck on the cheek. "I would do anything, learn anything, go anywhere for you. I think I've proved that." He swept his hand out at the infinite blue.

Elizabeth nestled her shoulder against his as they walked. "Yes, you've proved it."

"You wouldn't have to lift a finger. I'd cover every window with curtains to give you the privacy you want. Put in a high fence so no one could see you. Install three locks on every door to keep them out or none at all if it terrified you. You could sit inside and rest while I hired people to help me with the garden and the animals."

"You'd shut me away only for yourself?"

"Of course. It's what I've wanted to do ever since I met you."

Elizabeth and Lewis paused at the point in the ship's bow and gazed out through the glass. Amelia stopped, facing the rail in case they noticed her. As long as she could prevent them from retiring to their room before she knew Darius had left it, she could stand where she wanted.

Lewis quieted with reverence. "I'm sorry about Arthur. I never dreamed his death would give us a way to be together."

Elizabeth took a minute to answer. "How do you miss someone you saw less and less? I grieve for him as he was, but I can't say I long for the lonely evenings our marriage shrank into."

"You won't have to be alone. Or bothered if you want to be alone with your thoughts. I'll be as near or as far as you want me."

"I want you close, Lewis." Her words rushed together. "Always."

Elizabeth and Lewis walked away along the rail down the port side of the ship. Amelia stayed where she was, only partly listening to their conversation behind her.

Lewis spoke up with revived happiness. "What's the first thing you want to do in France?"

"Take a very long, hot bath. Wash the dust of New York off of me forever. Leave all the sneers and whispers behind us."

"We will."

Amelia started back the way she had come. Across the deck, the French doors of the windowed room swung open. Elwood and Dorothy hastened out into the open. Elwood carried a large dark case in one hand, securing Dorothy's grasp in the other. Tethered together, they struck out in Amelia's direction.

Now that they scurried toward her instead of darting away, Amelia made out their details. Elwood had a long, thin face, his nose echoing the same dimensions in the middle of it. His dirt-brown hair slicked down beneath his bowler, and his suit continued the drab color all the way to his shiny leather shoes.

Dorothy's face stretched as wide as the moon with broad, round cheeks. She held a parasol above her head, much higher than necessary to accommodate her velvet hat. What Amelia could see of her upswept hair seemed such a muddy mix of colors, Amelia was not sure which dominated, mousy taupe, dirty blonde, or cool brown. Lace adorned every hem and seam of her jacket and dress, giving her a grace and elegance Dorothy might not have otherwise possessed.

The couple arrived at the railing not far from Amelia. Dorothy collapsed her parasol and stored it against the bottom of the rail. Elwood set his case on the deck and opened it, lifting out the spyglass Claudia had mentioned. He passed it to Dorothy, who squinted through it, aiming the wider end down beyond the ship's rail.

Anxiety strained Elwood's courtesy. "Don't drop it." He unpacked a metal object which he unfolded into a tripod stand. He propped it on the deck floor and secured the spyglass on top of it.

Dorothy's hands flew to her hips. "As if I would, on accident or on purpose. If you're that worried about it, we can walk down to the glass. I like using it as much as you do."

"But you use it too much. Then it gives you a headache." Elwood bowed over and peered through the spyglass. He adjusted its slant. "Maybe you should try the painting lessons instead. The brochure said they're in the lounge on the second deck."

"I can paint anywhere. I came here for the view. Besides, I'd never drop the spyglass over." Dorothy scanned Amelia with disinterest. "It's the best thing you bought for the trip."

"It's the only thing I had to buy." Elwood stepped back and gestured to the spyglass. "There's still a lot of ocean left to cross, but you can see darkness out in the distance where Europe is."

Dorothy hunched over to view it through the glass, and Amelia touched the brim of her hat in greeting to Elwood. She stopped walking within speaking distance.

He tipped his hat in quick response. "How do you do, miss?"

"Fine, thank you."

"Elwood Molt." He gave a short bow.

Amelia fought back her satisfaction at already knowing so much about him. "Amelia Harlow. Smart idea to bring a spyglass on board."

"Yes. Well, we'll be able to see more than waves as we get closer to France. Portugal and Spain from this side. England on the other."

"You read maps?"

"In my spare time. There are a lot of maps used as decorations on the *Duchess.*"

"I hadn't noticed." Amelia had been too busy following Elizabeth and dallying with Darius.

"In the lounges mostly," Elwood added.

Dorothy stood up and prodded Elwood's arm. "Why don't you take a gander?" She shot a withering sneer at Amelia.

Elwood motioned to Amelia. "Would you like a try? As I said, there's not much to see yet, but it's exciting to notice the land coming closer."

Amelia's stomach tipped with uneasiness, and she took a step back. "No, that's all right. Enjoy the view."

"Ah," he remarked with understanding. "It's not for everyone."

Dorothy tugged on his sleeve, and Elwood touched the brim of his hat in parting to Amelia before he stationed himself at the spyglass. Dorothy sized up Amelia beneath drooping, suspicious eyelids.

"Good day," Amelia wished her, taking her leave.

Up ahead, Lewis opened one of the French doors for Elizabeth. Amelia kept her distance until they descended the stairs out of sight. She strode the rest of the way and let herself into the windowed room. Boot steps resounded below her, and she made up for lost time going down on the quiet fronts of her shoes.

Elizabeth's utterance drifted up to her. "Beautiful day."

Lewis' followed close behind. "Every day will be beautiful from now on. I promise you."

When Amelia landed on the first deck, Elizabeth and Lewis had only strayed half a dozen feet from the stairs. Luther rushed up to them, breathless, his hands quaking in supplication.

"Have you seen my watch?" He offered a prompt tip of his hat to Elizabeth. "Excuse me. It's just very expensive, and I bought it only a week ago."

Lewis blinked with concern. "No, I'm sorry. I haven't seen any watches that weren't mine."

Amelia grabbed the opportunity to get closer to Elizabeth and Lewis. She walked over and addressed Luther. "What was it made of?"

"Gold and silver, miss." Luther lifted his hat. "The face has the sun, moon, and stars on it under the hands."

"I haven't seen it, either," Amelia admitted with sympathy. She glanced at Elizabeth and Lewis to keep them anchored there. "When did you last have it?" she asked Luther.

"Yesterday at dinner. I must've seen it after that, but I'm not sure. I only remember admiring it in the dining room. When I went to find it in my jacket this morning, it wasn't there."

"Did you inspect the dining room?"

"Yes. I just came from there." Luther plucked a handkerchief from his pocket and dotted his glistening face with it.

The motion imitated something else Amelia had seen, Lorena drying Celia's dripping face with a napkin. Also in the dining room. And at dinner the night before.

Alvin had taken his time with conversation and apologies even though he did not know them. Luther had initiated the jovial contact of touching Alvin's arm, but Alvin had continued it. Everything Amelia knew about the arts of distraction and redirection unboxed from her memory.

So the clothing mogul's son was a pickpocket. What could he possibly want with the watch? To sell it? Keep it? Use it to keep the time or for divination as the spiritualists did?

Amelia resolved to make a closer study of Alvin if she were able. There was already one thief too many aboard the *Duchess*.

To Luther, she said, "I'll keep an eye out for it. Maybe it was kicked under a table or something."

"Maybe," Luther mumbled. "Thank you." He jogged off into the dining room.

With Darius still absent, Amelia debated the risks and advantages of introducing herself to Elizabeth and Lewis to buy him more time. He approached her from the nearest hallway on her left, freeing her lungs from their apprehension. To his credit, he did not greet Elizabeth, but he tipped his bowler to her with an impish smirk. Elizabeth met Darius' familiarity with disdain and guided Lewis away toward their room.

Darius lingered at Amelia's side. "Nothing."

"Yet," Amelia whispered. Darius flattened something metal against her palm, and she wrapped her fingers around the key. "My turn. Do you remember how to play the game?"

"Certainly."

Amelia spoke up so Elizabeth and Lewis could hear. "Mr. Wallace is keen on finding his missing pocket watch. I think with as much as it means to him, as many people as possible should help him acquire it."

Darius observed Elizabeth and Lewis sidelong as they headed toward their room. "Where is he now?"

"In the dining room. Scampering under all those tables, I suppose."

"Then he'll need all the help he can get." Darius called to the fleeing couple. "Mrs. Cole? Mr. Blakely, is it? We could use your assistance if you're going to nothing pressing."

Elizabeth and Lewis slowed to a stop at the entrance to the hallway. Lewis spun, his expression helpful and eager. Elizabeth took her time to circle around, eyebrows set in defense over perceptive eyes.

Darius ambled up to them and offered his hand. "Darius Shank. I'm sorry if I put you off the other morning. We got off on the wrong foot."

Lewis shook Darius' hand. "We've got time to search before lunch. What do you think, Elizabeth? Just for a few minutes?"

Elizabeth's face remained drawn. "Of course."

Darius beamed at her. "Thank you." He led them in brisk steps toward the dining room.

Amelia completed the deception. "I'll investigate under the tables in the lounge," she called after them.

No one replied, and within moments, Amelia stood alone.

Chapter Eight

Amelia slipped into Elizabeth's room and locked the door. Her hand scrambled for the chandelier's switch and grew its flames to half height. Her eyes flicked from item to object around the room, her heart racing as every second ticked by without reward. She skipped over the places she had explored before and singled out anything she had overlooked.

The map was worth hundreds of thousands if not more. Elizabeth had to know that, or she would have sold it with the rest of her husband's African collection. Amelia would have learned about a sale that groundbreaking.

Elizabeth also had to preserve it for the journey oversees. Would she have rolled it? Doubled it over? Inserted it in a pocket or some other ingenious hiding place?

Amelia scrutinized the pictures and paintings hanging on the walls. Flowers and houses and people. An obvious place would hide anything best. Amelia stepped forward and pulled one of the pictures off the wall. A solid wire strung across the back of the wooden frame. Several thin nails emerged from the frame, heads pointed inward to hold the picture in place. Amelia replaced it on the wall and moved to the next one. She investigated each frame around the room until she arrived at the last one.

Behind a painting of man and wife, a folded map nestled behind the exposed nails of the frame. Amelia could not breathe. She touched it, her eyes zeroing in on every word marking the page. *Cameroon Mountains. Congo River. Equator.* And the words that nearly stopped her heart. *Timber. Iron ore. Unexplored.*

Amelia pushed out a tremulous exhale. She could not stand around poring over the map all day. She forced herself to move, to think, to plan. Shifting the map slightly in the picture frame, she tore a shallow rip in one margin. Returning the map to its resting place, the division hid neatly behind a nail where Elizabeth might not notice it if she checked on it.

Amelia replaced the picture on the wall, hanging it as straight as she found it. She scrutinized all the paintings, each one meticulously square. Amelia started for the door, Elizabeth's jewelry box glinting at her. Amelia paused and opened it, examining the pieces anew. She lifted aside a silver peacock brooch, exposing a pair of gold earrings that stuck out for their size and glimmer. A round diamond dotted each post, three more following in a line. Dangling from the ends, diamonds hugged pear-shaped rubies in spectacular drops. Her eyes swept over to Elizabeth and Lewis' luggage, a plot tumbling in her mind.

Darius' voice shocked her from the hall. "Thank you for your time, Mrs. Cole. I'm sorry to see you rush to your room so soon."

Amelia closed the lid of the jewelry box and darted her eyes over the room. Only one possible hiding spot presented itself, and Amelia memorized its placement before dousing the chandelier flames. She moved through the blinding darkness until the bedspread trailed under her fingers for several feet. She flattened herself on the carpet and scooted on her belly under the side of the bed away from the door.

Elizabeth responded with chilly tension. "I don't mind helping someone who needs it, but I didn't board this ship to spend my time crawling around the dining room."

Amelia gathered her skirts under the bed as best she could without seeing them.

Lewis spoke up as metal clicked in the door's keyhole. "Good day, Mr. Shank. I'm sorry we couldn't be of more use to you and Mr. Wallace."

"Quite understandable," Darius allowed.

The door swung open, bathing the carpet in hallway light. Amelia arranged the bed linens falling past her face before anyone noticed them disheveled. She worked on taking even, silent breaths.

Darius seemed to call in through the open doorway. "We're bound to find it. It's probably a mistake, and Mr. Wallace will find it later *still in his room.*"

Amelia ground her teeth at his pointed words, and she covered her mouth with a gloved hand to keep from snapping at him. He knew their return stuck her in there with no way to signal him.

Elizabeth answered with dry dismissal. "I'm sure he will."

The lights brightened in the room before the door closed, and Amelia suffered several soundless seconds.

"What's wrong?" Lewis asked, pained.

"I despise that man," Elizabeth spat. "He'd shame me on my hands and knees all afternoon if he could."

Lewis remained gentle and forgiving. "I don't think he was doing that at all."

The mattress sank down over Amelia's feet. She squeezed her eyes shut.

Lewis continued, patient and coaxing. "He was just trying to help Mr. Wallace."

"I don't trust him," Elizabeth murmured.

Lewis hesitated. "You don't trust anyone since you got out of prison." In an instant, he added, "And I understand why. But you're out now. Things are different. People are different."

"Not all people. Somebody killed my husband, and that person's out there somewhere, probably not in prison like I was."

"We don't know that. Maybe he tried to rob someone else, and the police caught him."

The bed sprang up, and Elizabeth snapped. "Don't be so hopeful, Lewis. It doesn't help anything."

Amelia's eyes widened. Elizabeth's rant rendered her mind a blank.

Lewis' patience strained, taut. "I'm all you've got, Elizabeth. Your mother's gone. Your father won't talk to you. Or your sisters. Any friends you knew are back in New York."

"And they can stay there. Did you ever read the letters they sent me? Dahlia had the nerve to congratulate me on liberating myself from my less-than-fulfilling marriage. She always seemed quite the happy widow after her husband keeled over. Amanda said she'd pray for my soul, the condescending hypocrite. And Hetty sent me pictures of her cousins in case I wanted any of them to court me after my release. Without mentioning the murder incident, of course."

The mattress eased down a few inches closer to Amelia's head. "None of them visited me. Not one. All I got were apologies in the mail, saying how intimidated and frightened they were to come to the prison." Elizabeth's outcry scratched in her throat. "I know it was terrifying because I was in there!"

The bed lowered in a second place. "Don't cry. Please." Quiet pucker sounds marked the ensuing stillness.

Amelia tried not to picture Lewis kissing Elizabeth's face.

"A new life," Lewis encouraged her. "We're almost there."

"But what good is France if all of our memories and mistakes and pains haunt us?"

"They'll fade away. Didn't you ever have a nightmare when you were a child?"

"Yes. On a ride through the country, I saw a farmyard of chickens and roosters. I dreamed they were chasing me, trying to peck at my clothes and my ankles."

"But it doesn't scare you now. You got over it. Didn't you?" Lewis asked, tender and supportive.

Elizabeth sighed and sniffled. "Yes."

"Don't cry. It'll all be over soon. We have everything we need here with us. I made sure of it."

"We'll find someone to talk to about the map." Elizabeth blew her nose in wet but dainty bursts. "Arthur wouldn't tell me much about it except that it was important. He was so proud and sentimental about his artifacts. I wish he would've–"

Authoritative knocks sounded on the door. Amelia peered toward the door although all she could see was the bed frame and draping blankets. The newer weight lifted off the mattress above her, and the other wriggled away from the door. The wood parted from its jamb.

"Yes?" Lewis asked, slightly impatient beneath his politeness.

"I apologize for disturbing you, sir. Ma'am. The staff has received a report there may be a mouse or two on board. We just need a few moments to ensure the room's safety, if you don't mind stepping out."

The mattress flew up where it sagged above Amelia.

The man piped up in consolation. "There's a lovely lounge on the port side of this deck."

Elizabeth muttered. "Let's go, Lewis."

The pattering of boots trailed away until Amelia drifted in silence. She lay perfectly still, waiting for the man to leave and the door to close.

Darius murmured instead. "Thank you." A paper bill scrunched in a crisp crinkle.

The door latch clicked, and Amelia counted out ten seconds before dragging herself out from under the bed. She breezed to the door on light footsteps, listening for noise in the hallway. She swung the door in, whirled out of the cabin, and closed the door. She strode away toward the lesser-used hallway, too eager to retreat to her room to worry about catching her breath first.

Amelia rounded the corner. Darius listed against the wall facing her room, gleaming at her with pure enjoyment. Amelia arrived at her door with a huff. Darius stepped closer, and she let them both into her cabin.

As soon as the door was locked, Amelia glared at him. "I assume you could've gotten me out of there sooner."

Darius shrugged, his mouth tilting in amusement. "I rescued you. Eventually."

"You did a poor job of keeping them out."

"Not everything's a conspiracy. I couldn't keep arguing with Elizabeth to hold her in the dining room. It was obvious she wanted to bolt and hide in her cabin. She was already suspicious of me."

Amelia cooled, enjoying his falling out with Elizabeth. *"Despises* is the word she used."

Darius cocked his head in mock fondness. "She was talking about me. How perfect. But it wasn't my fault she shouldn't seek solace in her room because somebody was snooping there." Darius closed the gap between them and rested his hands on Amelia's sides. "What else did you hear? Was all of it cursing my good name, or did they move on from that to each other?"

Amelia pushed him away, but Darius' features remained uplifted in his joking. "They were talking about moving to France and Elizabeth's time in prison."

"So nothing good?"

"I think we should take more than just the map," Amelia said, firm enough to arrest Darius' interest.

"Why? What did you find in there?"

"Nothing as valuable as the map, but as long as we're borrowing one thing, we should take more. We have a key. We can have as much access as we want, especially if they keep walking the open deck."

"They're full of surprises, aren't they?" Darius wrapped his arms around her waist. "What's caught your eye, my sparrow?"

"She has an astounding collection of jewelry. Some pieces more expensive than others. I thought a pair of ruby earrings might be a nostalgic challenge for us."

"To wear or to sell?" Darius nibbled the upper ridge of her ear.

"Either one."

His bottom lip brushed her skin. "What's in it for me?"

Tingles spread through her neck, but Amelia ignored his effects on her. "I found a statuette wrapped up in her luggage. Bronze. Heavy. Good quality."

"What's the subject?"

"A woman in a dress. Your favorite one."

"Almost," Darius hummed in her ear.

Remaining serious, she met his eyes. "What do you think? A few extra takes for fun and profit. It's the game we like best."

"And one we're awfully good at, my dear." Darius pressed a kiss against her temple. "Let's go for it. The earrings will be easier than the statue, but I always did welcome a test of my skills."

"I know," Amelia assured him.

"I look forward to spending more time with you later."

"Of course."

Darius kissed her, his cologne suiting him well although she had never smelled it on him before. A splash of citrus, a sting of spice, and the allure of sandalwood. Amelia almost regretted him pulling away and setting his hand on the door handle.

"Your copy, please." She held up her palm.

The corner of Darius' mouth perked up. "Copy of what, darling?"

"My cabin key. I know you have one the same way you have one of Elizabeth's."

"Not necessarily." He settled in against the dresser behind him. "How do you know I didn't pick the lock the first time I came in here?"

Amelia broke into breathy hilarity. "Because I've watched you struggle to pick locks. You lack the precision for it."

"A lot can change in seven years." Darius sank a hand into his pocket and placed a key in Amelia's grasp. Her room number, 20, glinted on it.

"How did you get this?"

"Bribed one of the staff to bring me an extra from the crew's set. If you ask the staff to clean your room and no one does, that's why."

She bounced the key up off her palm. "You must've bribed him well. No one said anything to me about this going missing."

"You didn't have a problem with my copy of Elizabeth's key. Or with me asking you to break into her room, for that matter. The only good bribe is a high one." Darius winked and let himself out.

Chapter Nine

Amelia savored her lunch, treating herself to unhurried enjoyment of fresh, succulent shrimp cocktail. She filled up on herbaceous, roasted spring chicken balanced with mustard dressing drizzled on lettuce. Somewhere in the middle of devouring a bowl of sweet but nutty almond pudding for dessert, Lewis passed by her table toward the exit. Around the time Amelia set her spoon in the empty bowl with a satisfying ring, Elizabeth swept by her, disappearing outside the French doors. Amelia took the last few sips of cold iced tea before standing up and making her way out of the dining room. The outer hallway would provide a more direct route to her room, but she preferred to experience as much as possible when she could.

Claudia stood in the open area near the stairs, peering up at them and wringing her hands.

Amelia walked over to her. "Have you lost something?"

"What?" Claudia's eyes brightened while her frown remained. "No, it's Elwood. He always disappears right after meals. I can't eat as fast as they do. I think they do it just to run away from me."

"No." Amelia concealed her disdain for Elwood's actions. "They're just excited about the ship."

Claudia made a sarcastic cluck in her throat. "I wish I could believe you. You're sweet to say so." She rubbed Amelia's arm. "Where have you been for the last two days? I haven't seen you since I gave you the newspaper article on Elizabeth Cole."

"Avoiding the view."

"You don't like heights?"

Amelia shook her head.

"Poor thing. You picked a funny way of getting to France."

"I guess my bravery misled me when I bought my ticket on the ground."

Claudia hummed a note of sympathy. "Have you been dizzy and lightheaded from the altitude? The woman who signed me in at the station told me that might be a side effect. When Captain Barrett flew the *Duchess* to test its capabilities, he experienced them a little."

"Yes." Amelia touched lying fingers to her temple. "I've had to spend some time reclining in my room."

"You know, you don't even need to bother the ship's doctor. Just close your eyes and take big, deep breaths. It'll relieve you in no time. And if you take one of the washcloths and run it under the cool water in your room, lay it right across your forehead. It's better than a tonic on frazzled nerves."

"Thank you very much, Claudia." Amelia had to admit the matron's friendship and kind heart truly refreshed her.

"I hope in your condition you haven't spent too much time peering down from the ship."

"Hardly any at all."

"That's probably wise. Elwood and Dorothy must be spending a lot of time up there with their spyglass. That's where I imagine they are when I can't find them on this deck or the one above us." Claudia managed a wavering smile. "Anyway, they say Dorothy gets lightheaded sometimes from staring down so much."

Amelia said nothing, especially not that she had learned as much from Elwood and Dorothy while up on deck.

"They seem able to find fun anywhere." Claudia lost her enthusiasm, splaying her interlinked hands. "I have four days left until France, and I'm running out of ways to entertain myself."

Amelia remembered something else she overheard from Elwood and Dorothy. "There are painting lessons on board."

Claudia's eyebrows rose, but her lips pursed in uncertainty. "Really?"

"In the second-deck lounge. Not outside your usual walking scope."

"Very kind of you to mention, but I've never tried my hand at painting. I don't know how useful I'd be with a brush and colors. I probably wouldn't produce anything worth the paint and canvas."

Amelia kept her admonishment light. "What attitude is that?" She held her hands out from her sides, gesturing to the open area surrounding them. "From the time I met you, standing right about where we are now, you struck me as a woman who sets her heart on something and sees it straight through. You're already trying one thing that's unfamiliar. The airship. Why not set your sights on something else that could bring you hours of entertainment in the future or at least assuage your boredom for the next four days?"

Claudia beamed. "You're very right. I should give it a try. What have I got to lose? Better to attempt it here than at home where all of my friends would want to see what I painted. Would you join me?"

"No, thank you. But I'd like to see what you create."

Claudia hung on Amelia's arm. "I'm excited now. It's been so long since I picked up something new. Besides flying in an airship, of course."

"The details for the classes are in the brochure in your room."

"Silly me for not reading it all the way through! I better go see when the next class is. I don't want to miss it. Thanks for letting me know."

"No problem."

Claudia shuffled away, and Amelia helped herself to one of the couches in the nearby parlor. She picked up a boldly colored copy of *Natural History* from the side table and thumbed through it. Charles Darwin's name, along with pictures of African tribespeople and honeybees, flashed past her eyes. She needed time to think while she waited for Elwood and Dorothy to come down.

Elizabeth and Lewis had presented themselves as an unbreakable code, a solid front with no cracks or vulnerabilities. But their conversation while Darius' inaction left Amelia trapped under the bed proved otherwise. Lewis' helping, outgoing nature had made him agree to Darius' suggestion of aiding Luther in locating his pocket watch. Lewis must have known – or would have, if given time to judge the situation – that Elizabeth would not wish to participate. As Darius had surmised, Elizabeth wanted only to shut herself away, not degrade herself by crawling under tables.

By itself, it was hardly incriminating. An honest misstep on Lewis' part. He was young. Impulsive. Perhaps raised to lend a hand to strangers or eager to be around new people. But behind their closed door, Elizabeth had swung out at Lewis with an attack Amelia had not expected.

"Don't be so hopeful, Lewis. It doesn't help anything."

Instead of backing down, Lewis had crossed Elizabeth's most sensitive lines.

"I'm all you've got, Elizabeth."

"A new life. We're almost there."

Lewis' tenderness stabbed jealousy through Amelia's heart. Deliberate honesty drove his desire to support Elizabeth, not inexperienced naïveté. Their intense loyalty to each other must be based on true devotion to have lasted this long. Whatever happened between them the night Elizabeth returned home to her murdered husband, every event since then had dragged their lives into turmoil and anguish. Elizabeth had surely changed through her prison experiences, but what of Lewis?

He could not be the same man Elizabeth risked so much for. Was his reputation as tarnished as hers? Was he carefree and spontaneous once, careful and protective now?

Elizabeth and Lewis might have formed a tight bond, but Amelia inspected the weaknesses in their rapport. Lewis lived by different rules than Elizabeth, no matter how devoted and attentive he was to her. The only way to find out more about them and their schedule would be through Lewis. Elizabeth guarded herself, too defensive with strangers to let them approach her. And the only way to get clean, full answers from Lewis was to pry him away from Elizabeth, the woman who clung to his side.

Elwood and Dorothy clomped down the stairs. The dark spyglass case dangled from Elwood's hand.

Dorothy slid the pin from her hat and lowered it from her head. "It'd be the perfect place for a nap if someone would hold a parasol over me."

Amelia laid her magazine aside and stepped up to interrupt them. "Excuse me."

Elwood raised his eyebrows and doffed his hat. "Good afternoon, Miss Harlow. I didn't think we'd meet again so soon."

Dorothy's moon face puckered with annoyance and irritation. "Too soon," she muttered.

Amelia pretended not to hear. She pointed to the case in Elwood's grasp. "I wondered if I might borrow your spyglass for a little while."

"Had a change of heart about seeing Europe from a distance? It's quite a treat. You don't get views like this back in the States."

"I thought I'd better take advantage of it while I can."

"Sure." Elwood handed over the spyglass case although Dorothy's jaw dropped in protest.

"I'll take excellent care of it." Amelia took in their faces, frozen in the likenesses of the comedy and tragedy masks of theatre. "I should be able to get my lightheadedness under better control now. I met a lovely woman on board who gave me good advice."

Elwood's long face tipped up. "I'm relieved to hear it. I'd hate for anyone to miss out on such a spectacular view."

"It's sad, though. She's traveling with family, but she spends all her time alone. Claudia Molt. Is she a relative of yours?"

Elwood gulped. "Yes, I'm afraid so. My mother."

Amelia set her hand out. "I'm sorry. I didn't mean to meddle. Please don't tell her I mentioned it."

Elwood raised his drooping head, meeting her eyes. "I won't."

"I can see how apologetic you are. Perhaps you won't miss me borrowing the spyglass so much if you make up for lost time with your mother."

"Perhaps not," he echoed, lost in thought.

"It's awfully bulky to carry up and down those stairs so many times a day. Would you mind if I left it up in the windowed room when I'm done with it?"

Dorothy burst out with insistence. "Don't, please. Someone might steal it or break it."

Amelia forced an understanding but disbelieving laugh. "A thief on the *Duchess*? At the price of four hundred dollars a ticket? I should doubt that. As for breaking it, by the same token, anyone on board would have the funds to replace it for you."

Elwood considered his wife, sliding his lips from side to side. "We should spend more time with Mother."

"Do what you want, Elwood." Dorothy stormed off and disappeared down the hall.

"I'm sorry," Amelia said.

Elwood waved his hand. "It's all right. I should've brought more spyglasses, I suppose."

"The *Duchess* should come replete with them."

"Quite." Elwood tipped his hat and tucked his hands in his pockets. "I'll see you some other time. I have to find the rest of my party. You're free to do with the spyglass as you please. I'll collect it before I step off in Bordeaux."

"You're beyond generous, Mr. Molt."

Elwood bunched his lips up in preoccupied thanks and walked off in Dorothy's direction.

Amelia remained standing until Elwood passed out of sight. She reclaimed her seat on the couch, stashing the spyglass case on the floor beneath her. She picked up *Natural History* and resumed browsing its articles on hummingbirds and upcoming expeditions to Antarctica. She mulled over strange but lifelike drawings of an African okapi, its brown body resembling a hump-backed deer while its legs carried the black-and-white stripes of a zebra.

In time, Amelia heard the second pair of voices she waited for.

"They'll get over it," Lewis said from around the corner. "They can't expect you to spend all your time in your room."

Elizabeth countered with venom. "They'd like me to."

Amelia left her magazine on the sofa beside her and rose to her feet. Elizabeth and Lewis rounded the corner from the hall of cabins. Elizabeth's eyes darkened at Amelia, but she neither halted her steps nor verbalized her disapproval. Lewis tipped his hat, guiding Elizabeth toward the stairs at the same moment Amelia stepped toward them.

"Going up?" Amelia gestured to the rising, dark wooden banisters. "To the top deck?"

"We like the fresh air." In the strain of Lewis' answer and the mixed light in his eyes, the two parts of him warred. He tended towards the polite. He wanted to open up to strangers, but his faithfulness to Elizabeth and her wishes maintained a wall around him.

Amelia hoped her understanding would appeal to his more outgoing nature. "I like it, too. I was on my way up."

Lewis motioned her ahead of him.

"No, thank you. I'll follow you."

Elizabeth and Lewis started up the stairs. Amelia returned to the sofa and pulled the spyglass case out from under it. She flipped it open on the cushions and lifted the instrument free from its protective, molded velvet. Closing the case with the stand inside, she carried both of them to the stairs and ascended after Elizabeth and Lewis.

At the top, Amelia found Lewis holding a door open for her. Elizabeth stood past him in the sunlight, her arms braced across her stomach.

Amelia brightened in gratitude. "I'm almost there."

On the last step, Amelia made sure to catch the toe of her shoe on the edge of the floor. She fell forward, trying to keep the spyglass from crashing to the wooden deck. Lewis' hand shot into view, too late to catch her. The case smacked the floor, and Amelia used it to brace the jolting fall on her knees. She stayed on the hard boards a moment, listening to her labored breathing.

"Are you all right?" Lewis strode into the room, reaching both hands down. "That seemed terribly rough. Would you like some assistance in getting up?"

"I shouldn't have tried to carry so much." Throbbing soreness spread through Amelia's legs, and she cringed.

"Let me take this for you." Lewis slid the case towards him, careful to lend Amelia his support as he did so. "Do you think you can walk? Should I run for the doctor?"

"That won't be necessary. Just some bruises at the most. I should be fine. I'm mostly suffering from embarrassment at the moment."

"Don't be. It could happen to anyone."

Amelia took Lewis' hands with her free one and engaged the muscles in her limbs. With Lewis' steady pull, Amelia drew up to her feet. It was the closest she had ever been to Lewis, and the kind patience in his youthful face startled her. The afternoon sun, filtered through the room's clean windows, illuminated the variations in his cool brown hair. His eyes greeted her with concern, the color of bitter dark chocolate or strong coffee. A thin, trimmed beard freckled his soft cheeks and slender jaw, further enhancing his catch between innocence and maturity.

Amelia took a deep breath and pulled her hands away. "Thank you, Mr. Blakely. I'm sorry I haven't introduced myself. We've crossed paths several times now. I'm Amelia Harlow. I've known who you are since the day we boarded."

Amelia met Elizabeth's eyes, the woman whose husband's attack Amelia had witnessed. Arthur's barking orders – *"Who are you? Get out of my house!"* Knocking and banging as the two men scrambled, slamming into walls and furniture. The aggravated cursing of the intruder. *"Why won't this gun work?"* Amelia had climbed the stairs in time to peek around the corner at the frantic beating the thief dished out with the unloaded or defective rifle. She winced, the thief pounding harder with every blow. Arthur Cole fell to the ground, blood pouring from his head, holding up a wobbling arm in self-defense. The thief unfurled a length of rope from his pocket and lassoed Arthur's neck with it before Amelia fled unnoticed into the night.

"Mrs. Cole." Amelia addressed her with sympathy, almost reverence.

Elizabeth locked her arms tighter against her body.

Amelia extended a hand for the case's leather-padded handle. "Let me collect the box, and I'll be out of your way."

Lewis lifted the case. "No, I can't allow that. I'll carry it for you. Where would you like it?"

Elizabeth's nostrils flared. Amelia could not read the exact emotions behind her sharpened eyes. Jealousy? Impatience? Betrayal?

Amelia pointed through the glass of the doors to a random place along the portside railing. "Over there is fine."

Lewis drew the door open. "I'll be right back, Elizabeth. It'll just take a moment."

Amelia walked out onto the deck, and Lewis fell into step with her. His different sides intrigued her beyond the information she needed to mine for. She let several more strides separate them from Elizabeth. "I respect you. Both of you. It must be hard to live with so much speculation and gossip all the time. Even this high above the middle of the ocean, you can't escape it."

Lewis' index finger loosened from the case's handle to pick at it. After a long pause, he answered, "Yes, it is."

"It must've hurt to wait so long for her to be released from prison." Amelia thought of her parents, whom she had not visited since her accident in Prague despite passing through New York. Missing them made her chest ache and injected empathy into her admission. "I've spent time away from people I care about, too."

Lewis spared her a sensitive glance. "It's difficult, isn't it?"

Amelia tugged on one melon-colored sleeve. "You're pulled to them the same as if they were yanking on your arms."

He lowered his head. "Yes."

"I appreciate your rescue. I know Mrs. Cole isn't very trusting of the people on board."

"She saw a lot of terrible things in prison. Her friends and family abandoned her. The press have hounded her since her release, wanting photographs and statements. They misrepresent everything she says." Lewis bit his lip.

"I don't believe she did it, if it helps," Amelia admitted.

Lewis' arms hung screwed to his sides, and he relaxed them. "Yes, it does. Thank you for saying so."

Amelia wanted to ask more about his relationship with Elizabeth but shied away from the risk of him closing down communications with her completely. She tapped a fingernail on top of the case he carried. "Have you taken advantage of Mr. Molt's spyglass?"

"No. I didn't know it was on board."

They stopped at the railing.

"Is this a good spot?" Lewis asked.

"I think so." Amelia made herself take in the unbroken expanse of cerulean sky dotted with clouds. She dropped her focus to the water. It hung much lower than she expected, and her belly drew up as if gathered by a string.

Lewis set the case on the deck floor and popped it open. "I'm not sure how this works."

"I'll set it up. I saw Mr. Molt do it once."

"Are you sure?"

"As long as there aren't any stairs involved, I think I'll do fine."

Lewis stood up and swept a palm against the back of his neck. "I wish I would've known you were carting this up. I would've grabbed it from the beginning and saved you the trouble."

Amelia's thoughts scattered toward all the memories of situations Lewis could have improved with his forward, genteel accommodations. Her breathing hitched, but she kept any stirring personal feelings behind her front of self-deprecating reassurance. "I would've managed it if I hadn't been so eager to admire the spyglass out of its case." Amelia spied over her shoulder, finding Elizabeth's stiff form by the doors to the windowed room. Even from seventy feet away, Amelia could see the contempt blazing in Elizabeth's eyes. "I've kept you long enough. I'm grateful for your assistance, but it's time to send the knight back to his lady."

A bashful grin broke out across Lewis' face. "You're too generous, Miss Harlow."

"It was an honor to make your acquaintance, Mr. Blakely." Amelia touched his sleeve, her thumb giving his forearm a brief rub.

Lewis stayed within her grasp for a moment, still and obliging. He nudged his hat brim in farewell, his sparkling eyes dimming to a respectful glimmer, and strode away across the deck toward Elizabeth.

Chapter Ten

In the dim light of her room's chandelier, Amelia lay on her back in the bed. She left her naked body exposed except for a swath of sheet across her legs. She curled her fingers toward her to examine her nails, running her thumb across their uneven lengths with a frown. She twisted her body to snatch her nail file from the small table beside her, scrollwork decorating its sterling silver handle. Reclaiming her reposed position, Darius returned to her peripheral, seated in the chair to her far right, wearing only his pants. He squinted at the door, lost in concentration.

He tapped one hand against the other, his words low and wondering. "How do we steal the map? Elizabeth must keep a closer eye on it than she does on her talking toy."

Amelia ignored Darius' dismissal of Lewis' worth. "She's spending more time outside her cabin. Lewis' influence, I think." She grated off a sliver of nail, evening out its curve.

Darius made an offhanded sound in his throat. "*He* can always make his way back to her. The map, once it's out of her possession, might never find its way there again."

Amelia warmed at the possibility of owning the map. "Taking it might be the easy part. Making sure it's not missed will be trickier."

"The earrings will be a walk in the park," murmured Darius. "Small. One pair in a whole box of jewels. Simple enough to pocket them and walk away when the time is right."

Amelia zipped the file around a second nail and set it on the bedside table. She rolled toward Darius, supporting her head on her arm. She hated how attractive he looked with no shirt, his shoulders broad and sturdy. His strong arms flexed while he pondered the heist, one hand balanced against his chin.

Defined muscles covered him from his chest to his waist, soft only where the knife scar marked his abdomen. "So what's bothering you?" she asked.

"The statuette. Why did you have to pick something so bulky and irregular?"

"Isn't that what makes it exciting? If you like, we can ditch the idea and go straight for Elizabeth's cash. I'm sure I know where she keeps it." Amelia pushed herself up to sitting.

"It can't be terribly easy to access."

"We'd have to acquire her luggage keys or break into her other pieces."

Darius swept his eyes in slow reverence from her face down the length of her bare body. "Well... I'm not in favor of that. It's too risky and hard to cover up. A figure of a lady, you said?"

"Yes."

"Perfect, then. It'll give me something to remember you by when we're apart again."

Amelia hummed, not sure how seriously she wanted to take Darius' play at sentimentality. "All we need to do is obscure it once we have it."

"What about the weight? The space it takes up in her luggage? She'll miss it if we don't replace it with something."

"There's still time," she reminded him. She lay down on her side, propping her jaw in her hand.

"Time to steal the objects? Naturally." Darius got up and came over, perching on the bed. "Time to plan? A little smaller than I'd prefer."

Amelia shifted onto her back. "We might've been able to get closer to Elizabeth if you hadn't greeted her the first day on the ship. It disturbed her. If you use a disguise, it'll have to be a good one."

Darius trailed his fingers from Amelia's throat between her breasts to her stomach. "It won't make much difference." He rested his hand on her belly. "If you weren't making friends with everyone on board, it'd be easier to disguise you, too. How many people do you know by now? How many names?"

"Not all seventy-three. Not any of the crew, not like you."

Darius bent down and kissed her.

Amelia searched his face. "I only befriend those who can be of use to me."

Darius smoothed her hair away from her forehead with his fingers. "Those poor people."

"I know what I'm doing."

"You always have an angle, don't you?" His mouth arched in appreciation.

"Yes," Amelia answered, relishing the irony. "I do."

Chapter Eleven

Amelia savored each flavor of her mignon of lamb, delicate salt and butter punched up with black pepper and thyme. Creamy mashed potatoes piled high beside the filet, green peas glistening beside them. A bowl of steaming, amber consommé accompanied a small wedge of yellow cake on a dainty dessert plate. She thought over her time with Darius, lapsing into a shared concern about how to carry out her complex plan. Her mind tumbled every face and room and object she knew on board the *Duchess*, trusting the ship would eventually offer every solution she sought.

A gruff utterance burst into her thoughts, Rudolf Greisman's Polish-accented English. "Yetta, your bag."

His wife batted her hand through the air. "I always leave it on the table. Nothing's gone missing yet."

"I don't even know why you bring it in here."

"It's where I keep my extra handkerchief and my opera glasses. Hurry up, or they'll run out of sausages."

"We can eat sausages at home," Rudolf grumbled.

Amelia sought out the corner table the Greismans had probably vacated. She could not see the bag past the French couple and other passengers. When Amelia returned to her dinner, a hearty uproar engulfed her from the party on her right.

Luther clenched Alvin's hand in greeting, delight filling his face. "Dancing and drinks after?"

"Sure," Alvin said. "Sure."

Luther clapped him on the shoulder and moved on. Alvin remained where he stood, fixating where Amelia had just spied, toward Yetta Greisman's unattended belongings.

Alvin took a step toward the back of the room, and Amelia grabbed the plate closest to her. Rising in one quick motion into the aisle, she collided with Alvin's stomach, smashing the remains of her dinner against his suit. Alvin stumbled back, unsticking the plate from his body. The rest of Amelia's steak fell to the floor along with a confetti of peas and globs of mashed potato. Amelia's jaw dropped in earnest to see the slick stain of gravy bouncing light off Alvin's jacket.

Alvin threw his head back and launched into the loudest guffaws Amelia had heard since the captain's speech. He pointed to the smorgasbord clinging to his clothes, scanning the nearby tables to see who had witnessed it.

Amelia motioned to his suit. "Sir, I'm horrified." Inside, she congratulated herself for such a quick-thinking diversion.

"It's quite all right." Alvin almost brushed at the mashed potatoes on his jacket but lowered his hands instead. "I knocked a glass of tea across Celia's face last night at dinner. Did you see it?"

"I must've missed it. How do we get this cleaned up?"

Yetta interrupted with a gasp, approaching from the buffet. "What happened?"

"A little accident," Amelia answered.

Alvin chuckled. "Little? I'd like to hear what you'd call a disaster. A mere inconvenience, perhaps?" He pealed with delight.

Rudolf and Yetta continued on their way, and Amelia sighed with pride at protecting the older woman's reticule.

A member of the staff, a lanky man in black clothes and white apron, appeared with a short stack of plates in his hands. "Do you need some help, sir? Is everything all right?"

Alvin turned his elbows out. "Perfectly."

Amelia gestured to his jacket with her outstretched palm. "There's food all over your suit."

"If it was good enough to go in my body, surely it's good enough to stick to the outside."

The aproned man shook his head. "I won't hear of it. I'll tidy this immediately. What do you require, sir?" He took the plate from Amelia's hand and added it to his collection. He swept his attention over the food spilled on the carpet. "Another steak for you, miss?"

"Please." Amelia did not intend to go hungry for doing a good deed.

Alvin held his hand up. "Nothing for me, really. A jaunt to the lavatory, a change of clothes, and I'll be right as rain. Not to worry, miss...?"

"Harlow," she supplied. "Amelia."

The staff member darted away.

"Alvin Burgess." The young man adjusted his tie with short jerks. "Don't let the last name scare you. Just something I borrowed from my old man."

"The cotton mogul, am I right?"

"Oh, God." Alvin groaned and slapped a hand to his forehead. "You met him, didn't you?"

"No, I just overheard."

"Still. My apologies." Alvin stepped toward the French doors. "Do you dance, Miss Harlow?"

"Occasionally." She fought a thousand memories trying to flood into her head and her feet at once.

"If you ever wander upstairs to the ballroom, don't be shy. We should share a dance together. Unless, of course, it's *Mrs.* Harlow?"

"No. I'm not married."

Alvin pulled his chin up while he gave Amelia a quick scan. "Perhaps Father's right about one thing, and young men are fools. Anyway, I'm eager to see you there. Stepping on your feet is more like it. I hope that doesn't ruin my chances."

"It sounds wonderful." Amelia raised her volume to be heard as Alvin gravitated further away. "Then we might be even."

Alvin issued a cavalier salute and wove his way out of the dining room. Amelia made sure to step in the mess of mashed potatoes and peas on the floor, grinding them into the carpet with every step back to her table. She sat down only moments before the aproned man arrived.

He set a full plate of fresh food before her. "I apologize, ma'am."

"Don't," Amelia told him. "It was my fault."

"No," he insisted. "Thin aisles. Hot plates. Your steak didn't burn you, did it?"

"No."

"We'll take care of this right away." He scrutinized the carpet. "We'd better wipe off the bottoms of your shoes, too."

"That's really not necessary. Bring me a hot, wet towel, and I'll do it."

The man's eyes bulged. "I wouldn't dream of it. This is the *Duchess*. I can't let word get out we make our guests clean off their own shoes."

Amelia took a breath. In her life, she had polished her father's shoes, washed her mother's hair, and coaxed mud out of her own dresses. Just because she had since dined on caviar and afforded an expensive airship ticket provided no excuse to let the staff wait on her hand and foot.

"Please." The man bowed toward her. "I don't want to lose my job."

Amelia gave in to his logic. "I understand. If there's a can of Gold Dust washing powder nearby, use that. It should take the stains out."

"Thank you. I'll be back."

The man rushed off, and Amelia busied herself eating her second helping of dinner. Several couples sauntered by as the man returned, one figure against the flow of ebbing guests.

He steered them around the mess of food in the aisle. "Be careful not to slip." He knelt at Amelia's feet, and she swiveled towards him in her chair. He murmured with breathy assurance. "Just take a second."

A teenaged boy, solemn in his staff uniform, strode over. He held a bucket in one hand and an orange box of Gold Dust powder in the other. He showed it to Amelia.

She recognized it at once. "That's the one."

He dropped to his knees, reading the back of the box and pouring out some of the powder into the bucket.

The man at Amelia's feet swiped his rag over the toes of her shoes. "How are you enjoying your flight otherwise, ma'am?"

"Fine." Amelia kept eating, trying to ignore the man's bumps against her soles.

He sprang to his feet and doubled the towel over. "Anything else?"

"No, thank you."

The man jogged away. Very few passengers dotted the dining room now. The teenager scrubbed at the carpet with a brush.

"Excuse me," Amelia called to him. "Do you mind taking my plate away? I'm finished with it."

The teenager popped up, leaving the brush in the bucket of sudsy water. He snatched up Amelia's plate and silverware, carrying them away toward the station behind the buffet.

Amelia crept over to the bucket until she could snatch the box of washing powder. She held it low as she retreated to her chair, sinking her drinking glass below the tabletop as well. She poured a teaspoon of white powder into the glass and replaced it on the table. She leaned over into the aisle and set the box of cleanser back on the carpet.

The teenager dashed over to the mess and resumed his scrubbing. Amelia stood up and brought the glass with her, hung low at her side. She accessed the closer, lesser-used hallway at the front of the ship, only a short walk from her cabin. Through the windows in the French doors at the far end of the hall, Darius relaxed in one of the lounge's grand Louis XV armchairs. He spoke with someone Amelia could not see, his mouth perking up in a twisted smile. He glanced her way.

Amelia ducked down the second hallway and let herself into her room. She locked the door and went straight to her jewelry box. She dug out a black-and-white cameo ring, flipping the picturesque lid open to its hidden compartment underneath. A few knocks rapped at the door, and Amelia hastened to empty the moistened cleaning powder into the ring's vacant vessel.

"Miss Harlow." Darius drew the last syllable out and down, hinting at the thin pretense of her alias.

Amelia clasped the ring shut and closed it away in her jewelry box. She left the glass on the dresser and opened the door.

Darius propped his forearm against the door frame. "I thought I saw you pass by."

Her arms stiffened. "There was an accident in the dining room. I spilled my plate all over the young Mr. Burgess."

Darius' eyes narrowed. "Do you mind if I come in?"

Amelia let him pass by her and closed the door.

"It's been my experience that when you stay late in the dining room," Darius intoned, "it's because you've got something up your sleeve."

"Maybe," Amelia conceded.

"Something to do with the plan?"

"Of course."

Darius swept his eyes around the room, his eyebrows bunching at the glass on the dresser. He picked it up. "Forget to leave this behind?"

"No, I was finishing what was in it."

Darius sniffed at the contents. "Did you need to do some cleaning?"

"I borrowed some washing powder for my shoes. One of the staff cleaned them for me, but I wanted to be sure he didn't miss anything."

Darius set the glass down. "Keep your secrets," he said. "It makes it all the more interesting."

"As if you don't have secrets, too?" Amelia challenged, the night of the Archduke Stephan fire blazing in her mind.

Darius lightened into good humor and took her hips in his hands. "Perhaps one day, we'll learn to trust each other."

"I do trust you," Amelia lied, arranging Darius' ascot in a more pleasing drape.

"And I trust you, my dear. I trust you want the same things I do."

Amelia tilted her head to one side, tightening the loose knot of the ascot up against the base of Darius' throat. "And who taught me to want those?"

Chapter Twelve

Unlike most mornings aboard the *Duchess*, Amelia made a point to arrive early for breakfast. She moved through the buffet, selecting eggs Florentine, small sausages, and piping-hot griddle cakes. She relished every bite, keeping an eye on the other passengers as they entered the room and approached the buffet.

Only one figure strode straight in past the heavy, delicious smell of food. Elizabeth ducked her head as she raced down the aisle. Amelia did not acknowledge her, pretending to be more engrossed in combining a bite of sausage and egg on her fork at the same time.

When Lewis left the buffet line, Amelia dabbed a napkin to her lips and stood up to greet him. As usual, he carried two plates of food.

She clasped her hands together. "Good morning. I wanted to thank you again for your help on the deck yesterday."

Lewis' mouth curved up as he dropped his eyes. "Don't mention it. Did you enjoy your view through the spyglass?"

Amelia had avoided the ocean itself. She busied herself with far-off clouds and coaching herself through healthy breathing until Elizabeth and Lewis left the deck. With great relief, Amelia had packed up the spyglass and tucked the case in a corner of the windowed room. "Yes, it's an experience one can't get in urban areas."

"That's for sure."

"Even one as big and varied as New York City."

Lewis' eyebrows rose, his chest filling with elation. "Have you been there? Do you know it well?"

"Only a little, but I wish I knew it better."

Lewis settled into a more casual stance. "When you get back to New York, you should certainly stay there awhile. Between all the boroughs, you get as much culture and fun there as anywhere else." Lewis took half a step deeper into the room.

Amelia worried he would run off to Elizabeth if she did not keep him talking. She pored over the food on his plates. "Are you having eggs Florentine, too?"

"No." Lewis raised it an inch. "That's Elizabeth's. Mine is the ham-and-cheese omelet."

"Well, you can tell her for me it's delicious. I must've missed her when she came in. Where's she sitting? Can you see her from here?"

"The same table as usual, I suppose." Lewis stretched his neck up, gazing almost straight ahead. "Yes, she's there."

"Where?" Amelia set the tip of her thumb against the lid of the poison ring on her index finger.

Most of the people in the back of the room were already seated. Others walked around Amelia and Lewis, remaining on their feet as they set their plates at their seats.

Lewis raised Elizabeth's plate forward, indicating across the room. "Right in front of the big map. She's sitting alone."

"Waiting for you, and I'll gladly let you go as soon as I spot her and wave to her."

"The second table from the doors," Lewis provided, swaying a shoulder toward the back of the room.

The view between them cleared. With Lewis meeting Elizabeth's eyes with such unwavering intent, Amelia raised her hand past Elizabeth's plate. In one flick of her thumb, Amelia dispensed the dissolved glop of washing powder into Elizabeth's eggs. Between the creamy texture of the hollandaise sauce and the pure white of the poached egg, the cleaning agent all but disappeared. Amelia clicked the lid closed, setting her hand on her forehead in concentration. She let her eyes settle on Elizabeth, waving her other hand in solidarity.

Elizabeth clenched her jaw and averted her eyes toward the sunlight glaring in the windows.

Amelia rocked back on her heels. "I apologize for my rudeness. I should've invited you both to use the spyglass with me yesterday."

"That's all right. I'm not sure how Elizabeth would take to it."

"She likes the view from up here, doesn't she?"

"Well enough."

Amelia beamed at him. "It's much better through the spyglass. Mr. Molt told me we'll be able to see more and more as we get closer to the coast of Europe."

"That sounds charming."

"I'll be up on the open deck this afternoon if you'd like to join me. Mr. Molt has given us free rein of the spyglass until we land."

Lewis' fingers fidgeted under the plates he held. "How thoughtful of you both. I'll talk to Elizabeth and find out if she's interested. At any rate, we're sure to see you up there. Elizabeth gets so much refreshment from the air."

"I'm glad. Have a good breakfast."

Lewis started around Amelia to his table.

His steadfast loyalty tugged at her heart, but Amelia pushed past the regret of deceiving him. "I know the eggs Florentine smells wonderful, Mr. Blakely, but remember your manners. Leave Mrs. Cole's food for her. There should be plenty left for you at the buffet if you want to try it."

Lewis replied with a kind but fleeting upturn of his lips. "I'll remember."

Chapter Thirteen

Amelia forced herself to peer through the spyglass and hold herself there. With the first half of the *Duchess'* journey over, she remained comfortable hovering above the middle of the Atlantic so long as she did not witness evidence of it. After spending her time before lunch memorizing maps in the first-deck lounge, she was confident she could point out the coasts of various countries to Lewis.

A slight discomfort gripped Amelia. Only by the drift of the spyglass' scenery did she realize the ship was gliding to one side. She lurched for the rail and grabbed onto it until the sensation subsided, returning her organs to their intended places. She shivered and dabbed the heel of her thumb against her forehead.

She did not hear anyone approach until a pair of shoes sounded on the deck floor twenty feet away. She hoped it was Lewis and not Darius, Elwood, Alvin, or anyone else she knew on board.

Lewis traipsed up to her with his hands in his pockets.

His presence without his other half added to Amelia's relief, but a flutter whispered in her chest. This was her first meeting with him entirely alone, and she took a deep breath to fuel her mission past that fact. She checked around Lewis in false dismay. "Where's Elizabeth?"

"She's not well."

Amelia let her enthusiasm fall. "Is she all right?"

"Her stomach mostly. She's confined herself to our room for the afternoon."

"I'm sorry to hear that. Did you alert the doctor?"

"She didn't want me to. She's sure it'll pass."

"I suppose the stairs are too much in her condition?"

"I presume so."

Amelia sighed, casting her eyes over the deck. "The fresh air would do her good if she could get to it. There are lounge chairs and everything."

Lewis lifted his heels off the floorboards and rocked them back into place. "She was adamant about her seclusion, but I wanted to honor your invitation to come to the deck. I promised I'd tell Elizabeth everything I saw when she recovers."

"I hope it's soon."

"Thank you. She might want to have a peek for herself before we disembark."

Amelia motioned to the spyglass and stepped back from it. "There's only Greenland and Iceland from the port side. If you keep the spyglass where I have it, you can see the coasts of Portugal and Spain, not that you can see details. There are some tiny islands several hundred miles to the south of us. They mostly read like green dots in a sea of blue from here."

"Are you well versed in the layout of the world, Miss Harlow?" Lewis set his eye to the spyglass.

"A little. I've done some traveling here and there. I brushed up on my geography with the maps on the lower decks before I came up here."

"I wish I'd seen more of the world."

Amelia offered him a gentle reminder. "You're traveling now."

"We're moving. That's different."

"Aren't you excited to move to France?"

Lewis nodded, holding the spyglass steady on its stand. "Have you ever been to France?"

Amelia sidestepped the question. "It's a beautiful country."

"Hopefully, wherever we settle, whoever lives around us won't be too current with news events from the States." Lewis straightened up, gesturing to the spyglass with a raise of his eyebrows.

Amelia shied away from it. "No, thank you."

Lewis returned to his bowed position and swiveled the instrument across the horizon.

He had seen to Elizabeth's comfort and needs that morning at breakfast as he always did. Amelia could well imagine him regaling her with every detail of his experiences once her nausea subsided. Genuine curiosity moved Amelia. "May I ask you something personal, Mr. Blakely?"

"What about?"

"Why do you always leave the dining room ahead of Mrs. Cole?"

A subtle blush rose in Lewis' cheeks. "Elizabeth asked me to shield her from anyone waiting to ambush or ogle her because of her past."

"That's a wise decision. I didn't mean to embarrass you."

"I only hate that false accusations ruin every part of our lives." Lewis stood up and stepped back from the lens.

Amelia crouched to view the sky through the spyglass. "I commend you for sticking by her all this time. The prison sounds like an awful place, and the newspapers must've been relentless about the whole thing."

"They were." Lewis' tense shoulders relaxed in her peripheral vision despite his urgent agreement. "They hounded us then, and they swarmed us again when she was paroled. The nightmare that started the night Arthur died never ended."

"How did you know what to do all those years?"

"Elizabeth told me who to talk to and how to do everything. When the police arrested her, I posted bail. When the jury convicted her of Arthur's killing, his sister fought the execution of his will. She insisted his estate shouldn't go to Elizabeth as he'd promised. But the judge showed sympathy to our case and said the law had already dealt Elizabeth all the punishment it saw fit to give her. That didn't sit well with the public, either."

Amelia blinked with sympathy.

Lewis rubbed his palms together. "After that, I met with Arthur's partners and sold his share of the banks. I won't repeat to you the names they unearthed to call me. I sold off most of his artifact collections and the furniture. Sold their brownstone in Manhattan and bought a smaller house in Ithaca where I could be closer to Elizabeth in prison."

Amelia's mouth popped open. "That was smaller?" She strengthened her composure and explained herself. "I remember the pictures in the paper."

"I didn't want to buy anything second rate in Elizabeth's name. I thought she deserved the kind of privacy that comes with a high bill." He shrugged. "Obviously, the press still found ways of sharing her freedom with the world."

Everything Elizabeth and Lewis had been through humbled Amelia. "She was lucky to have you." His letters to Elizabeth, the content of which Amelia had skipped over, must have helped her through many a hard and lonely night. Such a thick collection of them, some maybe even from before Arthur's death, guarded as treasured mementos. It was more romance than Amelia had ever trusted to exist. Knowing Lewis better now, she was sure the letters were sincere and compassionate, not maudlin or brimming with empty promises. "A lot of men would've moved on or taken advantage of her. Rented her house for profit or kept the proceeds of the sales and disappeared forever."

"None of that ever occurred to me."

Amelia's heart pulsed a double beat, romanticism reducing her response to a murmur. "Very lucky indeed."

"I think it'll take a long time for her to realize nobody's after her anymore. We're halfway across the ocean. What's done is done. Everybody who formed a strong opinion about her is thousands of miles away. There's nothing left but to move on."

"That's a wise sentiment." Amelia raised herself upright and faced Lewis. The sun glowed against his simple, boyish features. "I hope you find everything you've waited for. You're questing an awfully long way to find it."

Lewis gave a shallow bow of his head. "I never asked why you're going to France."

Amelia's chest hardened at the name. "I'm just traveling." She wished, as she had a thousand times, the airship were headed anywhere but France.

Lewis shuffled his shoes against the deck floor. "Perhaps Elizabeth and I will do some sightseeing once we're there. I wonder what summers at the coast are like."

"I don't know much about the coast," Amelia admitted.

There was nothing she could do about where the airship docked, and Amelia accepted that. She would not loiter long once she arrived there, anyway.

Chapter Fourteen

Amelia made her way down the hall toward the dining room, a thick flow of fellow passengers ahead of her. She slowed her pace in the open area around the stairs, realizing she could not reach it any faster than the others were willing to move. She backtracked to linger at the end of her cabin's corridor.

Lewis' voice seemed welcome and familiar to her now. "I've got you."

Elizabeth's weary one surprised her. "A little soup will do me wonders."

Amelia stayed out of their way, half obscured behind the corner. When Lewis noticed her and waved, Amelia returned it, pleased with any measure of progress. Her chest warmed to see him. His kindness was an unexpected reassurance, and chatting about New York made it seem much closer to her. Amidst all the passengers excited about their mutual adventure, Amelia had not counted on meeting anyone else who yearned for home.

Darius strolled out of the same hallway moments later. Amelia abandoned her daydreams and hissed to alert him to her presence. He circled on his heel and joined Amelia around the corner.

"What have you got?" His eyes sparkled.

"Now's the time to take the earrings," Amelia whispered. Guilt tugged at her lungs, but she pushed it aside. "Lewis just escorted Elizabeth into the dining room for dinner."

"As much as I'd love to grab them as soon as possible, don't you think it's too soon?" Darius rested his shoulder against the wall. "She's got days left to notice they're gone."

"She won't notice," Amelia insisted. "She's got a box packed with jewels in there."

Darius inclined towards her. "Have you seen Mrs. Cole? Dazzling with diamonds every single day. She's going to notice, and what then? There's a purser on board, at least two security guards, and a quite able-bodied staff to back her up in hunting for it."

Amelia set her hand on her hip. "They raised no army for Mr. Wallace's expensive pocket watch. How much trouble do you think they'll go through for a convicted murderess who could've misplaced the earrings herself? That's supposing she trusts anybody enough to go to them with a problem."

Darius paused, the anger releasing from his face. "You've got a point. But what if the missing jewels make her suspicious? We don't need her locking everything up even tighter."

"She wouldn't."

"Why not?"

Amelia gauged the determination in Darius' eyes and finally offered a piece of her garnered information. "She'd blame Lewis before anybody else."

Darius blew out a breath of exasperation. "What are you talking about? They're inseparable. He does everything for her, and he'd probably do anything she asked if she discovered there was a problem. That's ridiculous."

"They have weaknesses." Amelia tried to convince Darius with the least number of facts. "They don't always get along, and they don't approach life with the same spirit."

Darius scratched the back of his head beneath his hat. "We'll try it your way." He corrected his posture, and the old veneration sparked in his eyes. "I know you sometimes see things I don't."

Amelia rushed to fill him in the rest of the way. "Elizabeth was ill earlier. I don't know if she'll stay in the dining room a long time finishing her soup or if she'll race to get out."

"Leave everything to me. If I hear their key in the lock, I know where to hide."

Amelia's jaw ticked. "I'll be in the ballroom after dinner. You can seek me out there when you're done."

Darius lifted her hand and kissed the back of it. He walked away toward the front of the ship, and Amelia strode off in the other direction.

She could hardly enjoy her Parisian chicken, roasted to golden perfection with white wine and shallots. Her colorful Creole gumbo, full of seafood, vegetables, and spices failed to move her. Buttered green beans came nowhere close to exciting her. Even her silken, indulgent vanilla ice cream left her lukewarm.

Deep, raucous laughter erupted at the next table. The spiritualists tossed their heads back in enjoyment, Alvin standing over them, awash in satisfaction. He met Amelia's eyes and parted from their table.

He directed his high spirits at her, a bowtie completing his sleek, black evening suit. "Are you coming up to the ballroom tonight?"

Amelia assumed Alvin was only seeking fun there. As usual, she hid a second motive. "Yes."

He bounced his palm off the back of the vacant chair in front of him. "Splendid. See you there."

Amelia dawdled in finishing her meal. She stood up at the same time as the spiritualists and preceded them out of the dining room. She climbed the stairs to the second deck and floated straight into the room on her left.

As large as the first-floor lounge, the ballroom tapered in an identical curve as it expanded toward the front of the ship. Two elegant chandeliers dazzled from the ceiling. Gold wallpaper accented in flourishes of jade green wrapped the space in elegance. In the far left-hand corner, a small chamber orchestra composed of two violins, a viola, one cello, and a piano produced long, repeated notes. All of the musicians were draped in black like elegant shadows. Closer to Amelia, several couches lined the walls. The French couple sat close together, murmuring back and forth. Edwin, Iris, and Priscilla perched near them.

Priscilla's muted soprano spoke up. "Why do musicians do that? Play the same notes over and over?"

Edwin supplied a boisterous answer. "They're tuning notes. Changes in temperature loosen the strings, and they need to be tightened to ensure each song sounds the way it should."

"But pianos don't have strings."

Edwin tilted his head, kindness curving his thick lips. "Not on the outside."

She grinned and ducked her chin.

Amelia stepped in further. On her right, halfway along the inner wall of the room, stood the bar.

Alvin propped his elbow on the dark wood surface, supporting his weight on it. "A rusty nail sounds like something that should send you straight into the hospital."

The bartender poured tequila into a cocktail shaker.

Alvin mulled over the wall of shelves behind the bar, filled with bottles cradling all colors of spirits. "Sherry flip reminds me of an impudent woman."

"Ha!" The bartender traded the tequila bottle for vodka. "What's your opinion on a velvet hammer?"

Alvin gave the slightest pause. "An argument carried out in whispers."

The bartender cackled and took a bottle of gin off a shelf behind him, its red-and-gold label making it recognizable anywhere.

Amelia sat down on a sofa to wait, the emerald silk fabric decorated with a pattern of golden crests.

The cellist plucked one string several times, similar notes sliding up and down.

Edwin winced, turning away from the musicians. "That's still a little sharp." His tone rippled with understanding.

"How can you tell?" Priscilla asked. "Just by listening? That's remarkable."

Iris sighed, casting slow blinks at the far wall. "He's pulling your leg, Priscilla."

Edwin puffed up his chest and adjusted his monocle beneath undulations of his thick eyebrow. "I trained at the Peabody Institute in Baltimore, Mrs. Coates. I can tell by listening when a note is sharp, in tune, or flat. If I can't, I hope I'll receive a partial refund of my substantial tuition there."

Priscilla's bright eyes wondered at Iris. "Haven't you heard of perfect pitch? I bet Edwin has that."

Sarcasm grated in Iris' long throat. "With an ego and a mouth to match. Only the musicians need perfect pitch, not him."

The musicians' notes and scales stopped one by one. The spiritualists, standing on the other side of the French doors from Amelia, applauded.

Alvin arrived in front of her. "May I have the first waltz, Miss Harlow?" He lowered his torso in a genteel bow over his arm.

"Of course."

Footsteps echoed in the near end of the ballroom as couples formed and fell into proper hold. Amelia stood up, her chest lifting out of practice, freeing up her breathing. She rested her left hand on Alvin's arm, letting him clasp her other hand. She kept her upper arms even to the floor, and Alvin slipped his free hand around to her left shoulder blade. They tilted their right sides toward each other, remaining near enough to talk.

Light chuckling filled the corner behind Amelia. She could imagine the spiritualists enjoying their obvious pairs – Luther and Celia, Harold and Lorena. Unless Edwin had invited Priscilla to twirl with him and she was tickled to accept.

The pianist picked up a slow, elegant melody. Amelia and Alvin began to move, Amelia stepping back in the mirror image of Alvin's gliding forward. Their steps and slides formed box shapes as they circled counter-clockwise to the swelling crescendos of chords and chiming keys. The piano pranced and strutted, the string instruments singing with it in light, sweeping notes.

Alvin strode forward too soon, and his shoe kicked Amelia's. He blushed. "Sorry. I dance for the fun of it, obviously, not to show off any technical skill."

"It's all right." As Amelia rotated, she could see the other couples spread across the inner end of the ballroom. The French couple flowed with effortless motion. Luther and Celia beamed even when they averted their eyes from each other. Edwin, Iris, and Priscilla remained on the sofa, providing an audience to the rest of the passengers.

Edwin sank back against the cushion, his eyebrows rising. "Brahms. Opus thirty-nine. Number fifteen. I'd know it anywhere."

Secure in Alvin's arms, Amelia floated away from the others as the tune lifted and soared. "Are you interested in attempts at flight, Mr. Burgess? What brings you on board?"

Alvin met her eyes for a moment. "Same thing as everybody, I suppose. The chance to get away, to experience something new. Isn't that why you're here?"

Amelia distilled her intentions to their purest form. "I'm looking for a new start, to be sure."

"What waits for you at home when you return?"

Amelia pushed images of her parents and their cozy, sprawling house out of her mind. "There's not much keeping me in the States. I'll probably stay abroad for a while in one country or another."

"So you've done a fair amount of traveling before?"

"Yes."

"And you enjoy it?"

"For the most part."

Alvin lunged to the side to catch up with the music. "Do you always travel alone?"

Amelia wondered how much Alvin had been watching her. "I prefer to travel alone."

"I've been thinking of trying it myself."

What would Alvin do on his own? Continue picking pockets and honing in on old ladies' reticules? Amelia could not discern his motives or his goals.

The song trailed off like a slowing music box into one final reverberating, tranquil note. Amelia and Alvin stopped moving as the orchestra burst into a more grandiose, dramatic opus.

Alvin tossed his head up. "Strauss. *Voices of Spring.* Even I recognize it. Shall we dance again?"

"Of course." Amelia was not sure whether she agreed more out of personal enjoyment or perplexity.

The music steadied into a rhythmic, frolicking pace. Amelia and Alvin repeated the same steps and rotations to the melodic, skipping tune of the violins.

"Are you returning to America soon?" Amelia asked.

Alvin hesitated. "I haven't decided yet."

"Did you buy a return ticket or not?"

"No. I can always buy one if I need it, right?"

Amelia gave no answer. She wondered if Alvin intended to rob her, but aside from her jewelry, she carried nothing of value on her person. Would he try for her pockets anyway? A bold maneuver in a dance where she could feel where both of his hands should be – one on her upper back and the other secured in hers.

Alvin made no move toward mischief. He responded to a crescendo in the music by letting her pass in a full, guided spin beneath his arm. Amelia pursed her lips, impressed and flying on the skipping of the instruments. Regaining their hold, he stumbled and corrected his posture.

Amelia caught a glimpse of Luther talking to Celia as they danced. "Do you know if Mr. Wallace found his missing pocket watch yet?"

Alvin's questioning sound barked like a startled grunt. "What?"

"Mr. Wallace over there with the brown hair and moustache. His timepiece got away from him."

"I..." Alvin gulped. "I didn't realize."

"Expensive little gem," Amelia added, putting on the pressure. "It's hard to imagine a thief riding on board with us, but he's had several people rummaging for it."

"It must've gotten kicked under a sofa or something," Alvin murmured.

"He's explored high and low for it."

Alvin shifted his neck in his black bowtie and white shirt collar. "It must be a thief, then. Any idea who it is?" He craned his neck to see the others in the room.

"An incredibly silly person," Amelia answered. "We're fifteen hundred feet above the Atlantic. There's nowhere for him to hide and only forty small cabins to dig through for it."

The flowing violins led the song into a more demure, light-hearted passage.

"What makes you think it's a man?" Alvin tilted his head at the other dancers. "Luther's gotten cozier and cozier with Celia. Maybe she lifted it."

"Maybe," Amelia played along.

"Or a member of the staff. Why should they offer to come in and tidy our rooms? It's only a six-day voyage. I can make my bed by myself." Alvin entertained his characteristic bright, broad smile. "I'm a big boy now, despite my inability to see a dance through without trouncing my partner."

Amelia inclined towards him. "You're doing fine."

The music swelled, flooding the ballroom with sharp, energetic interchanges of violins and bass.

A solemn breath huffed out of Alvin. "I can't wait until we land."

"You're not enjoying the ship?"

Surprise flashed in Alvin's cornflower-blue eyes. "The ship's all right. I guess I prefer solid ground under me instead of metal, wood, and air."

"It's a change, isn't it?" Amelia agreed. The music surged with liveliness and the upbeat soaring of the violins. "Perhaps we should just enjoy what we have, Mr. Burgess. Good music, good company, and good health."

"And good spirits." Alvin licked his lips. "Have you ever had a jubilee cocktail? Very tasty."

"Did you ever think that drinking and dancing might be the reason why you stumble?"

"Never." He winked. "And even if it was, it wouldn't stop me from combining them. It's best to distract yourself from life with not just one vice but two at a time. Much more effective."

Amelia wanted to ask Alvin what he needed distracting from when Darius drifted through the doorway. Instead, she gave in to her enjoyment of Alvin's cheeky philosophies and devoted herself more fully to the art of the waltz. She dipped lower on her forward and backward steps, lifting higher on her toes as she arced left and right. The music picked up with her movements into a rollicking pace.

"You're really quite good." Alvin wondered at her beneath raised eyebrows. "I was under the impression you didn't do this very often."

"Not much these days," Amelia admitted. She sought out Darius, who leaned against one side of the wide door frame. His brooding eyes followed her every movement, neither loose nor sharp. "It's been a few years since someone led me around the dance floor."

"I find you so mysterious, Miss Harlow."

"And I you."

The music exploded into grand, swift melodies. Amelia floated on every one. The romantic runs of soprano violins added further bounce and energy to their dance.

The stiff angles of Alvin's arms relaxed, and his straight back took on a more casual stacking. "I could waltz with you all night."

A white-gloved hand landed on his black sleeve, and Amelia faced the newly arrived Darius. He fixed his eyes on Alvin. "May I cut in?" he asked, more of a warning than a question open for debate.

Alvin's gaze flicked to Amelia. "Sure." His confidence faltered. "I could use another drink. Do you want me to order one for you, Miss Harlow?"

Amelia's earnest fun having spoiled, she kept her cool. "No, thank you." She had expected Darius' jealous approach but thought he might wait out the rest of the song.

The lively, promenading music continued without their participation.

Alvin pointed a low finger halfway to Amelia. "Save me a dance for later?"

"Yes," Amelia replied.

Directing another frown at Darius, Alvin walked away toward the bar. Darius slid into Alvin's place, clamping one hand around Amelia's and resting the other on the small of her back. Darius took his first forward step, and Amelia moved with him, the familiar intuition of the way they danced together.

Amelia's heart beat faster, swaying in the slow and even swirl of the dance until its final fast, triumphant bars. The crescendo concluded in several loud, unified notes of exclamation. Several people applauded from the corner of the room. Amelia stilled her limbs, her chest heaving with quick breaths, Darius holding her closer than Alvin had dared to.

The pianist began a slow, haunting melody graced by muted, bewitching chords. Darius returned to the waltz, Amelia gliding with him in perfect time.

"Moonlight Sonata," Edwin spoke up. "Of course, it wasn't called that until after Beethoven's death. He wrote it in 1801, one hundred years ago this very year."

Darius directed Amelia away from the others. The strings joined the piano, adding even more morose beauty to the tune. "Do you remember how many times we've danced to this?"

Amelia tried not to and gave no answer.

"All the different countries?" Darius' murmuring pursued. "England. Austria. Germany. France."

"How could I forget?" Amelia offered, tense at his presence but offhanded against his talk.

"I've always preferred the Viennese waltz to its western cousin. It's more formal, faster, directed. Less like a crowded barnyard."

Amelia ran through a quick count of the others in the room. "There aren't that many people in here."

Additional couples had filled in the dance floor, but plenty of room existed between them.

"Do you remember what we danced to in Vienna?" Darius prompted.

The tune popped into Amelia's head on cue. Blasts of horns of the orchestra followed by graceful, subtle violins. *"Be Embraced, You Millions!"* Amelia spoke the name.

"When it was almost new," Darius reminded her. "What great fortune we had to be in Vienna that year."

It was 1893, the year before the fire in Prague, but Amelia did not say it.

Darius' focus loosened. "No one hosts a ball like the Viennese."

"Perfectly lovely," Amelia had to agree. Gigantic ballrooms with lavish, gold accents lining every doorway and the top of every wall. In between stood grandly detailed paintings with life-sized subjects. Grandiose chandeliers cascaded in glittering crystals, supporting dozens of flames apiece. Jewels bedecked the women's upswept hair. They modeled dresses in bold canary yellow and serene turquoise silks adorned with white lace that graced their collar bones, sometimes leaving their shoulders bare. The men, occasionally in military dress, carried themselves with dignified, suave postures.

It was a year in which Amelia had known Darius to be a devil but had at least believed they stood on even ground. She had trusted him, albeit loosely. Enjoyed his presence. Fallen for him anew in the short time they played against each other in Vienna. Twirled and conspired across the dance floor for hours before slipping off into the night to devour each other in a shadowed garden.

As beautiful as these memories were, made even larger and richer by the passage of time, the accident in Prague burned them out. The first whiffs of smoke offended her nose as she stood alone in her hotel room. Expecting Darius back any moment, she waited for him until shouts and screams in the hallway roused her to action. This was no passing kitchen fire or cigarette singe. Dark smoke crawled along the white ceiling, and Amelia raced to dunk one of her scarves in the water pitcher on the dresser. She plastered it over her nose and mouth as she dashed into the corridor. Several people sprinted past her. One of the women hunched over, squealing in fear, tears streaking down her round cheeks. Amelia jogged around her, but the woman's fingers seized Amelia's arm.

"Where's Hector?" Her shriek split Amelia's eardrums.

Amelia shook her head to keep from using up oxygen as the smoke sank lower around her.

"What's this?" The woman grabbed Amelia's scarf. "What do you know that I don't?"

Amelia tugged to free herself. Thirty feet of hallway remained for her to run to achieve the staircase. Black smoke billowed up its opening.

"Give it to me!" The woman jerked on the trailing end of the scarf, scratching and kicking Amelia.

The scarf lunged away from Amelia's face. The woman slapped her in the temple before Amelia had a chance to kick back. The stranger pounded her with a tight fist, buckling Amelia as her head throbbed. Flames roared and crackled as they ate away the top of the stairs. The woman sprinted the other way.

Amelia's deep breaths of shock and exertion let the enveloping smoke rub her throat raw. She choked on it, fighting the needling lightheadedness to follow the other guests fleeing the stairs. The gold walls and pale floor tipped and swam around her, dim and fuzzy. She stumbled, passing out before she took more than a dozen steps.

Amelia woke up in more pain than had ever seized her. Searing nerves screamed across her face, and when Amelia howled for real, her throat burned, producing hoarse, raspy wind. Nausea rolled through her stomach, making her cringe at the waves of rising discomfort.

Nurses explained the floor had caught fire beneath her, burning her face and singeing her hair before someone pulled her out of the inferno.

Amelia managed to repeat one begging word over and over. "Chloroform."

In between the nurses' doses, she inquired about Darius. Pain and worry drove her to hysterics. Was he in the hospital? Nurses assured her he was not. Had he been carried away dead? Nurses brought in the newspaper for days and read her articles about the blaze while she recovered between Dr. Petzel's surgeries. None of Darius' aliases surfaced.

Amelia seethed. She cried and winced at the pain igniting her skin every moment she lay awake.

And for the next seven years, one question persisted. Did Darius walk away innocent, or did he leave her there to die?

His face provided a wall now, guarding his secrets. She let her accusations and bitterness shine through, her eyes piercing his stronghold.

The façade tempered as if he could read her thoughts. "They wouldn't let me back in. To the hotel."

"When?" she asked. "When did you try?"

The pianist struck the final haunting chord. As it died out, Amelia and Darius stopped circling. She meant to pull away, but his hand gripped hers.

He bent his head next to her ear. "I have the earrings."

"Good."

"Piece one of three is in place."

"Now we just have to wait."

A few taps landed on Amelia's upraised arm. Alvin offered her a dazzling, uninhibited gleam despite Darius' intrusive proximity.

The strings took up a playful, trilling tune accented by rousing chords of the piano.

Amelia relaxed her shoulders. "You're just in time. I have one more good waltz in me before I retire for the night."

"Lucky me," Alvin said.

Darius tensed his fingers against Amelia's back before he withdrew. He walked away toward the open doors to the hall.

"Friend of yours?" Alvin resumed his position mimicking Amelia's and took her hand. He settled his other palm in a light hold on her upper back.

"No." Amelia peeled her attention off Darius and placed it squarely on the young man in front of her. "Not a friend."

Chapter Fifteen

Amelia reclined on her bed, combing through the newspaper Claudia had given her three days before. In the rush of reaching and boarding the *Duchess*, Amelia had drifted away from the current happenings of her native country. A third-page article grabbed her attention entitled *Second Rematch Earns a Different Ending*.

A mere fourteen years ago, President Grover Cleveland's untimely death boosted Thomas Bayard from secretary of state into the limelight of the White House. Every election that's followed has driven us to the fronts of our seats.

No one alive will forget the divisive results of 1888 when President Bayard ran for re-election. Championing consumers won him the popular vote, but his loss of New York's electoral votes cinched the presidency for Benjamin Harrison. Other former presidents might have stayed home rather than endure once more the hard work and wide exposure of campaigning for the country's highest office. But Mr. Bayard rose to the challenge and reclaimed his prior title, several states tinting blue to support him. (An outcome many have lauded since President Bayard's diplomatic ways here and abroad no doubt stemmed the overwhelming economic crisis the following year.)

With the Bayard-Harrison rivalry scored at one to one, America sat poised for a new pair of competitors. Robert Pattison of Pennsylvania spurned suggestions of running for a senate seat, jumping from state governor into the 1896 presidential race. When the dust settled after many an argument about unemployment and workers' strikes, Mr. Pattison stood triumphant. And who could help but entertain the deepest levels of intrigue four years later when President Pattison went toe to toe with William McKinley for a second round? Would history repeat itself with a split record, or would President Pattison win back-to-back terms? In the president's own words, any lesser Democratic candidate might have lost the election against Mr. McKinley's iron platform. (A jab against former nominee William Bryan, perhaps? Whom President Pattison had once called "a sure loser" for the run of '96.)

Two months ago, we saw President Pattison sworn in, and he's already continuing his trademark pushes toward railroad reform and reduced national debt.

A quick rapping on the door snapped Amelia out of the article. Even if the visitor was Alvin or Claudia, Amelia had no wish for aimless chat.

"Miss Harlow," Darius hissed through the door.

Only his urgency, raw and real, made Amelia jump off the bed. She scurried to the door and swung it open several inches.

Darius kept his volume at a whisper. "You'll want to hear this. You were right. The lovebirds are tearing each other apart. Well..." He smirked. "Mama bird's dealing most of the damage."

Amelia's heart ached as she tossed the paper on the bed. She followed Darius down the outer corridor and around the corner toward Elizabeth and Lewis' room. Sharp undertones punctured the air from several doors away.

"You took them." Elizabeth's high pitch wielded a razor's edge. "You know Arthur gave them to me, that they were special to me."

Confusion warped Lewis' response. "I haven't seen them in ages. Why would I take them?"

"Because you wanted me to leave him," Elizabeth blasted back.

Darius nodded to the bench outside the women's lavatory catty-corner from Elizabeth and Lewis' room. Amelia sank down on it while Darius settled onto the bench across from her.

Incredulity strained Lewis' timbre. "I never said that."

"But you thought it. I know you did. We were always sneaking around. Lying to everyone. Fear plagued me every night I slept next to Arthur and every breakfast we ate together. I was terrified he'd find out about us and what he'd do."

"But I didn't take anything from you. Then or now."

"You're a fool, Elizabeth," she admonished herself. "A silly fool." She exploded anew. "You were hoping I wouldn't notice, weren't you?"

"No!"

"Those earrings were buried a little because I hadn't worn them. If I didn't knock this off the dresser, I wouldn't have noticed they were gone until we were in Bordeaux." Elizabeth paused. "That's it, isn't it? You were going to leave me once we landed."

"That's ridiculous."

Lewis' desperation crushed Amelia's chest.

"When did you take them?" Elizabeth demanded.

A young couple entered the hall from the open area but changed direction to hustle toward the other corridor.

Lewis' volume rose. "I didn't."

Elizabeth drilled him. "When I was sick? When you left my side to keep an appointment with that woman?"

Amelia's organs cringed for Lewis and herself.

"Miss Harlow has nothing to do with this, and neither do I," Lewis countered.

Darius' eyes inspected Amelia, judging her, boring into her. She maintained her composure.

"Why does she keep talking to us?" Elizabeth asked. "To you?"

"She's a friendly person. It doesn't spell foul play. Miss Harlow even told me, unsolicited, she believes you're innocent."

Elizabeth did not answer.

"Maybe it was the same person who took Mr. Wallace's pocket watch."

"No. He's out around people every time I see him. I don't understand how anybody could've gotten in our room, and my jewelry has been in here since we took off."

"Are you sure you didn't lose them before we left Ithaca?"

Elizabeth shrieked at him. "Arthur gave me those earrings, and I made damn sure I had them before we left!"

Lewis' comeback shriveled. "I can't believe you think I'd take advantage of you while you were ill."

Elizabeth's words ran cold. "Somebody robbed me, Lewis, and the worst of it is, you know what stealing means to me. It's the only reason a stranger would've been in my house, the reason Arthur was murdered. There's only one other person who uses this room. Not even housekeepers have been in here. I requested no staff come in this cabin."

Lewis met her with meekness. "Maybe you're mistaken. They could've bounced under the dresser."

The meat of a fist pounded on wood. "I've checked everywhere! How easy do you think it is to misplace two huge ruby-and-diamond earrings? They're nicer than anything you ever gave me. Get out of my room. My husband's fortune paid for it. Go! I don't want to see you again tonight."

Amelia leapt off the bench and strode toward her room before the first jiggles of the metal door handle. Darius sped along right on her heels.

"What now?" he asked under his breath.

"We wait for their next move."

Darius shot off into the short hall leading to the dining room, and Amelia curved away in the opposite direction. She returned to her cabin and picked up the paper. She dropped into a chair at bedside to give Lewis a little time to unwind. Then, she would make moves of her own.

Chapter Sixteen

Dreamy chamber music floated down from the floor above as Amelia left her room. The hallway stood empty, its residents enjoying themselves elsewhere or retired to bed early. Amelia tiptoed down the corridor toward the stairs, listening for any clues of where Lewis had gone.

She drifted past the staircase, finding no one in the parlor or the hallway she had last heard him in. Amelia intended to ascend to the second deck when ice cubes clinked in a glass. Although the lights spread a dim haze through the dining room, the tinkling emerged from inside.

Amelia crept toward the open door. When she recognized Elizabeth sitting in the near-darkness one table to her right, she wished she had ignored the innocent taps.

Elizabeth sat in full dress. A feathered hat above her black, braided hair. Glinting jewels dripping from her earlobes, neck, and wrists. White tailored jacket and silver dress. Her eyes stared off across the room, a glass tumbler graced with caramel-colored liquid supported in her hand.

Amelia took a step back to leave the woman in peace.

Elizabeth spoke, pinning her in place. "Have you ever really felt alone?"

Her detached monotone unnerved Amelia. She took a smaller step back toward the stairs.

Elizabeth sipped her liquor. "Do you know what it's like to live a life no one sees?"

Amelia stopped moving. She owed Elizabeth. She had slipped into her cavernous house to steal from her husband and neglected to stop his murder when she witnessed his attack. She never came forward to clarify Elizabeth's innocence, and she had boarded the *Duchess* with less-than-pure intentions of completing her botched robbery. She had stalked Elizabeth and Lewis their entire three and a half days in the air.

Amelia inched forward to the doorway. "I know both."

Elizabeth's eyes showed little recognition of Amelia's admittance, just a subtle change in their yellow highlights. "I've never been truly alone until now. Lewis has always been there. At least, in some way."

Amelia spoke, almost under her breath. "What really happened that night?"

"The night I murdered my husband, although I was clear across Manhattan at the time?" Elizabeth gave a wry twist of her lips, but her haughtiness faded. "When I met Arthur, he was just an errand boy for his banker father. He wasn't even sure he wanted to go into his father's business. All those papers and coins. They didn't mean anything to Arthur. Yet."

Elizabeth slurped her drink, and Amelia eased through the doorway. She sat down at the nearest table and faced Elizabeth.

"First, he decided to learn the business." Elizabeth's story picked up speed and emotion. "After we were married, things kept changing. Arthur's closest friend, the explorer, Theodore Stockell, left for his first expedition to Africa. When he came back with stories and discoveries, everyone treated him as a hero." She sighed, lowering her scrutiny to the contents of her glass. "It altered Arthur forever."

Elizabeth's silence unraveled until Amelia surprised herself by prompting her forward. "How?"

"He became obsessed with money." Elizabeth flicked her eyebrows up in emphasis of her disapproval. "He spent more and more time at the banks. Talking to his father. Learning everything he could. Meeting and appeasing anyone who could further his career.

"But it didn't make him happy." Elizabeth frowned at her melting ice cubes and downed the rest of the liquid. "He was overworked. Exhausted. Any little noise or imperfection threw him into a rage."

Elizabeth set her glass on the table. Her strength wavered with raw regret. "It wasn't the life I wanted. He hired servants to do everything around the house." She shook her head. "The sheer number of them made me uncomfortable just to pass them in the hallway, let alone when they'd speak to me. Always wanting to know what they should do next or if I needed their help. They wouldn't leave me alone."

Amelia cut in. "How did you meet Lewis?"

"I started going out by myself. Arthur gave me my own carriage. The house was lonely for me. How much worse could the city streets be for me? But the boroughs were kind to me. Manhattan embraced me. There was fresh air for my lungs and shopkeepers to talk to. I drove farther and farther from home until I found myself in Brooklyn. It was a hot day, and relief filled me to see an ice cream vendor with his cart in the street."

Elizabeth fought a smile. "It was Lewis in his cap and suit. Other than the children around us, he had no one else to scoop ice cream for, so we talked. He was much the same way then as he was when he stepped on this ship. At least, as far as I could see. He was performing a lower job than any Arthur had ever worked, but he didn't care. Lewis was simple. Generous. Willing to spend more time talking to me than Arthur had in years."

Amelia glimpsed Lewis through Elizabeth's eyes, knowing exactly what had made Elizabeth adore him. The unspoiled optimism. Legitimate charity. Easy-going hospitality.

Elizabeth drew her gloved finger around the rim of her glass, falling solemn again. "I always worried Arthur would find out about the affair. I don't think he ever did. He would've mentioned it to me if he'd entertained any suspicions. My comings and goings were already so common, the servants didn't notice anything new. I was careful to the point of paranoid when I met with Lewis. Planning everything. Meeting in neighborhoods where nobody knew me." She sat up straighter. "But you asked about the night that changed everything."

Amelia laid her hands on the clean white fabric covering the table. "I've read the papers. I know what the prosecution claimed."

Elizabeth slid a silver pin free from her hat and set them both on the table. Her extra poise and polish went with them. She could have been any woman Amelia had ever spoken to. "I was at a hotel with Lewis, like I always said. I feared his neighbors would spread rumors or try to find out who I was if we always met where he lived. I left, torn as usual. My heart stayed with Lewis, but my duty was at home, by Arthur's side."

Amelia shifted in her seat, images of Elizabeth's illicit night with Lewis trying to conjure in her brain. She fended them off.

Elizabeth met Amelia with a stronger connection. "I sometimes wondered whether his reputation would survive a divorce, but I doubted it. I struggled with it." She glided her glass across the tablecloth in aimless swirls. "I wasn't eager to arrive home that night, so I spent a few hours by myself, driving the streets of Manhattan. The worst I had to worry about out there were drunken men and the stench of horse manure. I came home, and the servants were screaming."

She pried her hand off the glass and set it over her face, thumb at her temple and fingers bridged over her eyes. "I can hear them every time I think of it. I opened the door, and even from downstairs, I heard them shrieking with horror."

Amelia winced. The most she had heard from the servants were complaints about the head maid, confirmations that certain chores had been completed, and invitations to take a break.

Elizabeth exhaled, lowering her arm to the tabletop. "I told the truth, thinking it would save me. Lewis had several people to confirm his whereabouts, but since I'd been trying to conceal who I was, I had no one. The drunks who sang and vomited in the streets weren't going to remember me or my carriage passing by them. Lewis vouched I'd been with him earlier that night, but even he only had my word that I didn't ride straight home and kill my husband.

"My lawyer did a good job." Elizabeth tapped one foot on the carpet. "He was a fantastic speaker, and he told the jury everything about my state of mind. He reconstructed that night for them, how I spent some time in quiet contemplation before arriving home to mayhem and murder. There were too many different fingerprints on the rifle to exonerate me using Francis Galton's analysis on shapes and patterns." Elizabeth tapped the fingertips of one hand against her thumb. "Everyone who visited Arthur at home wanted to touch his collection. I had no idea where that rope came from. My lawyer proposed the murderer was a thief who brought the rope to tie up any meddling servants. They sat cloistered together in the kitchen, gossiping or drinking or playing cards. Instead, the thief alerted Arthur, reading in his study. The thief had to fight his way out, grabbing whatever he could get his hands on. Those African guns barely worked when they were loaded, so Arthur didn't bother. He just liked them on display because they were gifts from Theodore."

Elizabeth tipped the tumbler towards her but frowned at its emptiness. "Some of the jury believed him. I could see sympathy or doubt in some of their faces. But every time a

witness proved the prosecutor's version of the story..."
Elizabeth dropped the glass' bottom onto the tabletop. "It killed
every chance I ever had."

The full reality of Elizabeth's night with Lewis forced
Amelia's jealousy into check.

Elizabeth's eyes sharpened. "He was tough. A little man
with a monumental ego driving him to win. He constructed a
scenario in which I left Lewis that night tired of keeping up our
charade. He insisted I flew home on the devil's wings with the
singular intent of murdering Arthur. With the servants
distracted, all I had to do was return home a second time and
feign surprise at his violent death. The prosecution beat that
story into the jurors' heads until there was no hope for my
professions of innocence. He claimed if I could lie to my
husband, my family, and my friends for a year, I could commit
perjury to the jury for a few months. He paraded my friends,
my neighbors, my sisters, my servants up to the stand. They
attested to Arthur's declining interest in anything but the
banks and his worsening disposition." She pushed her glass
away. "Once the jury saw Lewis sitting there, twenty-one and
insisting on my innocence, they bought everything the
prosecutor sold them. What woman wouldn't trade a business-
obsessed ogre for a gentleman, even a poor one?"

Amelia's question almost stuck in her throat. "They didn't
entertain enough doubt to acquit you?"

Elizabeth reposed against her chair. "He destroyed my
credibility the way a bored child obliterates the sandcastle he
spent hours building. There was nothing I could say to defend
myself, so I quit trying."

She slouched down as much as her corset and dress would
allow her. "My silence convinced the jury I'd been lying, but in
the end, it served me well. No matter what the papers or
gossips say, I caused no trouble as an inmate. I served my time

with the most dignity they would allow me, which was a mere sliver of what I enjoyed in my free life. I kept my anger and my despisement inside. It would've done me no good to show anyone a violent or unsteady temperament." Her upper lip rippled. "Who did I have to talk to in there, anyway? Most of them had committed crimes before. Uneducated. Dangerous. Conniving. Yet I pitied them because we were all in there together at the mercy of the guards." Elizabeth swiped her fingertips under her eye although no tear had fallen. "I'm out now, and it's over. *That* part of it, anyway."

Elizabeth pushed herself up in her chair, drawing the empty glass closer to her. "Do you realize this is the first time in nine years I haven't known where Lewis is? He's always told me where he was or where he'll be. Working, pushing the ice cream cart. Washing his laundry. Waiting for me. I have no idea where he is, except that he's on this ship."

"And that's why you feel alone," Amelia guessed.

"No." Elizabeth's tone flattened. "To leave everything I've ever known behind except for Lewis, and to have him betray me a thousand feet above the middle of the ocean. That's what true loneliness is."

Amelia sorted through all the different things she could say. The paralyzing shock of her own first betrayal. The agony and heart-wrenching solitude that burdened her every step between the hotel fire and sitting in that chair in the dim dining room with a woman she had only spoken to in passing. Seventeen years without seeing her parents or former acquaintances, letters sent from all corners of the world dying out long before the altering blaze.

In a stranger world – perhaps a better, more civilized world – Elizabeth could have become Amelia's greatest friend. In the world that existed, Amelia stood up and walked out of the dining room. Elizabeth, true to her past, said nothing, and Amelia started up the stairs to the upper decks.

Chapter Seventeen

In the descending twilight of the open deck, one figure leaned forward against the railing, gripping his hat in his hands. Amelia almost did not go to him. He deserved his privacy, his time alone to sort out the ugly things Elizabeth had launched at him.

Amelia let the French door close with a muted thud behind her.

"Oh." Lewis straightened up, arranging his grey trilby on his head. He patted a handkerchief to his face and tucked it away. "Miss Harlow. How's your evening?"

"I don't want to talk about mine." Amelia's heart ached for him as she strolled towards him. "I heard you got into a fight with Elizabeth."

He hung his head and turned away. "That. Is everybody talking about it already?"

"Not everybody." Amelia stopped at the rail beside him.

"The sunset's hard to see from here." He gestured to the back of the ship. "It'll be completely dark soon."

Amelia obliged him by sharing the view. Beyond the widest berth of the ship, mauve streaks gave way to blazing, cherry-red clouds and orange sky. "It's beautiful."

"They erected the Statue of Liberty in New York Harbor when I was fourteen. It took the workers months to assemble it. The platform was already there waiting for it, and I was, too. As long as I lived in Brooklyn, I used to watch the sun sink down behind that massive icon."

His longing spread to Amelia. "And in Ithaca?"

"No statue. I saw the sun set over the neighbor's house if I caught it at all."

"You must miss New York."

"More than anything. You're not from the city, though, are you?"

Amelia hesitated less than she would have with anyone else. "Seneca Falls."

"I know where that is. It's close to... other places I've been."

In a beat of silence, Amelia thanked him for not mentioning the town where Elizabeth had served her time. "Do you have family in New York City?"

"Some aunts and uncles and cousins. My parents moved out of state after the trial."

"It must've been difficult for them."

Lewis lowered his hat and held the brim in tight fingers. He doubled over the rail and set a hand on it to push himself up. "How could she...?" His face scrunched up. "How could she just accuse me like that?"

Amelia's thoughts implicated her for the schemer she was, and she brushed off the nagging guilt. "Like what?"

"Like... I didn't mean anything to her." Lewis swept his hat out to his side. "Like we haven't been through hell together. I believed in her innocence. I helped her interview lawyers and scoured the city for any possible witnesses. I waited for her. I bought the tickets for the *Duchess*. Sold the house in Ithaca to leave the country forever. I've done everything she's ever asked of me."

Lewis combed his hair back with his empty hand and put his hat on. "I never thought I'd have to sleep alone again after she got out. Now, after everything, she doesn't want to see me. There's a sofa in one of the lounges with my name on it, I suppose."

"What did she accuse you of?" Amelia pretended with every fiber of bone and muscle she did not know. She laid her hand on Lewis' arm.

"Of taking some earrings her husband gave her years ago." Lewis threw his free arm up in exasperation. "What would I want her jewelry for? Because Arthur gave it to her? I don't care. Arthur's dead, and I'm the one who's here." He jabbed his thumb against his chest. "I'm still here. I'm alive. And until this evening, that was good enough for her."

"She must've been confused, Mr. Blakely," Amelia persuaded. "Mrs. Cole never would've assaulted you in her right mind."

"Her right mind?" Lewis wondered at her from a crooked expression. "Elizabeth hasn't been the woman I met since her husband died. She was widowed, tried, and sentenced to prison within a year. I was naïve to think her parole would give her back to me. She belongs to more people than ever. Arthur's memory, me, and all the guards and inmates she was at the mercy of these last seven years."

"You must know her temper," Amelia suggested, laying her other hand on his arm as well.

Lewis grunted. "Never has she spoken to me like that before. I've seen her angry – at her situation, her servants, the newspapers, the boring eyes. But never has she directed her wrath at me. I didn't think it was possible. I feel stupid about it now."

Amelia squeezed his arm. "Don't. You shouldn't. Maybe she wasn't really mad at you, just upset at losing the jewelry."

Lewis shot out a breath. "I wish that were true, but you weren't there. You didn't hear what she said to me. Blaming me, blaming you for even talking to us. It made no difference you believe she's innocent."

Amelia softened her approach. "Was she mean to you?"

Lewis' head bobbed. The anguish scrunching his cheeks made him appear younger, but his rising anger aged him. "She made it pretty clear she doesn't trust me. I never thought she'd question my loyalty after everything I've done for her."

The fantasy of a partnership with Lewis wrapped itself around Amelia, stealing a fragment of Elizabeth's life for herself. "You've done so much."

"I wrote to her. I visited her when her own friends and family wouldn't do it. The whole place terrified me. They built that building with white walls like that would make it more cheerful, but it was still all guards and gloom. It used to be an asylum. I only had to be there for a couple hours. Elizabeth had to live every second of those years in there." He took a breath, thinking. "Her lawyer only stopped in to talk about appeals and trying for parole. I was the one who knew she wasn't capable of murder. I carried out every errand she needed for eight years to the letter. If I was honest about her husband's business and her fortune, why would I take a pair of earrings now?"

"You wouldn't," Amelia said, knowing full well who had.

Lewis lifted his hat and ran his fingers through his hair before setting it on his head.

Amelia folded her hands in front of her. "You did more than anybody could expect from you. How much you sacrificed I don't think anybody could know. Seven years is a long time."

"I was prepared to wait longer," Lewis confessed. "Her lawyer was good, but not expert enough to keep her out of prison. I thought parole might not be possible."

"You stood by her anyway."

Lewis' resolve hardened the muscles along his jaw. "It's true."

"You were young, romantic, sensitive. She wasn't the only woman in New York." Amelia relaxed some of her seriousness. "No matter who crossed your path, whatever beauty batted her eyelashes at you, you waited for Elizabeth."

The corner of Lewis' mouth perked up. "I did."

Amelia entertained a little playfulness. "Are you remembering someone in particular?"

He shrugged, but a roguish glint played in his eyes. "It doesn't have to be."

"Come on. I can see right through you. Who was she?"

"Just a girl." Lewis ducked his head.

"Did she like you, or did you like her?"

"She liked me. I bought eggs and cheese from her all the time in Ithaca. A man has to eat. I had to buy food from someone."

"Maybe she just welcomed the business. Ithaca's a lot smaller than New York City."

"Nahhh," Lewis countered in a long, cheeky dismissal. "She always told me how handsome I looked in my suits."

Amelia wished she had the same opportunity. "The other people you bought from didn't say that?"

"No. Not the other women, and certainly not the men."

"Did you see her often?"

"Once or twice a week."

"Was she pretty?"

Lewis exhaled, bending his hat brim down to cover his forehead.

Amelia touched his arm. "Never mind. Of course, she was. Did you tell her that?"

"No."

Amelia moved closer and teased him. "So you never kissed her?"

Lewis squirmed. "No."

"Did you want to?"

Lewis met her gaze in the draining daylight. "I wouldn't let myself. It wouldn't have been fair to Elizabeth."

Amelia raised her eyebrows. "So you gave up a sure romance with somebody who liked you to wait an indefinite amount of time for Mrs. Cole? Who later asked you never to see the city you love again and move to France with her. And she rejected you, accusing you of stealing from her before you even arrived there?"

Lewis nodded in subtle movements, his eyes preoccupied, unseeing.

"That's terribly sad, Mr. Blakely," Amelia murmured.

His eyes searched her, his volume dropping. "You like me, don't you, Miss Harlow?"

"Yes," she whispered, the truest word she had uttered in years.

Lewis cradled Amelia's jaw in his hand, sweeping his thumb across her cheek. He bent his lips down toward hers. Shadows engulfed them as their mouths met. His approach was light, almost like wings brushing her skin. He did not rush, did not press, did not presume. Even though Lewis' attention gave Amelia an answer she had always needed, his tenderness posed it more like a question. She savored every second, every connection with his lips until he pulled away.

He spoke before she could. "You look very beautiful. Your eyes remind me of tiger's eye, brown and gold."

"Thank you." Amelia wished she could tell him how much she had been through to achieve that face, certainly not the one she had once traveled the world with. The one she had attracted men and broken hearts with.

Lewis' composure melted, and he kissed her.

"Lewis," she said, breathing his first name to him for the first time. "Please don't assume you have to make up for lost time with me. Just because I like you and I'm here."

His eyebrows tensed. "I'd never." He took Amelia in his arms and kissed her. Her high, poufy bangs brushed her forehead between them, and her closeness shifted his trilby. Lewis stepped back and lowered the hat from his head. Seizing it by the narrow brim, he flung it out beyond the ship's railing.

Amelia's mouth sprang open, and she jumped against the rail with her fingers outstretched to try to catch it. The wind ripped it away, sailing it in swirls and rises toward the rear of the ship. "That was a perfectly good hat!"

Lewis set a hand on her arm. "Amelia, you've been kind to me beyond words. I can't tell you how much that means to me."

Amelia met him partway. "Everyone deserves a good friend." Her deceptions stuck in her throat.

"You might be the only friend I have left on board." Lewis kissed her with more perceivable intent, long and lingering.

Pinned between Lewis and the ship's rail, Amelia could have spent the rest of the night there in contentment. But as Elwood had once said of his shared cabin with Dorothy, Amelia's room was the only place she had a key for that promised privacy. Hopefully a place Darius could no longer access. "You don't have to sleep on a sofa, Lewis," she told him. "You're welcome in my room."

"You don't think anybody will see?"

"It's at the end of the hall. Far enough away from... the room you're used to."

Lewis cupped Amelia's face in his hands. After a prolonged pause, he said, "Show me."

Amelia took a steadying breath and led Lewis to the stairs. She yearned to grab his hand but could not afford herself that luxury. They descended with quick, light steps to the second-level deck. From the ballroom on their left, the pianist flew through the rollicking, fanciful *Minute Waltz* by Frédéric Chopin. Clapping and laughter marked every measure. Amelia and Lewis continued down to the first floor, where she glanced around for Elizabeth as they crossed the open space. Darkness encased the dining room. No one hung around the parlor or the halls. They hurried down the corridor to Amelia's room, where she trembled working the key in its lock. She ushered him in, and the click of the bolt securing the door settled her nerves.

No matter what Darius could do, or if he could procure another key, at least she had gotten one copy from him.

Lewis spoke up with tentative honesty. "I've only ever been with her."

Amelia distracted herself with the furniture and details of the room, easier than facing him. She had caused the rift with Elizabeth, and only pure selfishness guided her actions. "I wish there was a sofa instead of the chairs. You can take the bed, Lewis. I'll find out if the staff stores extra blankets on board."

He inched towards her. "Did I misjudge your feelings for me?"

"No," Amelia answered honestly. Self-servingly.

"Just because I'm inexperienced doesn't mean I don't know... that I don't want you." Lewis reached for Amelia's hand, vulnerability constricting his words. "You didn't invite me down here just for sleeping, did you?"

Amelia thought very carefully about her next move. She should leave her intimate knowledge of Lewis at a few kisses on the open deck. She should abandon him this very moment, find the purser, and ask about extra accommodations. She could set everything straight in five minutes if she wanted to, but she did not. Amelia slipped her hand into Lewis'. "No, but it's not my place to ask that of you. This is the only fight you've ever had with her."

Lewis stepped forward. "Of this magnitude. We've had our tense discussions before. It's hard keeping an affair secret from everyone you know." He pushed his chest forward, his words picking up with insistence. "She cast me out. That was her decision, and I don't want to talk about her anymore. All I've done for nine years is think about her." Lewis swept stray wisps of hair off Amelia's forehead. "I want to think about me and you. Everything we'd be giving up if we didn't..."

He trailed off and kissed her. Amelia gave up fighting with herself. She held onto Lewis' arm, his thumb stroking her cheek. She moved his other hand to her hip, kissing him with the desperation that had grown for him over the last two days. Lewis' hand alighted high on her jacket, slipping down to its low row of three buttons. She set her hand on his chest, the rustling of him opening her jacket deepening her breath.

She let their clothes fall where they did, her short jacket then his long one, his stone-grey vest, his white shirts, and her champagne-colored dress. His light grip traced the corseted curve of her waist. Close together, they each maneuvered toward the bed until they bumped against it.

Amelia sat down on the coverlet, and Lewis crouched to slip off her red silk shoes, a black bow adorning the toe of each one. He stood up and kissed her, Amelia helping him slip off her flowered petticoat and ribbon-laced corset cover. Lewis joined her on the bed, Amelia returning his favors. She pulled off his polished shoes, socks, and black pants.

They reclined together, each clothed in one small, thin layer. Lewis trailed his fingers from the patterned lace on her blue-and-white corset to the frilly drawers of her chemise down her black silk stockings. Amelia slid her covered knee over his bare thigh and back, biting her lip as she tempted him further.

Lewis set a kiss against her forehead. Amelia steered his hand to the clip holding up her stocking, attached to her corset by a pink silk ribbon at her hip. He unclasped it, Amelia rolling onto her back to let him unhook the other one. He slipped his hand under the band of her stocking and rolled it the length of her leg. He guided the other one off, exposing the yellow bruises she had earned beneath her knees to get closer to him. Amelia unfastened the first few hooks on the front of her corset. Lewis met her face to face, kissing her as he loosened the rest of them.

Amelia pressed him onto his back, devouring his slender neck and sturdy chest. Lewis pushed the strap of her chemise-and-drawers combination off her shoulder, kissing her collar bone where the light cotton had covered her skin. He planted kisses up her neck, lowering the other strap. He slipped the all-in-one from her body, stopping at every exposed curve to grace it with his lips.

Amelia slid the silk drawers off his hips to the floor, nothing left between them but a measure of shyness and determination. She stroked the soft, straight lines of his stomach. They lay down to face each other, and she drew her leg up over his. She scooted closer, their hip bones bumping together. Lewis caressed her face, his forehead mirroring hers. He eased into her, Amelia squeezing his arm, both their breaths hitching at the concentration of pleasure. Lewis deepened inside her, his movements as gentle and gradual as everything else he had done. Amelia stopped urging him forward, giving in to his rhythm, his patience, his reveling in every sensation that trickled through their bodies.

Amelia wrapped her arms around Lewis' neck, planting his bearded jaw line with affection. He splayed his hand against her lower back, their chests touching. In the slowest build of anticipation she had ever waited for, Amelia lost herself. She was no longer an international traveler and thief, betrayer, liar, seducer, and survivor. She was not the innocent young woman she had once been but something new, someone who could almost be herself. Someone she had almost forgotten.

The pleasure widened in Amelia's body. Lewis ran his hand down her side, her tension releasing into ripples through her muscles. Lewis kissed her more insistently, Amelia matching his desire while she remained in his arms. He pulled away and set his forehead against hers once more.

Conviction strengthened his words. "I love you." Lewis glided his hand up her bare arm. "Not that I know what will happen tomorrow or the next day. You remind me of a home I'll never see again. I like being alone with you. Is it all right if you're important to me?"

Amelia blinked, beholden to Lewis in the same way. "Yes."

"I don't want to move. I'm afraid I'll ruin everything."

Amelia stroked his cheek, his beard satiny across its broad surface. "Nothing could tarnish this. Not now."

Lewis' fingertips traced the muscle along her shoulder, looping around to the dip behind her collar bone. "I didn't think I'd meet anyone like you on board. I assumed there'd be others from New York flying out, but I expected all stuck-up, high-society types. Not anyone I could really talk to or even want to."

"There are enough of those with us already."

"I'm still not used to it. I used to sell ice cream from a cart for pennies. I came from nothing to be here."

"I only came from a little bit of something."

"Yet here you are. We both are." Lewis took Amelia's hand and kissed her naked palm. "I don't want to go to sleep."

"We have to." She combed her fingers through his hair. "I don't want to, either."

"At least we'll be here next to each other."

Amelia got up and dimmed the chandelier light to its merest glow. She pulled the blankets back from the head of the bed, and Lewis stood up to help her. They climbed in toward each other, arranging the blankets up to their waists. Amelia curled up against Lewis' side, draping her hand across his chest. She delighted in the pressure of his arm encircling her back, sweet for now, a bitter memory for later. He nestled his temple against hers.

"Lewis?" she whispered in the dark. "I care about you, too."

Chapter Eighteen

In the morning, Lewis' half of the bed held only wrinkled covers. He sat in the chair furthest from Amelia, putting on his shoes. His black suit fit over his body, hiding his contours and exact shape. She could remember every muscle, the heat of his skin against hers. The closeness of limbs and desires and emotions.

"Are you leaving?" Amelia knew it was inevitable. He belonged to her no more than she belonged to him.

Lewis cleared his throat. "Yes. I thought I'd inquire with the purser and find out if there's an empty room I can stay in the rest of the voyage." He pressed his lips together as he stood up. "Amelia—"

She sat up, pinning the sheet under her arms to cover her breasts. "There's nothing left to say. The ship's enormous, but the decks aren't that big. We're bound to run into Elizabeth sooner or later."

Lewis crept to the door. "I'll let you know what I find out."

"I'll leave the door unlocked for you."

Lewis cracked the portal open and slipped into the hall. The click of it closing formed a lonely, hollow sound that almost surfaced tears in Amelia's eyes. She shoved her self-pity down and pulled her shoulders back. Her stolen night was over, replaced by a more solemn and practical day. She tossed the covers aside and dressed herself by the time Lewis returned.

His cool brown eyes surveyed her black-and-white outfit. "That's a pretty dress."

Decorum restricted Lewis' compliment, and Amelia's acceptance rang with the same formality. "Thank you. What did the purser say?"

"There's no extra room for me. All the spaces are taken."

"You're welcome here. We don't have to..." Amelia could not bring herself to put a name on their actions the night before.

Lewis' expression tightened. "I've already taken advantage of your hospitality. I wouldn't want to damage your reputation by staying in your cabin any longer than necessary."

"It's probably for the best." After the flare of jealousy Darius had shown Alvin in the ballroom, Amelia dreaded what he might do to Lewis. The threat of Darius' violence did not make speaking the truth any easier. "Do you know what you're going to do?"

"I should talk to Elizabeth." Lewis brushed his hair with his hands. "I should at least find out if she's willing to let me share the cabin I arranged for."

"If she isn't?"

Lewis rubbed the back of his neck. "Perhaps there's a berth in the lower deck for me."

"Among the crew?" Amelia considered his choices. "I hope for your sake she's cooled her temper down."

His eyes found hers. "Are we still friends, Amelia?"

"Yes."

"Are you flying back to the States after we land?"

"No, but I'm not staying in France long, either."

Lewis hesitated and extended his hands. Amelia tucked hers inside his grasp. "I hope our paths will cross again, no matter when. No matter where."

Amelia thought it unlikely. She moved around often and would have many tasks to carry out after her time on the *Duchess*. She wanted to avoid Elizabeth as much as she could but fixed the possibility firmly in her heart. "I hope so, too."

"I'll always remember you. Especially the way you sparkled in the sunset on the upper deck last night."

He would just as likely recall Amelia in his arms and in her bed, but she accepted his more genteel selection. "I'll remember you throwing your hat out into the wind." The final glimpse of its swirling curved her lips with fondness.

Lewis squeezed her hands. "I can't believe I've only known you for a few days."

"This isn't goodbye," she reminded him. "We still have two days until we land."

"I know, but it feels like goodbye."

More emotions filled his eyes than Amelia could pinpoint. Gratitude. Uncertainty. Regret. Longing. Nothing she did not suffer herself. "You should go to her. She's probably wondering where you are."

Lewis gave no answer.

Amelia memorized his face, still youthful for all the years he had spent worrying and waiting. She yearned to fight for him, to cast doubt on Elizabeth's character and build up her own. She wanted to throw her arms around him and kiss him until she was the only woman left in his memory. They could disappear in France or any country in the world, never to hear of Elizabeth Hunting Cole again.

Lewis centered on Amelia as well, and for a moment, she wondered if he would kiss her. He dipped his chin almost to his chest, and she knew the opportunity had passed. She circled her arms around his waist. Lewis wrapped his arms around her back, and she rested her eyes shut. She could see the remainder of the trip play out as if the spiritualists had divined it for her.

Elizabeth would welcome Lewis back into her cabin and into her life. He could not live without her, and she would wander painfully adrift without him. Amelia would continue to see him on board the *Duchess*, maybe wave or exchange a few words. But this was goodbye in the deepest sense, and it was the last time she might ever touch Lewis Blakely.

He pressed the side of his jaw against her forehead. In one motion, he left a kiss on her temple and pulled a full step away. "Good day, Miss Harlow," he bid her stiffly, blinking moisture from his eyes.

"Enjoy your breakfast, Mr. Blakely," Amelia said. "I hope they're serving omelets today."

Lewis swallowed hard. With a sharp inhale, he opened the door and disappeared through its opening.

Amelia sat down on the end of the bed. The scent of buttered eggs and peppered sausage wafted in. Her stomach growled, but she would eat later when she was sure most of the dining room had emptied out. She had no wish to see Lewis in Elizabeth's presence. At least, not yet.

Chapter Nineteen

Amelia gorged herself at lunch, too intent on eating all the courses around her to follow the other passengers' latest dramas. She scooped shrimp bisque into her mouth, tender vegetables, sultry herbs, and sunny citrus suspended in a creamy broth. When her spoon scraped the bowl clean, she moved on to the mound of chicken salad atop a spray of bright lettuce leaves. Every mouthful carried juicy meat, crisp celery, and biting onion. While most of the dining room guests wandered out to other parts of the ship, Amelia took her time with her oysters Rockefeller. Butter sweetened her tongue, garlic stole her palate, and blended greens evened out the effects. For dessert, she welcomed her bowl of rice pudding, silky, sweet, and satisfying.

Amelia pushed the china away, remaining in her chair even after a teenaged steward carried her dishes out of sight. The flight was not over yet, and despite their earlier advances in her plan, she and Darius still had much to accomplish.

A staff member with white highlighting his short, silver hair walked by. He paused beside her table. "Was everything to your liking, miss?"

Amelia managed a brief uplift of appreciation. "Yes."

"Can I bring you anything else?"

She pushed herself up from her seat with a resigning sigh. "No, thank you. I'm fine."

He walked on, collecting silverware from the table behind her with clinks and clunks.

Amelia traipsed out of the dining room's main doors. Luther and Harold sat in the parlor, interrupting their conversation to acknowledge her with amiable bows.

Harold tapped his feet on the floor. "Except for the loss of your pocket watch, it's been well worth the trip, hasn't it?" He sank back against the sofa cushions. "We can always find you another one in France."

Luther clenched his hands together, rubbing one thumb against the other. "The French make some handsome ones. But not as fine as the Swiss."

Harold speared a finger high into the air. "To Switzerland, then, to buy my friend a timepiece."

Amelia continued past the stairs and through the lounge's doors. Cora sat at the nearest writing desk, a pen in one hand and her other fluttering at Spencer towering over her.

His low pitch growled. "The children don't care what you ate for breakfast, Cora."

"Just a minute, please. I'm almost finished."

"That's what you always say. Then it transforms into another page of blithering description."

Amelia strode on, eager to pass out of earshot of Spencer's verbal assault. Glimpsing Lewis and Elizabeth standing at the windows slowed Amelia's pace. The fullness of her meal hit her with a wave of sluggishness and discomfort, and she wished she had not helped herself to so much of it. She tried not to stare, but of the handful of guests scattered throughout the long room, no one seemed to notice her.

Lewis draped his arm around Elizabeth's waist, his other hand pointing down at the angled glass. "England will pass by on this side when we fly close enough."

"Isn't it much safer to extol it from here?" Elizabeth joked, almost jovial. "We don't need the wind to rise up and snatch your other hat."

"No, we don't." Only the barest tension of his lies flattened Lewis' humor.

"Do you think the *Duchess* will ever catch up to it?"

"No, it's gone for sure. It took off like a bullet."

"Perhaps that's what happened to Mr. Wallace's pocket watch. The wind grabbed it."

Amelia fixated on how comfortable they were, not just with each other, but at the view out the window. They might stay there awhile, giving her and Darius the opportunity to sneak ahead with their plan. She slipped away before they noticed her, ducking out the far doors of the lounge into the outer hallway.

At the opposite end, by the back doors to the dining room, Celia and Lorena clustered in close confidence. Only years of practice listening in on others around her let Amelia understand their hushed conversation.

Celia appealed to her with insistence. "I couldn't help myself."

"After all your jokes and jabs at my expense?" Lorena shot back in a harsh whisper. "I can't believe you, Cee!"

Celia's shoulders sank back. "Luther's quite charming. He's a beautiful dancer."

Lorena knotted her arms together, jerking her chin up. "And quite charming when he's alone with you, I surmise."

Amelia considered taking the long route to Darius' room but continued on toward the next hallway. She averted her eyes from the two women as she approached them.

Celia dropped to a fierce murmur. "How dare you judge me? After all the times you and Harold ran off together."

Lorena's hands jumped in frustration. "To play cards or sightsee from the upper deck."

Celia locked her arms at her sides. "Playing cards where Luther and I can't find you?"

"Yes. Activities you can only normally perform sitting or standing *upright.*"

Celia slapped Lorena's face in such a quick, arcing motion, Amelia almost missed it. Lorena's jaw dropped as she covered her cheek with her lavender-gloved hand. Celia swiveled on her boot heel and strode away, passing Amelia with a beet-red complexion.

Lorena's mouth closed in halting increments. She adjusted her modest height, smoothed the skirt of her yellow dress, and advanced out of the corner. "How do you do?" she addressed Amelia, composed but haughty. Her cheek stung as red as her fiery hair.

Amelia shared her dry sarcasm. "Fine. You?"

They veered down the intersecting hallway together.

Lorena jerked her pointed, upturned nose into the air. "Never better." She continued past Darius' room and the lavatories, sweeping toward the parlor on determined legs.

Amelia stopped at Darius' door and knocked. She did not know if she would find him here or in what mood, but attempting his room now made more sense than wandering the rest of the ship first.

Darius opened his door, fully clothed with an amiable lightness relaxing his mouth. He raised his forearm and propped it against the jamb, setting his temple against his wrist. "Good afternoon. What do you have in store for me today?"

"I need to talk to you." She remained solemn, refusing to play into his mischievous attitude.

"Sounds urgent." He stepped aside, gesturing her in with a flourish of his hand.

Amelia stepped into Darius' room, giving it a subtle scan. Unlike hers and Elizabeth's cabins, no jewelry box graced the dresser. No dainty gloves or embroidered reticule lay ready for use. Darius closed the door, and Amelia faced him.

He spoke first. "Did you want another dance?" he teased.

Amelia's mouth twisted. "Maybe later. We should make a move on Elizabeth's room."

"Did she leave it all by herself, or did the injured robin fly back to the nest?"

The truth wounded Amelia, but she directed herself to the task at present. "Elizabeth and Lewis have patched things up after their quarrel."

"The lovebirds snuggling again." Darius wrung his hands together. "How nice."

Amelia ignored his deprecation. "Will you guard the door for me while I go in?"

"It's your turn, I suppose." Darius moved to the dresser and opened the top drawer. He dug under his clothes and held Elizabeth's key out to Amelia.

She took it, her fingers brushing his. "And the earrings, please."

Darius froze, his eyebrow cocking. "What?"

"I'm going to exchange them for something else."

He pointed to the door. "After you told me to sneak in and steal them?"

"Trust me. Everything will work out exactly as planned. The earrings you took need to go back in their box."

Darius closed the top drawer and fished around in a lower one. He dropped the diamond-and-ruby earrings into Amelia's outstretched palm. "I don't know who you're fooling more, me or them."

Amelia adopted some of Darius' condescending charm. "Don't worry, darling." She set her fingers under his chin. "For the moment, it's them."

Darius took her hand and kissed it. "Then I pity them. Where are they now?"

"The lounge on this floor."

"So they could come from either direction. I'd better take up the bench in the hall to be safe."

Amelia moved closer and gave Darius a subdued but smoldering kiss. If he suspected complicated motives, he did not mention it.

"Go," he suggested, his tempestuous eyes glowing. "Before we lose this chance. We're running out of time."

"No," Amelia assured him. "We have all the time we need."

She cracked the door open, listening before she stepped out into the hall.

From beyond the end of the corridor, resentment sharpened Lorena's chatty remarks. "I'm sure she's just a little stressed. Four days without her feet on solid ground must be taking its toll."

Luther's bass spoke up. "Maybe I should check on her."

Lorena clucked her tongue. "If you can find her." She sweetened into a more obliging tone. "Yes, why don't you go? Harold will keep me company, and I'm sure Celia would love to see you."

Amelia slowed her pace between the lavatories. Luther crossed the open space up ahead, disappearing from view before his shoes sounded on the staircase. Darius exited his room, taking a seat on the bench beside Amelia with a book in his hand. She unlocked Elizabeth's door and hid herself inside.

There was no need to draw her actions out. Amelia opened Elizabeth's jewelry box. A worn copy of *Wuthering Heights* and a pair of Lewis' white gloves beside it distracted her. The proof of Lewis' lodgings made Amelia bristle at the tale of lost, complicated love. Elizabeth had secured the relationship she wanted, and Amelia had not. She plucked several pins and pendants from the sparkling collection, nestling the stolen earrings amongst the remaining jewels and forms. The book and the paradox of its satisfied owner vexed her anew. As a petty present to herself, Amelia dropped a bracelet into her pocket, each square silver link dotted with a white freshwater pearl.

Amelia returned the rest of the jewelry and retraced her steps into the hallway. Darius remained on the bench, right beside her as she locked the door.

He kept his eyes on the pages of *The Count of Monte Cristo*. "How did it go?"

"Fine. Any sign of them?"

"No."

"Then I'll see you later." Amelia walked away toward the outer hall.

"I'll find you. You can't go far."

Chapter Twenty

Amelia faced herself in the lavatory mirror, one of several hung on the wall above the sinks. The private water closet doors behind her remained closed, giving her a few moments of privacy in the shared space. Amelia had taken years to get used to the face Dr. Petzel created for her, avoiding its reflection for months before forcing herself to scrutinize it. In the end, she adopted the attitude of accepting what she could not afford to change. Her old nose was smaller, daintier. Eyebrows higher and thicker. Cheeks rounder.

Amelia's hair, darker than the honey brown she was born with, wrapped around her head. The rest of its length rested on the nape of her neck, sagging in a slight droop on one side. Her nimble fingers pried a few pins loose and speared them in at different places, the solemn line of her mouth remaining a constant.

The even dusting of Amelia's rice-and-pearl powder gave her a paled, flawless complexion. Her fingertip traced the scars she knew it covered. Down both cheeks. Above the right side of her upper lip. Across her forehead. As she had many times, she gave begrudging thanks to changing social trends. The cosmetics ostracized in her youth had grown into enough popularity to give her an easy, flattering way to hide them.

Water running behind her signaled Amelia's privacy drawing to a close. She cast her keen eyes over her appearance and opened the door to the corridor.

Iris and Priscilla sauntered past her, and Amelia stopped herself from striding right out into them.

Priscilla adjusted her gloves over her wrists. "I wonder what's on the buffet today?"

Iris maintained her deadpan drone. "I hope they serve the crab meat garibaldi with avocado. It's the most delicious thing I've eaten all week."

"Don't let the chefs hear you. They won't know what to do with a compliment from you."

Amelia took a deep breath and let it out, resigned to following them into the dining room. She heard a knock on a door behind her and sought out who made it.

Lewis stood stationed in front of her room.

Amelia walked over to him, surprised and confused. "Mr. Blakely?"

Lewis faced her, his tense shoulders relaxing. "I thought you might've gone to dinner."

"I was on my way when I noticed you here." Amelia struggled with the right words. "Is there something I can do for you?"

"Just a word. In private, if you can."

"Of course."

Amelia let them into her room. Closed inside with Lewis once more, she realized what a mistake this might have been. She set about moving the conversation forward along the tracks fate and choice had already laid for them. "How are things with Mrs. Cole?"

Lewis' answer sounded casual but flat. "Better than I thought they'd be."

Amelia was glad he kept any elation at Elizabeth's forgiveness to himself.

He gestured to the door. "She's already in the dining room. She's getting more used to being by herself. That's good, I think."

Amelia encouraged him with a double hum.

"Amelia," he sighed. He licked his lips. "I wanted to apologize. I can't help thinking I acted too forward yesterday."

She wanted to reach out to him but held her hands back. "No."

"I believe I might've done both of us a disservice. I showed a lack of inhibitions. I didn't think things through."

"We can't take it back now." Practicality did not stop Amelia from wondering a few more things about Lewis. "Would you if you could?"

"No."

The last time Amelia had seen Lewis, he had attended to Elizabeth with his usual support at the lounge's window. "I noticed you with Mrs. Cole this afternoon. You seemed happy."

Lewis drooped, running a hand through his hair. "I can't say I'm not glad to have made up with her. I am." His troubled eyes met hers. "I regret it for your sake. I'm sure I behaved rashly, inappropriately towards you last evening."

Amelia stepped forward. Her hands felt heavy and sluggish as she laid them on his arms. "You didn't. We both played a part in it. You've done me no wrongs."

Lewis held her gaze steadier by the second. He raised his head up straight. "I'm proud to call you a friend. It was never my intent to entangle you in our lives or take advantage of my argument with Elizabeth."

"I understand." Experience put extra emphasis behind Amelia's insistence. "She's lucky to have you."

Lewis took a deep breath and let it out. He spoke with resolve although his uncertainty belied it. "My place is with Elizabeth."

"I think it is. At least for now."

Lewis dipped his chin. "I told her a few lies about last night. I claimed an odd wind blew over the rail and snatched my hat. I let her believe I'd slept in one of the lounge's arm chairs all night."

"You did what was best." Amelia's stomach soured, not entirely convinced. "I know you wouldn't have lied to her before."

"I never did, not even about her hats. If I didn't like one, I said so, but she's always had impeccable taste. And so do you."

Amelia thanked him with patient silence.

He grimaced, caught between humor and guilt. He rubbed his arm. "Do you know the darndest part about the whole incident? The earrings she accused me of stealing weren't even gone. She just found them in her jewelry box hunting for something else. There was no reason for her to be mad at me in the first place, which I told her several times."

Amelia tried to hide her missing surprise. "I'm thankful it's cleared up. She must've called herself silly for blaming you."

"She must've put them away without seeing them."

"Be sure to tell Mrs. Cole not to doubt you anymore. You've proven your devotion to her time and again. She doesn't need to keep such a close eye on her belongings. The ship is quite secure."

Lewis raised an index finger. "Except for Mr. Wallace's timepiece."

"I'm sure he'll find it unpacking his suitcases when the trip is over."

"I hope so."

Amelia drank in Lewis' burgeoning confidence and maturity. She was changing him, hopefully for the wiser not the sadder. But he had carried out an affair with a married woman. He was not completely innocent when she met him. "I wish you and Mrs. Cole a happy life together. You deserve it."

Lewis clasped Amelia's hands between his. "Best of luck wherever the wind sends you."

"Will you stay in France?"

"Probably."

Amelia slid her hands away and stepped toward the door. "Marry her, Mr. Blakely. You've waited long enough."

Sheepishness perked up Lewis' lips. "Perhaps, when we're settled in the countryside."

"Sooner," Amelia suggested. "As soon as possible."

"Do you think it's a good idea?"

She made herself nod, even if she only half believed it.

He tucked his hands in his pockets, his chest caving in. "You wouldn't be there to see it."

"No."

"Maybe if I think of you hard enough, you'll know we've done it. That's what the spiritualists would say, isn't it?"

Amelia warmed at her connection to Lewis. "I'll know."

"I'm sure I'll see you a few more times before we disembark."

"Probably."

"Until then." Lewis' stomach creaked. "I better go see what's left at the buffet."

"Take care of Mrs. Cole. She needs you."

Lewis fixated on the floor. "One argument isn't going to erase the years we fought to be together. We've persevered through worse situations than this." He shifted toward her, his eyes sad and longing. "Talking to you always makes me feel better."

Amelia slipped back into the truth. "I'll miss you when the flight is over."

His volume quieted. "This is the way it has to be, isn't it?"

"For the time."

"Maybe someday... a little Paris café."

Amelia winced at the name, dissecting her like a sharpened saber.

Lewis jutted his chin up. "The country, then."

Amelia painted the broader picture of their shared dream. "You're surrounded by farmers' daughters. Cows lowing. Horses prancing in their fields." Steaming sunlight, fragrant breezes, and wide open spaces. "I'll bring you eggs and cheese at your gate."

Lewis offered a genuine smile, and Amelia opened the door for him.

He stepped into the hallway, but she remained in her room. "Aren't you hungry?" he asked.

"I had a large lunch. I'll be there in a minute."

Lewis walked away, and Amelia clicked the door shut, crumpling against the inside of it.

Lewis had burrowed deeper into her heart than anyone had crawled in a long time. No matter how many years might pass, she would find his cottage amidst the rolling hills displaying carefully tended vineyards. She would carry a basket of brown eggs and hard cheese, whether her hands remained agile or had gnarled with age. Lewis met her at the gate of the fence stretching around his property, any grey in his beard not coming close to obscuring his identity from her. He welcomed her with a friendly greeting and a kiss like no time had passed since they last spoke.

Amelia squeezed her eyes shut and let the butt of her fist drop against the door. Eight years ago, she had learned of Theodore Stockell's map of Africa and forced her way into the Cole house to steal it. She had waited to procure that piece of paper as long as Lewis had waited for Elizabeth's trial and sentence to be over. Stealing the map might hurt Lewis in the long run, but that was not Amelia's concern.

Whether they ever saw each other again or not, they had different destinies to forge in the present. What Amelia needed to do would wound Elizabeth, enrage and disappoint her as badly as being convicted for a murder she did not commit. Just as with her missing earrings, she would surely seek someone to blame – Lewis, Amelia, Luther's pickpocket, the passengers, crew, or fate itself.

Despite Amelia's deceit, she had given Lewis and Elizabeth a gift no one else could give them. She had offered them the chance to discover the reasons they stayed together besides past loyalty and shared struggle. They had gotten what they wanted – renewed faith and respect for each other – and Amelia was just as determined to get what she wanted.

Nothing was going to stand in her way.

Chapter Twenty-One

After a light supper, Amelia wandered out of the dining room wondering where to spend the rest of her evening. She paused in the open area near the stairs, waiting to see where the other passengers ended up. Luther and Celia strolled past her toward the lounge. The French couple, chatting in their native language, moseyed in the same direction. Priscilla and Edwin walked by, her vibrant eyes pinned to his face.

Her cadence dragged with mesmerism. "The *Minute Waltz* isn't actually meant to be played in one short minute?"

Edwin tilted his head back. "Oh, no. It's a test of technical skill at that speed, to be sure, and quite entertaining to hear. But impossible to dance to without falling."

Iris followed along behind them, her heavy eyelids lowered in irritation. The trio climbed the stairs to Amelia's left. Elwood and Dorothy pattered up after them.

Harold and Lorena bounded toward the stairs. Harold planted a quick kiss on Lorena's cheek before he called behind them. "Are you coming or not?"

Alvin jogged into view from the dining room. He slowed his pace when he saw Amelia and twirled the silver cufflink dotting one of his sleeves. "I don't know. That depends. Are you dancing with us this evening, Miss Harlow?"

"No, thank you." Even though Amelia and Darius had many subjects to discuss, she had no desire to revisit her earlier evening in the ballroom. Or make it so easy for him to find her.

"What else is there to do?" Alvin tapped one fist on top of the other. "Have you tried shuffleboard? Very popular back home."

Amelia had spent numerous nights in dark pubs cutting her teeth on the table version. Questionable adversaries helped her test many a strategy. "I learned to play in Boston. I haven't tried it on board yet."

Alvin beamed, his eyes widening as he clapped his hands together. "That's practically my backyard, especially where worldwide travel is concerned. What business did you have there? Or was it pleasure?"

"I was mostly passing through."

"Where haven't you been? To the top deck, then?"

Amelia gestured to their dinner dresses and black suits. "In our best clothes?"

"Of course. Why not?"

Amelia pursed her lips in agreement. "I'll play."

Alvin poked Harold's arm. "Are you up for it? We can play pair against pair. Two shoves apiece."

Lorena grinned with a light smugness as if Amelia had not witnessed Celia slap her face. "I'm in."

Harold motioned Lorena ahead of him, and Alvin gestured for Amelia to precede him. Amelia climbed past the pictures and articles framed on the walls.

Harold's brogue echoed from below her. "Who's this fellow with the wiry beard? He reminds me of my grandfather." He laughed. "I can't believe how high they built the scaffolding just to construct the ship! That took some courage climbing all that towering metal." Amelia spied back at him as he saluted the portrait of Captain Barrett. "You're doing a great job, captain! You barely notice the winds blowing against us."

Amelia stepped up into the windowed room.

Alvin joined her, peering through the glass panes on either side of them. Elwood and Dorothy played on the starboard side. "That court's taken. We'll use the other one."

Harold propped one of the doors ajar, and the other three ushered past him onto the deck.

Alvin opened the cabinet fixed to the outside of the windowed room. He handed out long, wooden cues and painted metal pucks. "Green for Miss Harlow and me. Yellow for Harold and Lorena."

Lorena eyed the crescent-shaped end of her cue and tested the heft of her discs. "I've never played."

Harold elbowed her arm and wiggled his fingers. "Too busy with the spirit world," he joked.

Amelia surveyed the expanse of deck over her shoulder. As she had hoped, Lewis, Elizabeth, and Darius were nowhere to be seen.

Alvin tapped Amelia's arm. "Why don't you go first, Miss Harlow? So Lorena can see how it's done."

Amelia stepped up to the nearest line in the long, rectangular court. In front of her stretched a six-foot by three-foot oval. White lines split it into eleven sections, each one marked with a scoring number. An identical area on the far end of the court provided her target. She dropped one of her green discs in front of the starting line, tossing the other out of play.

Alvin pumped his fist in the air. *"Bonne chance."*

Amelia positioned the end of her cue behind the disc, where the hollow curve of it nestled the round metal. With an aimed and purposeful shove, Amelia's cue launched the disc into the far half of the court. It skimmed over the nearest ten-point scoring end of the oval and the nine-point square, lodging on the central zone marked for five points.

Alvin whooped. "Great shot, Miss Harlow!"

Amelia wrinkled her nose as she stepped off the court proper. "I pushed it a little too hard."

"You were aiming for the ten?"

"Of course."

"Ambition." Alvin aimed a finger at her. "I like that in a shuffleboard partner."

Harold stepped up to the line. "Follow my lead, Lorena." He slid his extra disc aside and set the other inside the line. He butted the curved end of the cue against his playable puck.

"But I don't understand–" Lorena chirped at the exact moment Harold pushed his cue forward.

Harold's stick jerked. Lorena gasped, letting her cue roll into the crook of her elbow. She covered her mouth with both hands. Harold cringed as his disc flew off the court, hitting the deck railing and skidding to a stop.

Lorena's hands fell, and her shoulders wilted. "I'm so sorry, Harold."

Alvin hunched over in guffaws, holding his hand out. "Lorena, let me explain what just happened." He pointed to Harold's wayward disc. "That's out of bounds and earns no points. What Amelia's puck landed on is halfway to the lowest score afforded by the board, and we're in the lead."

Harold bucked his chin up. "Go ahead, then. Let's see what you've got. I bet you're all bum and parsley."

"How can you even understand him sometimes, Lorena?"

She settled her weight into one hip, considering Harold. "Inflection, I think."

Harold winked. "You're both havering. And Alvin, failing means you're playing."

Alvin placed one puck out of bounds and the other by the white strip. "Here we go. Let's see who's closer to failure this time." He lined up his shot and sent his disc careening across the court. It slowed to a halt at an intersection of lines just past the ten. "Darn it!"

Harold hummed in amusement.

Lorena spoke up with tentative softness. "Isn't that good?"

"No points," Alvin grumbled. "The puck has to be a clean landing in one of the spaces. Of course, Amelia could knock it clearly into the seven with her eagle-eye precision."

The French doors parted and thumped closed. Darius approached, and Amelia tried to accept his intrusion. He wandered where he wanted, but she did not have to give him a reaction.

Alvin tipped his hat to Lorena. "Your go, my lady."

Harold took Lorena's extra disc from her. "Just like we showed you."

"Do I aim for the ten?" She stepped up to the line.

Darius stopped a foot behind Amelia and Alvin. "That depends on your strategy." He lifted his bowler to all in attendance.

Lorena blinked at him over her shoulder, waiting.

"If you land on the ten now, another disc could knock it away and earn you nothing. By the same token, you could try for one of the other spaces or try sliding Miss Harlow's onto the one."

Contempt for Darius' suggestion compressed Amelia's chest, but she kept it to herself. "I didn't know you played."

Darius purred. "I'm full of surprises."

Lorena took a small step to her left and focused on the disc in front of her. With a push of her cue, she sent the disc sailing across the court. It collided with Amelia's, leaving Lorena's yellow on the five with Amelia's disc sliding off the targeted zone.

A hush fell over the group.

Lorena searched their faces. "Did I do well?"

Harold clapped her on the back. "Well done!"

Alvin glanced at Amelia. "Not to worry. You can knock it away."

Amelia sized up Darius. "Did you want to play, Mr. Shank?"

"No." He settled his hands in his pockets. "I'm content to observe."

Amelia stepped up to the court and let her foot slide her second disc into position.

"Although," Darius spoke up, sending an unwelcome rigidity seizing each bone of her spine, "there's an interesting argument erupting in the ballroom."

Lorena fielded the remark. "Between whom?"

"You know Iris Coates and Priscilla Banks? Their husbands and Edwin Ames."

Amelia lined up her cue with the two discs in play at the other end of the court. "I didn't realize the ladies were traveling with their husbands." She drew her cue back and forth in practice.

"Neither did I. The gentlemen figured on each other's company and left their wives to do the same. They've finally gotten wind that Edwin Ames has transformed the two wives into a threesome."

Alvin's participation surprised Amelia. "Mr. Coates has nothing to worry about with his missus' winning personality."

Amelia shoved her cue, the disc taking off across the court. It slammed into Alvin's puck, running it into Lorena's. Amelia craned her head to the side, seeing that her disc sat squarely on a line but Alvin's had claimed the five with Lorena's on the farthest line.

Lorena moaned. "I'm out?"

Harold patted her hand. "It's only the first round."

Amelia sighed at Darius' continued presence. She handed her cue to Alvin. "Do you mind finishing up without me? There's some business I should attend to."

"Of course not." Alvin's eyes flicked sidelong at Darius. "Fantastic shot. At least I'm starting out ahead."

She laid a hand on his wrist. "Win for us."

"I'll try my best." Alvin tipped his hat.

Amelia resigned herself to walking away with Darius at her side. She spoke through gritted teeth. "If you ever advise against me in a game again, I'll trip you in front of the nearest moving vehicle."

"I'd expect nothing less." His tone hardened. "I looked everywhere for you."

"It appears, like you, I can be full of surprises."

Darius took Amelia's hand and threaded it through the loop of his arm, where he held it in place. "I hoped you deemed it time to tell me what's going on with the jewelry you had me take."

"It's not the setback you think it is," Amelia told him. "Elizabeth's already found it, and as far as she knows, all is well now in her world."

Darius rubbed his palm against the back of Amelia's hand. "Complacency has always been our greatest ally. Did you borrow a little something in return like you wanted?"

"Something she hopefully won't miss as much as the earrings."

"It was an honest mistake. Do you know how we're going to proceed?"

"I have a few ideas."

Darius stopped at the rail, admiration filling his eyes. "It's been too long since we worked together. Forgive me if I forget how cunning your foresight can be."

Amelia cocked her head to one side. "Did you think I'd leave this ship without everything I came for?"

"No." Darius supported his lower back against the rail. "I resolve never to doubt you again."

Amelia scrunched her cheeks up. "What a lovely lie."

No matter how much they had changed, trust was not a part of Darius' enduring nature.

Chapter Twenty-Two

Amelia traversed that same stretch of deck the next morning. She arrived at the rail, taking a big breath before viewing beyond it. True to the chatter and outbursts of the dining room during breakfast, the *Duchess* was nearing land. Two hundred miles away, the northwestern coast of Spain jutted into the ocean, lush and green, spotted with beige beaches and low-lying cities. Beyond them rose rolling hills and grey, rocky mountains.

The French door banged open behind Amelia, startling her. Elwood and Dorothy hurried out onto the deck.

"I want to use it first." Dorothy steadied the small hat perched atop her nest of nondescript hair. "I don't care what she says."

Elwood carried the spyglass case with him. "I'm sure there'll be plenty of time before she gets here."

Dorothy narrowed her eyes at Amelia. "Oh, great. The woman who started it all."

Elwood offered a genteel lift of his hat. "How's the view?"

Amelia wiped her sweating palms against each other, trembling as she did so. "Magnificent, Mr. Molt. I'm sure it's even better through the spyglass."

Dorothy tossed her nose up. "If it's even in the case."

Elwood knocked the knuckles of his free hand against the hard valise. "Who would steal a spyglass? No one else seemed interested in using it."

Amelia patted the top of the railing. "This is a good spot to set it up."

Elwood jogged the rest of the way, crouching to lay his case on the deck floor. "I'll have it propped up in a moment."

Dorothy stood over him, crossing her arms over the white lace of her pink bodice. Satin bows and ruffles at each wrist did nothing to soften her appearance.

Elwood unpacked the stand and secured it upright. He fixed the spyglass in place and bent forward to use it.

Dorothy bumped him out of the way with her hip and took the spyglass for herself. She peered through it, adjusting its direction at the view below.

Amelia tugged her sleeve cuffs farther over her wrists, choosing to address Elwood instead of his wife. "Are you excited to land?"

"Yes, I think so." Elwood cast praising eyes over the sky, the green glass partition, and the deck. "It's a beautiful ship, but I've never been off the ground for so long. It'll be refreshing to stand on solid earth."

"And your lovely mother. How is she?"

"She's on her way up. I told her we could get better details out of the coastline from the spyglass than the dining room windows."

Dorothy spoke up from her angled position. "I don't know why you'd have to convince her of that. It's simple science."

Amelia debated pulling the stand out from under Dorothy's nose.

One of the doors swung closed, and Claudia ambled towards them. She flapped her hand high in the air. "I'm here, Elwood." She squealed with delight. "Amelia! I haven't seen you for days."

Amelia shuffled her feet. "I'm sorry."

"No, dear, the fault's all mine. It's those painting classes you told me about. They've improved the outlook of my entire trip."

"I'm so glad." Amelia hoped her rapport with Claudia made Dorothy squirm inside. "Have you seen any of her paintings, Mr. Molt?"

Elwood raised his eyebrows high. "They're all right. Really."

Claudia tittered. "Amelia, you ask the wrong person. They're elementary at best. You should join me. We can learn together."

As much as the invitation won Amelia's heart, too many forces pulled on her already. "I'm afraid I'm better at waltzing than art. But I promise to stop by the classes and see what you create."

Claudia took a deep breath and ran her eyes across the sky. "What's passing below us today?"

Dorothy issued a singsong answer through clenched jaws. "You can find out in a moment."

Disappointment clouded Claudia's face before her eyes brightened. She lifted her chest. "Come on, Amelia. We can see just as well over the rail."

Dorothy clamped her teeth tighter together. "You can't. It's science."

Amelia stepped over to the railing next to Claudia. The strip of sandy beaches highlighted the ridge where the land met the ocean.

The older woman gestured with her hand. "Spain, they tell me, then Portugal. And France is on the left. Am I right?"

"There's a bay there." Amelia pointed. "North of Spain. That's where we're headed."

Claudia stretched her chin down, impressed. "You could fly the *Duchess*, you know. You're so knowledgeable. Have you been to Europe or France before?"

Honesty slipped out of Amelia. "Europe, many times. France, only once."

For the first time since reading in the *Chicago Record* that Elizabeth was fleeing to France, Amelia's mind drifted back to her misfortunes there. She had been seventeen when the romance and charm of Paris ran wild with her imagination.

"What would you like for a birthday present this year?" Her mother's dark eyebrows rose in curiosity and encouragement as she folded towels in the kitchen. "Make it a good one, Kate. One that will last you. Something special."

Amelia held up the postcards her close friend, Sophrona, had sent her from Paris. A couple walked along a bridge suspended high over cliff walls and trees. Slender streets zigzagged, lined with houses. Wide boulevards sported five-story buildings replete with thin chimneys. "I want to fall in love, Mama. Here. In Paris."

Her mother plucked a postcard free, switching her bewildered gaze between Amelia and the picture. "Traveling is good. It'll introduce you to new places and new people. Your father will be pleased. It's a practical choice."

Amelia advanced a half step toward her. "I only want to see Paris. There's so much life there. Sophrona has only the best stories about it. Music and art and dancing and people. Anybody who's anybody has been to Paris."

Her mother set her mouth in a firm line and held onto the postcard. "We'll wait and ask your father. Why don't you pass the time with your embroidery?"

Amelia trudged upstairs to her bedroom, adding new stitches to an emerging picture of roses in white thread on a white silk reticule. The passing hours only sharpened her resolve instead of distracting her, her wandering mind leaving her to prick her fingers numerous times with the needle. The moment the front door opened, Amelia dropped her embroidery and descended on her father.

She pressed her palms together in front of her. "May I please go to Paris for my birthday?"

From other rooms, her sister sang unintelligible words to herself off-key, and her brother intoned with plodding precision.

"Three times one is three. Three times two is six. Three times three is ten."

Her mother interjected with stern patience. "It's nine. Try again."

Her father closed the door, his bushy eyebrows tensed in skepticism. Amelia prepared herself to spend the rest of the evening changing his mind.

Over a small supper of vegetable soup and corn bread, Amelia's parents disrupted their usual discussions of schoolwork and good manners to dissuade her from her choice.

Her father continually shook his head. "I don't like it. There's no reason to travel. You'll be spending the rest of your life in Seneca Falls. Seneca County at the very most. You don't need images and memories of Paris getting in the way of your happiness here."

"But I'll never be happy here." Amelia knotted her arms in two punches of her limbs. "I can't stake roots anywhere until I see Paris."

"How do you suppose you'd get there?"

"On a steamship. Like Sophrona and her family."

Her father cocked an eyebrow. "You want me to disrupt this entire family's operations to take you to a place you don't need to go?" He zeroed in on his other two children, who scuffled with each other next to Amelia. "Stop that, both of you! Stop pulling her hair, and quit trying to poke him in the eyes."

Her brother's elbow speared Amelia's side as she attempted to quiet her mind and assuage her insistence. Solemn reason would convince her father, not a maudlin argument. She sat up straighter. "Father, that's not what I'm suggesting. I would never ask you to make such a sacrifice. I'll go by myself."

His eyes and mouth popped into circles. "Young lady, that's preposterous. Do you think there's only middle-class people on those ships? You'd be a stone's throw away from the likes of people you've never seen before. I'd sooner pay you to walk through the roughest parts in town."

Amelia held her countenance steady. "I know about the different people who might be on board. Sophrona told me everything about it. I would stay in my cabin or in the dining room designated to my class. I wouldn't even go out on deck if there was a chance of unsightly characters being around."

Her father sighed, tossing his hand with his spoon dangling from it. "Wouldn't you rather have a fur coat or a pretty hat? A new pair of shoes?"

Amelia regarded him with metered patience. "I only want to go to Paris. If you're going to spend money on a birthday present for me, shouldn't you let me decide what it purchases?"

Her father opened his mouth.

Her mother leaned towards him. "She wants to fall in love, George. That's why she wants to go."

Her father slammed his empty fist down on the table. The china and silverware jumped, as did Amelia, her siblings, and her mother. "Gosh darn it, Katherine! It's a silly idea that wants to ferry you across the Atlantic, is it?"

Amelia clenched her jaw, surprised she could form intelligible words through the vice of it. "Call it silly if you want. You and Mom fell in love once, at the vista of the great Niagara Falls, if I'm not mistaken."

Her father scowled, setting his spoon in his bowl. He positioned his hands on their blades two feet apart on the table. "There's almost literally a world of difference between Niagara

Falls and Paris. I'll gladly send you to Niagara by train as a compromise."

Amelia swiveled her head in perfect rhythm. "Mom asked me to pick something special as my present. This is what I want. I'll accept no substitute."

"But alone? It would take at least a week to get there. The same length to come back. Plus the time you spent there."

"I'll be eighteen, Dad. I can take care of myself that much."

"How much is a ticket?"

"Second class costs forty-five dollars. I don't need any better than that."

Her father swept a palm down his ruddy face. "That's not cheap, Katherine, but I'd pay it if I knew it was contributing to a good cause."

Amelia licked her lips. Her siblings' renewed roughhousing shoved her, and she ignored it. "It'd be an education. I already know a little French. I could learn so much more, right from the people who speak it every day. I could become a teacher or learn how to master French cuisine."

"How long do you plan on staying there?"

"I don't know."

"How much money were you planning on requesting from me to visit there? You'll need a hotel, food, carriage fairs."

Amelia's heart picked up a little. She had counted those expenses in the back of her mind, but faced with her father's economic realities, she had to admit she had not accounted for every possible expenditure. "I can work while I'm there." She scooted to the front edge of her chair. "If you pay for my ticket overseas, I'll take care of everything else. I have a little money of my own, and I can earn the rest. Even my ticket back if I have to."

Her mother stretched her hand across the table and wrapped her fingers around her husband's arm. "Don't do it, George. She'll only be eighteen. It's too far."

Amelia pressed her case. "Forty-five dollars, Dad. That's it. That's all I'm asking for. To give me a firm foundation for the rest of my life."

Her brother crashed against her arm, jolting her. He wriggled against her, his head thrown back. "Katie's going to marry some smelly old Frenchman!"

Amelia stayed locked on her father, intent on keeping his hard-won attention. "I'm not. There are plenty of Americans in Paris I can meet and talk to. I'll come back in a couple of months at the longest."

Her mother tightened her grip on her husband's forearm. "It's a dream, George. What if she can't find a job? She's never gone to another city on her own."

Amelia's sister clanged her spoon against her bowl. "Katie's going to get robbed, gosh darn it!"

Their father pointed a thick finger at his youngest daughter. "Watch your mouth. Nobody's robbing your sister."

Their mother spoke up, her soprano trembling. "Somebody really could, George."

Amelia's heart raced as her father filled his chest with a deep breath. "Katherine, I'm going to meet you on your own terms. I promised you a gift, and if this is what you choose, I'll grant it. But I'm only giving you the ticket to get you there. Everything else will be your responsibility."

Amelia closed her eyes in disbelief. "Yes, Father. Absolutely. I'll make all the arrangements."

"I expect you to write home and tell us how you're doing. I want honest reports, young lady. Where you're going. Where you're staying. Whom you're making friends with. And God forbid, any man you set your sights on to fall in love with."

"Perfectly reasonable."

Her mother extended herself toward her husband's ear. "What's the point of it, George? Forty-five dollars to send her away where we can't aid her if she needs us."

George Harrington plucked his wife's fingers from his arm and set them next to her soup bowl. "That's the point, Sylvia. You wanted her to have something practical. Here it is. The skills she'll learn surviving in France will never leave her. It's time she learned exactly what the world is like without her parents to cushion its blows."

Amelia cut off any more negativity her mother might express. "You won't regret it. Either of you."

Within two weeks of her birthday, Amelia packed her suitcases and boarded a train for the port of New York. She wrote a page to her family every day of the voyage across the water, sharing her fears and excitement as the rocky shore shrank away behind the ship. She minded her manners and kept a sharp lookout for anyone her father would disapprove of her befriending.

Amelia had never felt more mature than arriving in Le Havre by herself and riding an extra one hundred miles by train to Paris. Walking out of the station, the northern neighborhoods of the city unfurled like thousands of Sophrona's postcards glued together. Amelia could not stop staring as she took it in. Only one week removed from her family, she found herself immersed in a different world. Gone was the English language, the American accents, the genteel hard workers of central New York. Fallen away were conversations centered around little more than the falls, the businesses it attracted, and the fight for women's rights. All around Amelia, poised and stately people chatted. Every woman, it seemed, carried herself with natural confidence, draped in a colorful dress adorned with bows, lace, ruffles, and buttons. The men, topped

with hats and completed with spats, did not always wear their
gloves. They murmured to the women with suggestive wiggles
of their eyebrows, earning titters from beneath the twirling
parasols. Amelia grabbled in her mind for the translations to
their French. Some made her heart melt and some fired wanton
red into her cheeks.

Intoxicated all the same, Amelia filled her lungs with a
centering breath. A myriad of smells competed in her nose.
Exotic spices and ingredients from restaurant chefs. Thick,
cloudy incense both earthy and musky. Flowery, sweet
perfumes from women passing by. She set out to prove her
mother's anxiety wrong and her father's trust correct. Amelia
could make it on her own, and every step she took needed to
help her achieve that goal.

The sounds of Paris built layer upon layer in her ears.
Glasses clinking and men bellowing in bars. Accordions and
hurdy-gurdies sending sensual, upbeat musette music rollicking
out of a dance hall's open windows. The bubbling of
conversation from cafés where men and women drank steaming
beverages.

"Garçon!"

"Monsieur!"

"Un café, s'il-vous-plaît."

Amelia relaxed amidst the chaos. Despite the assault on her
senses, the foreignness of the people and their environment,
she reveled in it.

I really am going to enjoy Paris, she thought, more
confident than she had been even when trying to assure her
parents of the same fact.

Her first stop was in a small hotel, not as fancy as others
she had passed but clean and well kept. She carried her single
trunk up to the dark-haired man behind the counter. *"Une
chambre pour une personne, s'il-vous-plaît."*

His eyes roamed over her face and dress. "American?"

Amelia blushed. "Is my accent that bad?"

His French accent made his English laze. "No, it's good. I have a knack for guessing." He consulted an open record book and slid his finger down the page. "We have a good room for you. Upstairs."

"I'll take it." She pressed against the counter as he wrote in the book. "I'm staying for a few months. Do you know where I could find work close to the hotel?"

He quoted her the price of her first week, and she paid it. He stored it out of sight. "There's the tea room, many pastry shops. Printemps department store." His black eyebrows twitched. "The Folies Bergère."

"What's that?"

"A place people go for entertainment. You should apply to be on the stage, a pretty girl like you."

Amelia swallowed and backed away. "No, thank you. Your other suggestions have been most helpful."

He held out her room key.

She snatched it and picked up her trunk. She headed for the stairs on her left.

He called after her. "There are hundreds of artists who would pay you to sit for them."

Amelia assaulted the stairs two at a time and shut herself inside her room. She stood panting inside until she settled down. Elongating her spine, she descended to the lobby like a lady and exited the hotel.

Although the tea room did not need Amelia's help, she followed the owner's advice on finding the other establishments the hotel clerk mentioned. Faced with the two-story façade of the Folies Bergère, Amelia could only gawk at it from the sidewalk's farthest edge. Tattooed men, jugglers, strongmen, and dancing women covered the posters plastered to the walls and windows. She walked on, entering the department store instead.

She approached a clerk in a dark brown suit. "Manager, *s'il-vous-plaît?*"

The man pointed her further into the store. Amelia walked the main aisle between sections, inquiring with every employee she saw. "Manager?"

They gestured her on her way.

A gentleman dressed in a fitted black coat and striped dusky-blue pants stepped up to her. His wide moustache bristled from side to side, and he laid a hand on his chest. "Manager. *Bonjour.* How may I help you?"

Amelia rubbed her hands together. "I don't know much French, and I've never sold anything in my life, but I'm interested in a job."

He hummed with amusement. "Charming. Honest."

"Do you have an opening?"

"We can always use extra help at Printemps." He motioned for her, and she moved into step at his side as he walked. "Many of our customers speak some English. I'm sure you could help them without too much trouble."

"What would I sell?"

The manager stopped by a rack of hanging suit jackets, trailing his long fingers down a dark sleeve. "Men's clothing."

Amelia's mouth dropped open. "Sir, I can't. I don't know the first thing about it."

"We only stock the best premade suits they make. Just be yourself, add a touch of flattery and good taste. Our tailors and cashiers will do the rest. Would you like the job or no?"

Amelia pushed past her apprehensions. "I'll take it."

That evening, Amelia walked back to her hotel on sore, tired feet. Her lips turned up despite her sleepy mind, and a sigh of accomplishment escaped her lungs.

She wrote to her family as she said she would, mailing letters almost daily. She gushed about her manager's praise of her sales and newly acquired French phrases. She racked her vocabulary to describe the foods, beverages, and pastries she filled herself with at every meal. When an attractive young man bought three ties from her, she ended the story with a joke. *I may marry him and stay in Paris forever! (Just kidding!)*

Every evening on the way to the hotel from her job, Amelia passed the Folies Bergère.

Sometimes men stumbled out, supporting each other on buckling legs. Their disgruntled whines echoed in the street.

"Pas terrible!"

"Le pire!"

Other times, a group of artists stood outside the door, comparing their sketches and techniques. Amelia tried to peek at their work, but humility for the ignorance of their craft always kept her at a distance.

One night, a lone figure reclined against the wall of the neighboring building, and Amelia blinked to clarify the details of his face. The young man who purchased ties from her regarded her with curiosity, his eyes sparkling in the light of the streetlamps.

Just as she walked in front of him, assuming he did not intend to speak to her, he tipped his hat. "How do you do?" His clean, natural pronunciation struck her more in the street than it had the few times he had spoken English in Printemps. "Isaac Washburn."

Her mouth hung open. "You're American." Her manners caught up to her. "Pleased to meet you. Kate Harrington. I just arrived a few days ago from New York."

"I arrived three months ago from... all over." Isaac beamed with a charismatic tilt of his head. "Have you moved to Paris permanently?"

"No, it's only for a few months."

"That surprises me. You fit in so well. What about your job at Printemps?"

Amelia lowered her chin, humbled and flattered he would remember so much about her. "It's temporary so I can afford my food and hotel."

He ducked his head to find her eyes. "Did I embarrass you? I'm sorry."

"I didn't expect you to know who I was."

"Shy, then?" He peeled away from the wall. "Don't be. You should be used to people remembering the pretty girl who helped them pick out three of the best ties in France. I'm wearing one of them now." Isaac unbuttoned the top of his brown overcoat and pulled the wool aside. A silver silk tie marked with a pattern of black hash marks hung from his collar.

"It suits you nicely." Amelia's face flushed. She could not think about her reason for coming to Paris without her thoughts scattering like cockroaches from the light. "I'm not used to working."

"I'm not fond of work, either."

Amelia pointed to his outfit. "Then how can you afford silk ties?"

"Lucky, I guess." He arranged his coat over his chest. "Are you on your way to where you're staying?"

"Yes. I was going to stop off for soup and pastries on the way."

"Do you mind if I join you? I can pay my own way. It won't come out of your salary." He winked at her.

Amelia wobbled with a faintness that had never touched her before. When her corset squeezed her too tightly, it could make her lightheaded, but this was different. Had love found her already, her first week in Paris? How quickly she might prove her parents wrong. "You may walk and eat with me, Mr. Washburn."

Isaac snatched her hand and wrapped it around his arm. "This is for your own protection, Miss Harrington. Other men will see us together and refrain from throwing themselves at you."

Amelia tried to keep her head but a wave of giddiness swept over her. A boldness she rarely exercised overtook her manners. "What about you acting forward with me?"

"That I plan to continue until you ask me to stop."

She beamed as wide as her cheeks. Amelia wrestled her mouth into a more solemn shape, resolving to better behave herself. "I'll keep that in mind in case you say something too brash."

Isaac squeezed her hand where it stretched around his arm. "Don't you love the city at night?"

"I haven't spent much time out at night. Do you frequent the Folies Bergère often?"

"A few times a week. I don't care what they say. Entertainment is fun, whether the act stinks or does well."

The front desk clerk of Amelia's hotel had mentioned the place with questionable motives. "Someone told me I should work there."

Isaac frowned. "A man, I suppose?"

"Yes."

Isaac's arm tucked her hand closer against his ribs. "You don't belong with that crowd. Printemps suits you fine."

"How do you know? You've barely met me."

"I have a knack for knowing people. You seemed at ease in the department store, talking to customers. Up on stage or serving drinks at the bar of the Folies Bergère?" Isaac hummed in disagreement. "That's not your scene."

"Tell me more about myself," Amelia invited, having never met such an insightful, intuitive person before.

Isaac rubbed his chin, muttering to himself as he inspected her hat, her face, her clothes, her gloved hands, and her gait. He *tsked*. "I'm afraid I must diagnose you with a horrible case of romanticism."

She gasped in a war between surprise and offense. "How can you tell that?"

"Because, as you said, we barely know each other, and yet, here we are." Isaac gestured to the street around them with a flourish of his free hand. "Walking close together on our way to dinner before I see you safely to your hotel."

Amelia could not argue with his evidence or conclusions. "I believe I can trust you."

Isaac laid his hand over hers on his arm. "Forget the soup. Let me take you to the best croissants in the city."

"In the whole city? At this hour? How far away is it?"

"A five-minute walk."

Amelia could find no reason to refuse. "Lead me. I only know a few streets in Paris without a map."

"Miss Harrington, I will gladly be your guide."

Within the half hour, Amelia and Isaac relaxed outside a bakery enjoying better croissants than she knew existed. Each flake of dough landed as light as a snowflake on her tongue. Every bite flooded her taste buds with butter and weightless bread. They ate until they could taste nothing else, and Isaac wrapped Amelia's hand around his arm once more.

"Come on." His eyes shone with warmth. "I'll walk you home."

Amelia's real return would take her by train back to Le Havre, then rolling across the ocean's vastness to her waiting house in New York. *"Home* is thousands of miles away. Or can you walk on water?"

"I've never tried. Shall we head south to the Seine and find out?"

Amelia giggled. "No. I haven't seen the Seine yet."

"What about the Jardin de Luxembourg?"

"No. I haven't been anywhere but the train station, the department store, my hotel, and any place in between."

"Then allow me to be your escort, your personal ambassador from Paris to you."

"But why? You're not Parisian."

"I belong to any city I love. And I sense you love Paris, too."

"I do."

"So tomorrow, I'll show you the Seine, and on your next day off, I'll take you to the gardens."

Amelia swelled with appreciation. "That sounds wonderful."

Isaac ushered Amelia into the lobby of her hotel and tipped his hat. He narrowed his eyes at the desk clerk and walked out, the street's shadows obscuring his coat. Amelia waltzed up to her room, suspended in the dream of meeting someone who was at once her admirer and her guide. Her stationery, adorned with lilies and a bird in the upper corner, lay out on the mahogany desk's green felt top, but the thrill of meeting Isaac and the extra walking had left her too happily exhausted to set anything down in script that night. She changed into her white cotton nightgown and climbed into bed.

True to his word, Isaac appeared outside Printemps for her the next evening.

She walked at a natural pace at his side. "I sold more suits today." Her preoccupied eyes followed the lines between the stones of the street. "Sometimes I think they buy from me because they're intrigued or take pity on my poor French."

Isaac pouted. "No other men asked your opinion on ties, did they?"

Amelia's heart fluttered. "No. A woman came in with her grandfather, but he wasn't interested in me."

Isaac crowed loud and clear. "Miss Harrington, you charm me. Every man you see is enchanted by you, even if they don't show it. Perhaps, especially then."

Amelia doubted it. They wandered another fifteen minutes, and a paved square opened up, centered around the largest artifact she had ever seen. Her eyes followed the grey stone obelisk skyward, scenes and images carved into it for seventy-five feet. Its four flat surfaces united into a point at the top.

Isaac's vision scaled it, too. "It's Egyptian. Have you seen hieroglyphics before?"

Amelia could only shake her head. The clear, simple pictures and lines stole her breath away, eyes, birds, and symbols she could not make sense of. Amelia retired to her hotel room that night before she realized she and Isaac had never made it to the river. She had inspected the obelisk for a marvelous eternity and then moved on to exploring the sprawling Jardin des Tuileries. She dropped into the desk chair, determined to write at least a brief note to her family.

Dear loved ones – visited an obelisk and a large garden tonight with a friend. We meant to see the river, but I was too intrigued by what stood along the way. Soon, the Jardin de Luxembourg! All my honest affections, Kate.

On Sunday, Isaac arrived in front of the hotel in the back seat of an open, hired carriage. Amelia climbed up beside him, nestling against his side as the spring breeze swept her downy bangs back from her face. She did not care how long the ride lasted. The sun caressed her skin. Birds warbled, and she rested her cheek against Isaac's shoulder. The carriage crossed one of the stone bridges spanning the river, diverting Amelia from her companion for a few moments. *I finally got to see the Seine,* she remarked in passing.

At the garden's entrance, Isaac tapped the carriage driver on the back. "Wait for us here." He passed a few paper bills to the man.

He counted them with quick flicks of the money through his fingers. *"Oui, monsieur."*

Isaac stepped down from the carriage and lent Amelia his hand as she descended. Statues, fountains, and greenery dotted the landscape in every direction. A puppet show delighted children and adults alike. At the end of everything stood a cream-grey stone palace grander than any building Amelia had ever seen, two stories in the middle and three on each end. Even its roof fascinated her, rising in a number of navy peaks flanked with chimneys. Above the column-adorned façade, statues and etchings stood under a rounded roof. A gazebo-like structure topped it, graced with the waving French flag.

In the evening, Isaac and Amelia returned to the carriage. Isaac addressed the driver in quick, quiet French. Instead of steering toward neighborhoods more familiar to Amelia, the carriage traveled further into the heart of the city.

Amelia peered into Isaac's contented face. "Where are you taking me now?"

He grinned like a cat enjoying a bellyful of the neighbor's parakeet. "You'll see."

After several blocks, the carriage stopped, and Isaac guided Amelia down to the sidewalk. In the middle of a fountain rose the most detailed collection of statues Amelia thought possible, more real than life itself. Four pairs of bronze horses reared on their back legs, kicking amidst the spray. Their mouths opened in whinnies Amelia could almost hear. Around the scalloped perimeter of the fountain, sculpted fish spewed streams of water from their mouths. Metal turtles hovered at the surface of the pool, shooting sparkling jets back up and over the fish. On a tiered and decorated platform in the center of the wonder, four young women danced as they supported an ornate, cage-like globe above their heads. Their faces represented different backgrounds of the world, and they bared their soft, strong bodies completely except for swaths of cloth covering their hips. Amelia tried to take it all in, overwhelmed into dizzying silence by its boldness, grandeur, and representation of everything she had experienced in France.

Isaac took her arm and guided her to face him. Amelia expected him to tell her the name of the fountain, but his hand stirred against her hair, pinned in numerous sections of curls to the back of her head. He kissed her tenderly, releasing her with the same gentleness. "I hope I haven't gone too far."

Sincerity filled his grey eyes, and she could barely speak. "You haven't."

Her heart threatened to burst, full of every romantic song and poem she had ever read. She could scarcely imagine a more perfect, lovely scene. Isaac aided her into the carriage and saw her to the hotel lobby without accident or incident.

Amelia floated up the stairs, no longer walking but levitating from one destination to the next. As she did every night, she saw her stationery sitting on the desk in her room. She wanted to laugh and scream and cackle and gloat. She would keep her affair a secret from her family, at least for now. She had succeeded in her goal, and all she wanted was to bask in Isaac's affections.

Chapter Twenty-Three

Weeks passed in a daze of selling menswear and meeting with Isaac. They fell into a routine in the evenings of sharing croissants and sipping wine before Isaac walked Amelia to her hotel. On Sundays, free from her duties at Printemps, she traveled the city in a rented carriage next to Isaac. Since sightseeing proved so inexpensive, her nest egg grew to make her proud. Having never earned so much money of her own before, Amelia's impulses pulled her in opposite directions: save it or spend it?

In the interests of enjoying better quality time with Isaac, Amelia splurged more than she had her first few weeks in the city. She paid for older, fuller wines. She picked out chocolate truffles in place of strawberry and raspberry tarts. For their outings under the June sun, she bought a white silk parasol covered in layers of intricate lace to shade herself with. Of all the art, music, and monuments Isaac shared with her, the Fontaine de l'Observatoire where he first kissed her remained her favorite.

Unable to top the fountain and its meaning to her, she resisted his offers of visiting other tourist attractions, especially if they cost money. An increasing number of coins jingled amongst the crisp bills in her reticule, begging to be spent. In time, the shops around Printemps beckoned Amelia towards them.

Isaac stood with her on the sidewalk while she browsed store merchandise through the windows. Sometimes he joined her in peeking inside. Most of the time, he gauged her enthusiasm and reactions. "You know I'd buy you everything in there if I had the money," he said.

"I know." Amelia fluttered inside to hear him say it. "I don't need all of it. I want something special I can take with me when I leave."

"You're still leaving Paris?"

"Eventually. I don't like to think of it, either, but I promised my family I'd only be gone a few months."

Isaac bent his head toward the glass and the objects displayed behind it. "What strikes your fancy? The music box? Trinket box? The clock?"

Amelia tingled with possibilities. "Let's go inside and find out."

Isaac swung the door open, and Amelia swept into the shop, surrounded by dozens of articles vying for her interest. She took her time considering the ones that really spoke to her, moving past paperweights and porcelain figurines she might have snatched up in her youth. A marble clock stood sturdy and decorated on a shelf, its gold accents flashing like fire in the lamplight. Amelia picked it up, measuring its heft in her hands. Horses reared up on either side of its round, ivory face. A neat, golden bow added charm above it.

Isaac's voice rumbled near her ear. "Do you own anything like it?"

"Not even close. It's heavy, though. How would I travel with it? To the hotel, then all the way to New York?"

"You'd manage it if you really wanted it."

"It's beautiful."

"How much do they want for it?"

Amelia found a sticker adhered to the back of the clock showing the handwritten price. She sucked in a breath and lowered the timepiece. "Much more than my ticket to France."

Isaac nudged her. "Can you afford it?"

"If I stop eating truffles and drinking good wines, I can buy it and remain in my hotel."

"You should treat yourself." Isaac's bare fingers brushed Amelia's spiraled locks off the back of her neck. "You deserve it."

Amelia's skin trembled, and she held the clock closer to her. "I'll buy it, then."

Isaac made sure to keep it safe for her through the rest of the day, laying his coat across its paper bag in the carriage to hide its presence from prying passersby. He reminded Amelia of it so she would not kick it or trip over it. At the end of the evening, Isaac directed their driver back to the Fontaine de l'Observatoire, where he walked with her through the flower-perfumed garden flanked by rows of robust chestnut trees.

Amelia clung to Isaac, whether they strolled arm in arm or paused to embrace in the shadows of the magnificent boughs. She could not bear the thought of leaving him for the night or when her time in Paris was over.

He escorted her into the hotel lobby, ferrying the clock under his free arm. "Would you like me to carry this upstairs for you?"

Amelia answered right away. "Yes, please."

Isaac accompanied her up the stairs, and Amelia unlocked the door to her room.

He opened it before she had the chance. "Did you think I'd forget my manners?" he joked.

Amelia stepped in before him, a decision preoccupying her mind. "You can set it here." She directed him to the nearest surface, the desk's felt top. "Where I can treasure it whenever I'm here."

Isaac lifted the clock out of its bag and unwrapped the paper around it. He set the timepiece on the desk, angling it so it could be cherished from almost anywhere in the room. He folded up the bag and paper. "Good night, Kate. I'll see you tomorrow."

Lightheaded with her own forwardness, Amelia closed the door with the quietest of clicks. She met Isaac's blinks and askew eyebrows with a quick kiss. She pressed her door key into his palm. "I don't want to say goodbye. I want you to come and go as you please."

Isaac laid the brown paper on the desk and set his hand against her lower back. "What if I don't want to go?"

She eased toward him, whispering. "You stay."

Amelia had never acted so brazen in her life, but she followed her heart where it wanted to go. Isaac led her through the fumbling of buttons, the shedding of layers. The last ones made Amelia shy away, but with Isaac's mutual nakedness, she could hardly stay embarrassed. He guided her to the bed, uttering only the sweetest of compliments, and the coupling of their bodies bonded Amelia closer to him than anyone else in the world.

In the morning, they shared knowing smiles over breakfast before Isaac walked her to Printemps. He met her in the evening as usual, using her key that night to let them into her room.

On Tuesday, the ritual repeated itself.

Wednesday morning, a tangle of street musicians played beneath a house's open window. A woman sticking out of it waved dirt out of a rug, shooing them away. The musicians remained, and yelling at them flushed the woman's face crimson from chin to forehead. Amelia and Isaac chuckled about it as they walked the next several blocks. In the evening, Amelia exited Printemps to a street crowded by many people but could not see Isaac. Perturbed that he had her room key and concerned something might have delayed him, she waited outside the store for over an hour. Through all the foot traffic and horse-drawn carriages, he did not appear. Amelia followed the street down to the Folies Bergère, where every man who was not Isaac Washburn loitered outside its walls. She pressed on to her hotel, barreling past the desk clerk and jogging up the stairs to her room. Perhaps Isaac waited there for her. Maybe he had fallen sick or injured himself in an accident.

Amelia tried the doorknob, and the door popped open. She stepped in one foot at a time, peering around the room, which appeared exactly as she had left it. Except the desk. Beside her stationery lay the room key she had entrusted to Isaac. And next to them, an empty space where her marble clock once sat.

Chapter Twenty-Four

The summer she was twelve, Amelia smashed her thumb with a hammer. Her father had hired a repairman to replace a squeaky step at the bottom of the stairs, and his collection of tools fascinated Amelia. When everyone else cleared the room, while her father settled his bill, she copied the motions she had witnessed. Pretending to hold a nail to a stair between the banister spindles, she struck the hammer down. Its direct hit shot pain and shock through her flesh. It swelled and darkened while she cried, finding some solace in her mother's soothing. Her father took a block of ice from the icebox and chipped at it, a succession of its frozen pieces wrapped against her hand trading numbness for the sting.

Until the day Isaac disappeared with her heart and her clock, Amelia would have said her throbbing thumb gave her the worst pain of her life. It faded into a distant memory now, and she would have gladly struck her thumb a second time in exchange for never knowing Isaac Washburn.

She curled up in bed for days, clenching her pillow and sobbing into it. Only when her hollow stomach ached for food did she drag herself out of the covers. She did not bother arranging her hair or putting on a fresh dress. The desk clerk gawked at her as she passed him, once to buy food and again to return to eat it in her room.

She lived in the dark. She left the curtains drawn across the window although she hated their white-and-pink floral pattern on the muted red background. It reminded her of who she had been – romantic and carefree. She despised her earlier inclinations, cursing the ideas of love, travel, and happiness. She would never be the same. She acknowledged it deep in her soul, if it was still there, lurking amidst her shriveled heart and quivering lungs.

Amelia's money reserves shrank by the day until fear roused her. She hauled her carcass out of the covers, washed herself, and shuffled her feet down to Printemps.

Her manager waved her away, his moustache bunching. "*No*. I am done with you. You left me without help in your department for days."

"I have no other job." Every syllable came as a breathy, exhausted effort. "I need the money."

"Where were you when I needed you?" He motioned her toward the door with both hands.

Amelia slunk away, and in an instant, she realized where she would end up. She traversed the long road to the Folies Bergère, and for the first time in her two months in Paris, she opened the door.

"I'll do anything," she swore to the owner. "Sweep floors. Serve drinks. I think I can sing a little."

The man eyed her with perceptive but unimpressed scrutiny. "We'll stick to the first two. We'll let you do the third if we need talent for the night."

Amelia conversed with no one unless she had to. She avoided customers' eyes when she served drinks at the white-marble bar, and she tucked her chin when she cleaned up after the shows. The few times the owner persuaded or begged her to take the stage, her wholesome songs in English made the crowd groan until Amelia refused to remain in front of them.

Amelia meandered to her hotel by herself, shoulders hunched forward, arms wrapped in a tight bundle against her stomach. Any man who tipped his hat to her or offered a word of greeting she sneered at. Any woman offering her a friendly tilt of her parasol she pitied.

There are no reasons for joy in this life, she thought. *They'll learn that soon enough.*

Leaving the hall one night, a glimpse of Isaac standing across the street spooked Amelia like a ghost. Unlike how awe had paralyzed her during her arrival to Paris and loss had frozen her those first few days after Isaac's betrayal, Amelia's lungs took their first bellyful of healthy air in weeks. She strode across the white-stoned road, aimed at Isaac like a revolver's fired bullet.

Isaac raised his eyebrows in casual familiarity. "You're still in Paris."

Amelia swung her hand full force, smacking his cheek in a sharp *clap* that stung her palm. His face snapped to the opposite side. He vacillated his jaw and turned his head to meet her directly. Amelia reeled her other hand back and slung it at him.

Isaac raised his arm, blocking her wrist with his. He wrapped his fingers around her forearm, his grasp close but loose. "Once is enough."

"It's not enough!" she hissed. "Do you know what you've done to me?"

"What have I done, Miss Harrington?"

"You broke my heart!" She wrenched her arm out of Isaac's hand. "You pretended you'd miss me when I left, then you abandoned me here. You talked me into buying a clock I could hardly afford, and then you stole it behind my back."

"Will you listen to yourself?" He acted as if she had never assaulted him. He motioned to the French men and women strolling past, muttering to themselves. "Will you listen to them? Everybody's wondering about the two crazy Americans fighting in the street."

"I'm not crazy. I'm going back to America as soon as I can afford it."

"Do you really blame me for leaving you alone? You were alone when you traveled here. I merely returned you to your original state."

Amelia snarled in his face. "Without a word. No notice at all. You don't care about me."

"That's not true, but let's talk about the clock. It's such a tiny thing in the grand scope of the world. Is it worth all this anger and violence?"

"You knew what that clock meant to me. What did you do with it? Why did you take it?"

"I sold it. I needed the money."

Amelia groaned with aggravation, wanting to strike him again. "I would've given you the money if you asked. There's no way you earned what it was worth. Tell me. Were you planning to steal from me when you encouraged me to go in the store or right from the day we met?"

Isaac pursed his lips. "Don't give me that much credit. Don't you believe in spontaneity?"

"I believe in not running away from people who care about you and showing up at their place of employment to gloat about it. We're done, Mr. Washburn." Amelia spun on her heel and fled toward her hotel.

"That's all well and good," he called after her. "But my name isn't Washburn. It's Broots. Charles Broots."

Amelia paused and gawked at him. "You told me it was Washburn. Isaac."

He shrugged. "It's Broots. Now."

Amelia stomped over and planted her feet in front of him. "You didn't even give me your real name?"

"No."

She scrutinized every cocky muscle in his face. "You're not telling me the real one now, either. Are you?"

"Are you angry?"

Amelia huffed. "I've never been so livid in my whole life."

A challenge glinted in the murky-grey irises of the man in front of her. "Would you welcome a chance to get even?"

"Even?" Amelia had never heard a better-sounding word. "You bet I would. I wish I knew where to begin."

In fragments of one smooth movement, he reached out, closed his fingers around her wrist, and threaded her hand around his arm. "Come. Eat supper with me. I'll teach you everything you need to know. You can play the game better than me one day if you try."

Amelia set off with the man at her side. She crushed his arm against her ribs out of the desire to punish him rather than her former endearment. "I hope so. I'd love to beat you at your own tricks."

His eyes simmered. "I'd love to watch you do it."

Chapter Twenty-Five

At the rail of the airship *Duchess*, Amelia squinted down fifteen hundred feet at the Spanish coastline she had first spotted from the deck of the steamliner *L'Amérique*. After France, Germany, England, Austria, Bohemia, and several places in between, she liked to think she had nearly perfected Darius' game.

But she had never revisited Paris. She read of its accomplishments and news from other cities across the globe. The mass-attended funeral of the writer Victor Hugo, for whom the city draped its impressive, inspiring Arc de Triomphe in mourning black. The construction of the Eiffel Tower. The hosting of the previous World's Fair, the Exposition Universelle, the year before. Although Amelia would have loved to see these marvels and more, to think of returning, even seventeen years later, crushed her heart.

The man who now called himself Darius Shank had toyed with her in the street outside the Folies Bergère, confident and amused. She had often wondered during their times together and apart how many others he had betrayed before her. How many had he robbed? Misled? Manipulated? How many hearts had he smashed with his conceited ambition? How many young women did he jilt before he found one willing to use his own tactics against him?

And the deepest question of all, one Amelia knew Darius would never answer: what had happened to him to forge him so cavalier and ruthless? To delight in the torture and deception of those around him. To punish anyone who came too close and aim to profit from them in any possible way.

Perusing the periwinkle sky and darker ocean, Amelia was glad Darius' history remained a mystery to her. It kept her from entertaining too much sympathy for him.

Theirs was a game she believed them each willing to play until one or both of them died. Or, as one day might be the case, they killed each other.

Claudia leaned out over the rail, shielding her eyes with her hand. "I wish I could see Paris from here. Did you visit it? Was it beautiful?"

The gardens. The fountains. The monuments, cafés, and grandiose royalty. "Yes," Amelia admitted.

"It should be with all the work they put into it. I remember seeing pictures in a magazine. Simply breathtaking."

Dorothy stepped back from the spyglass. "Maybe you can see it through the scope."

Claudia rushed to the eyepiece and doubled over to access it. She rotated the little crank on the side to adjust its focus. "Oh, I see it, Amelia! I can see the Eiffel Tower from here."

Every muscle from Amelia's hands and arms through her shoulders and chest seized into armor.

"I thought it'd be too far away. Great choice of a spyglass, Elwood."

Elwood stepped toward his mother. "I think the least expensive one on the market could pick it up. It's the tallest building in the world."

Claudia motioned Amelia to the spyglass. "You should see it. Even from here, it's really something."

Amelia swallowed an impressive lump in her throat. "Go ahead and enjoy it. I will in a moment."

"If you insist." Claudia swiveled the device on its stand. "The coast is striking. The boats have more details through the lens."

Dorothy coughed into her gloved hand, sputtering. "Science."

Claudia straightened up from the eyepiece. "You should see it for yourself, Amelia. How many chances will you get to spy Europe from the air?"

Amelia stepped up to the instrument. "All right, but I do have a fear of heights."

"I'll hold onto you, dear." Claudia rested her hand on Amelia's arm.

Amelia trained the lens along the coast of pale beaches, green vegetation, and red roofs. "What are you afraid of, Mrs. Molt?"

Dorothy made a questioning sound like a hiccup. "Why?"

"We both know your mother-in-law's mostly afraid of being abandoned on family trips." Amelia hid her disdain in a casual drawl. "It'd be rude to inquire the same of Mr. Molt. So tell me. What scares you?"

Elwood chortled. "Spiders, and that's just for starts."

Dorothy remained silent until Amelia witnessed her fuming, puckered expression. "I hate rats and mice and all those. Doesn't everybody?"

Amelia pushed out an irritated sigh. It would be hard enough to find spiders on board, let alone vermin. If the staff had found any, they would have taken care of the uninvited pests by now. "All right. What do you like?"

"Like?" Dorothy spat.

Claudia graced the air with delighted exhales. "Don't be a rude parrot, Dorothy. Answer the question."

Amelia tried a new approach. "What do you like to eat? How's that?"

The bad mood twisting Dorothy's features wavered. "Cake. Chocolate cake. As much as I can get."

Elwood tapped Amelia's arm. "That's no joke. She'd have it for every meal if she could with a little steak and potatoes on the side."

Dorothy pouted, souring. "Why do you want to know?"

Amelia aimed her view further to the left, glimpsing what little she could of the Bay of Biscay's dark blue waters. "You've all been so kind to me. Making me feel welcome despite my traveling alone. Letting me use your spyglass at my leisure. I'd like to thank you before I leave the ship, if I can find a way."

Gloved hands appeared in Amelia's peripheral as Dorothy's most pleasant timbre oozed beside her. "Might I help you find the Eiffel Tower?"

Amelia wrestled her smirk away before meeting Dorothy's wide, expectant eyes. "No, thank you. Everything else is quite enough for me."

Chapter Twenty-Six

Sketches across the open pages of the magazine showcased large-brimmed hats adorned with ostrich feathers, black for winter and tan matched with pink flowers for spring. Long-sleeved blouses billowed in gold, amethyst, and topaz silks. Amelia tried to settle on the best cut and color for herself when a few knocks on the door roused her out of her daydream. She set her borrowed copy of *The Delineator* aside and opened the door. Darius' appearance failed to surprise her.

He kept his volume low. "May I come in?"

Amelia detested the lyrical, hinting quality of it, fueled by the fact he knew she would say yes. She stepped aside without answering and secured the door behind him. "Was there something else we needed to discuss?"

Darius considered the magazine's blue-and-gold cover on the bedspread. "Sorry to interrupt your deepest, most intimate thoughts."

Amelia perched on the foot of the bed. "I've been thinking about our plans, too."

"Have you stolen anything else?"

She shook her head.

Darius supported his arm on the dresser beside him. His nostrils flared, and his jaw made tight, pensive movements. "Why not?"

"I have a plan," Amelia assured him. "I just need time and patience to carry it out."

"There's less than a day left before we dock."

"I know." She observed him, relaxed in pose and agitated in spirit. "You know some things are most successfully stolen at the last minute, like my gold-and-marble clock."

Darius lowered his arm from the dresser and adjusted the cuffs of his jacket. "So on the eve of losing access to Elizabeth's room forever, we still have nothing we originally agreed to steal."

"Correct."

"Do you want me to take them?"

Amelia worked to keep desperation and urgency out of her answer. "No. I'll do it."

"I'm worried you've let yourself be sidetracked by some of the people on board. Elizabeth, Lewis, the upstart you were waltzing with. The spiritualists."

Amelia reclined on her elbows. "I'm collecting information. Nothing more." But Lewis had joined with her in that very bed. Picturing herself in his arms quickened her pulse, and she averted her eyes so Darius could not read their changes.

"Very well. Might I ask what you're planning to do with the objects once you have them?"

"I suppose I'll hide them in my luggage and disembark with them. We can arrange a place to meet in Bordeaux to decide what to do with the map. Splitting up the other items will be easier. I know what I want, and you can have the statuette."

Darius sat down next to her, setting his hand on her leg, thumb stroking her tweed skirt. "When I said I trusted you, I meant your brilliant, plotting mind, not your possession of the goods."

"What do you propose, then?" Even though devious and manipulating, Amelia could pinpoint her attraction to him. The sure, even brows. High cheekbones and sharp jaw. The depths of his eyes and muscled lines of his neck. She wished for a moment the game did not exist, and they were simply two people resting on a bed.

Instead, Darius drew his fingers in slow, halting circles and patterns across her thigh. "Before we leave the ship, you give me the bracelet you're so wild about for me to safeguard for you. Since you've intrigued me with your description of the statue, once you take it, you can hold onto it for me until we meet again. As for the map..." Darius gave her leg a gentle squeeze and met her lips with a tender kiss. "Do you still plan to share that with me?"

Amelia breathed in his earthy, spicy cologne. He never aimed so low as to merely smell good. Only the heights of seduction would please him. After so many years of his different colognes, she kept her head and answered his query. "Of course. I plan to share all of it with you. I didn't have to tell you about the map in the first place." She graced his angled cheek and firm jaw with kisses. "I didn't have to find other items of value to us, either."

From the brass speaker by the door, a man's baritone burst into the cabin. "Greetings, passengers! This is Captain Silas J. Barrett inviting you to tour the lower deck. As we'll be landing tomorrow and no harm or danger has befallen us, I'm proud to offer you this most unique of opportunities. I'll be showing off the engine room, map room, and steering room shortly. Another round of guests can join me for a second tour of the same locations prior to dinner." He paused. "Thank you."

The speaker and the room lapsed into heavy silence. Amelia and Darius remained close.

His temple touched hers. "Let's be honest for once." His words fell close and clear in her ear. "We don't trust each other. Holding the object the other one wants might be the only way to discourage us from double-crossing each other."

"You don't believe that," Amelia murmured. "It'd work fine as blackmail if we actually cared. We could just as easily take off with what the other person wanted – without batting an eye – as stay to retrieve the object we want. It'd leave the other person with nothing worth the trouble."

Darius lifted his hand off her thigh and planted it on her arm. "If you give over the bracelet and hold onto the statue for me, I'll let you guard the map until we meet in Bordeaux."

Amelia lingered at the crossroads Darius laid out for her. The map tempted her, drawing her toward any thin thread of permission to safekeep it, but she had to be smart. She knew it was his last-ditch effort to win her over, to tie her to him in case she was planning to keep the map for herself despite her claims. Yes, she wanted the bracelet, but if she was able to outsmart Darius the rest of the way, the map would never leave her hands. With its sale, she could buy all the jewelry she could ever want.

It was one of the biggest gambles in her life but the easiest path Darius could possibly offer her.

Amelia planted a long kiss on his stubbled cheek. "I'll give you the bracelet." She got up and opened her jewelry box.

His words plodded with deliberation. "I know how much it pains you to lose things you like."

She narrowed her eyes at him, trying to tease out how much of his tone was apology and how much was exacerbation. "Of course you do. Otherwise, you never would've suggested it." She picked through her jewelry, an eclectic collection of gold and silver, cameos and gemstones. She lifted out the silver-and-pearl bracelet, memorizing its squared design before holding it out to Darius.

He took the bracelet from her and grasped her hand. "Amelia—"

"Don't."

Knocks stole her attention to the door.

Darius droned above a whisper. "Whom are you expecting?"

"No one."

Amelia closed the lid of her jewelry box and opened the door. Alvin greeted her, rocking up and down on his heels.

She swung the door wider ajar. "Mr. Burgess."

He tipped his hat. "I hoped I'd find you here." His gaze wandered past her, where it stuck on Darius. Alvin frowned.

"Is there a problem?" Amelia moved toward him, hoping to distract him from Darius and smooth over both men's presence.

"No." Alvin fixed his pale eyes on Amelia. "Did you catch Captain Barrett's announcement? He's giving tours of the lower deck. In honor of it being the last day before we land and everything."

Amelia caught some of his youthful enthusiasm. "That sounds nice."

"Would you like to go with me?" His blinking stuttered.

"I would." She propped her hand on her hip and addressed Darius. "Will you join us?"

"No." He stood up with languid grace. "I have other business to attend to."

Amelia and Alvin stepped back from each other to let Darius pass between them. His fingers trailed across Amelia's sleeve as he did so, troubling her. Darius had never screamed or made demands in his jealousy. He stewed, he smoldered, and he went out of his way to remind her of who he was to her. He made her who she was, and he did not intend to lose her to anyone. Not a German scapegoat, a Cuban cabana boy, the doting Lewis, or the outgoing Alvin. But Darius' long fuse did not mean he held himself above exploding into violence with quick fists and broken china.

Amelia joined Alvin in the hallway and locked her door. Darius strode away the length of the corridor, veering right in the open area toward the lounge. Amelia tucked her hand around Alvin's arm and mustered the most genuine happiness she could. "Lead the way."

Alvin guided her up the hall. His rare silence bothered her, and she broke it.

"How do you feel about the flight, Mr. Burgess?"

"Fine. As long as it gets me to France in one piece, I think it's a marvelous invention. Three cheers to Captain Barrett for getting us there without so much as spilling a drink with his steering amidst the breezes. Of course, I can spill a beverage without his help."

Amelia flashed through tipping hot black coffee over Darius' lap at breakfast years before. With a shout, he had leapt from his chair and given her the chance to stab him for the Berlin rubies. "I can, too."

Alvin raised his eyebrows. "You? I don't believe it. You're too graceful."

"Accidents happen. Did you forget I dumped my entire dinner on you several nights ago?"

"That was my doing, I assure you. I was in a rush. I'd have to see another of these so-called accidents of yours to tell whether you cause them or not."

They exited the hall into the open area around the staircase. Rudolf steadied Yetta as they arrived at the top step and descended. The French couple followed behind them.

The slim woman's sparkling eyes roamed their surroundings. *"C'est plus excitant!"*

Amelia recognized how fascinated she was but cut herself off from listening in anymore. She had not accepted Alvin's invitation to ignore his company.

"Are you interested in the crew's rooms?" she asked. "Or just trying to escape the same old floors?"

"A little of both. I don't mind the lounges, and I adore the ballroom. But something's going on with my new friends, and no one will tell me what it is."

"The spiritualists?" Amelia tried to sound engaged and ignorant of everything she had witnessed.

Alvin stopped by the stairs, letting other couples advance in front of them. "It was obvious from the time I met them who had eyes for each other. Mother says men never notice things like that, but I think a blind one could. I wasn't going to break up those couples. Celia's an expert in a variety of subjects, which I always admire, even if she is much older than me. Lorena's passionate about her channeling, and she's lovely to look at. Not that you aren't."

His compliment and swift recovery made Amelia smile.

Alvin cleared his throat and scratched his blond head. "They seemed like such good friends. Now they can't stand the sight of each other. Different tables at meals. They're never in the ballroom together. I can't understand it."

Amelia decided to show only part of her hand. "Sometimes a misunderstanding is all it takes."

Alvin started for the stairs but wondered at Amelia. "Do you know about their quarrel?"

"I know about the ones I've had." Amelia had written numerous letters to Sophrona about her extended stay in France, her tangled infatuation with her many-named suitor, and their subsequent trip to London. Sophrona's replies grew more callous by the page.

You only write me these stories to make me want your life! Sophrona accused in packed, scrawling script. *No one calls on me for tea, even the boys I would never marry in a million years. Yet you stayed on in France for months when I had to hurry home after two weeks because of Father's business. He says we'll be lucky to ever see London the way sales have been. And you get to travel with a handsome rake? Your father would kill you if he could reach you.*

The letter arrived the day Amelia skipped London, leaving her rake behind with barely enough money for a hired carriage. She mailed a response before she sailed out of Portsmouth.

My dear friend Sophrona – I never intended to spite you. I'm leaving England now, and I'm going alone. I don't know where I'll end up or when I'll set a course for home. This will be my last letter to you. My advice is to burn them all. That way they can't hurt you and my father will remain blissfully unaware of the complicated paths my life has taken. Farewell – good health – good husband!

Amelia struggled with how to sign her name. She could not bring herself to sign *Kate* anymore. The girl she had been would not have stolen a five-dollar bill or abandoned even the newest of acquaintances in such a manner. She settled on her initials, looping the ink into a large *KAH* before sliding the letter into an envelope. Of all the lies Darius' influence sparked her to tell, she kept her promise to Sophrona. She never relied on her childhood companion to keep her secrets again or supplied her with a more current city of address.

Walking down the stairs of the *Duchess* on Alvin's arm, the loss of Sophrona's friendship gaped like a fresh wound in Amelia's chest. She pulled his arm closer to her. "How many people do you think will join us for the tour?"

Alvin checked over his shoulder at the footsteps behind them. "Hopefully not too many. I'm not sure the captain meant to squeeze more than three dozen people down here at a time."

Amelia tried to lighten her mood with a joke. "He shouldn't have invited the whole ship, then."

Alvin rewarded her with a chuckle.

Behind them, Iris snarled. "Good riddance, if you ask me."

Timidity slowed Priscilla's words. "I thought Mr. Ames was nice. He knows an awful lot about music."

A man near her gave a throaty harrumph. *"Awful* is right. If I had to hear about that Peabody place one more time, I was going to string him up by his ascot."

Priscilla spoke up with a tremble. "It's an institute. In Baltimore."

The man growled in response.

Alvin spoke up, pulling Amelia back into her own situation. "I didn't think you knew him that well."

"Who?"

"The man who's always near you."

"Mr. Shank."

They descended to the bottom of the stairs, unable to move forward for the still, standing crowd in front of them. The clean white walls proved far less engaging than the ones upstairs covered in detailed, formal paper.

Amelia quieted to keep their conversation as private as possible. "It's complicated."

"You said you weren't friends."

"We're not." Amelia found a glimmer of confusion and sadness in Alvin's eyes. "Sometimes when you travel, you meet the kinds of people you wouldn't have met staying at home."

Alvin gave her hand preoccupied pats where it rested around his arm. "That's certainly true."

Captain Barrett, in his sleek black-and-white hat, stepped out of a doorway to meet his captive audience. "Welcome, kind passengers!" He raised his hands into the air. "Can all of you see me?"

The crowd replied with a medley of words and hums.

"Can all of you hear me?" A knowing guess at the answer warmed Captain Barrett's question.

"Yes," the passengers responded as one.

"Glorious. Let's proceed. Now, you needn't let the crew quarters unnerve you. I'm sure you'll recognize the same layout as the decks you're used to. I hope you'll forgive me for not showing you everything. The crew cabins and mess room aren't prepared for public viewing, I assure you, and you're hardly prepared for them. I'll guide you by the kitchen first."

The mass of people flowed forward and to the right. Amelia and Alvin moved with them, trapped in their midst.

Pride filled Captain Barrett's announcement. "Here's where all your first-rate meals are prepared. We can't go in. We wouldn't fit, and we wouldn't want to disrupt the activities that will create our dinner. So if you'd like to peek inside, be my guest, as we move on to the rooms I promised you."

The couples in front of Amelia did not budge, and she tensed at being surrounded with no easy exits. Her sharp vision sought them out, the slim crevices between bodies that would let her slip through if needed.

Behind Amelia, Priscilla continued her campaign. "I don't know what you don't like about him. He's been perfectly polite and pleasant."

"Showoff," Iris grumbled.

Their husbands offered terms of their own. "Bore."

"Philanderer."

Alvin dropped his head close to Amelia's. "For what it's worth, I think you could do better for a friend or a non-friend than Mr. Shank. And you probably should."

Amelia told him the truth. "I didn't think he'd be on board." Knowing Darius' history, she derided herself for failing to assume he would buy a ticket. But with the journey nearly over, she had little choice but to forgive herself just as quickly.

"Can't you tell him to go away and leave you alone?" Alvin suggested.

A miniscule space opened in front of Amelia, and she crept forward. "The ship's not that big. I avoid him when I can, but he knows he can find me."

"Like when you're trying to dance or win a game of shuffleboard."

Amelia read deeper into Alvin's expression. His eyes, light and bright, revered her, but a crease of concern furrowed his forehead. Like Lewis, Alvin showcased no ulterior motive for his good intentions. On the other hand, she had witnessed some of his less-than-honorable deeds, and Amelia could only admit to herself how much he baffled her. Why did a liar and a pickpocket care whom she associated with in the air between shores? "I can handle Mr. Shank."

"Maybe, but you shouldn't have to if you don't want to. He's not the friendliest fellow. I doubt anyone knows what brought him to the *Duchess* or why he's going to France, except maybe you."

Amelia held her tongue from pointing out the same proved true of Alvin. She tried to steer him away from his interest in Darius. "I think most of our motives are hidden from the other passengers. Why are any of us on board? To see a foreign country. To have an experience on the *Duchess* most people will never have. And to earn bragging rights about all of it once we return to the States."

"That's true."

Amelia and Alvin stepped up to the kitchen doorway. Long wooden countertops like Amelia had never seen before held glass canisters and stacks of soiled dishes. Large spoons and gleaming silver pots hung from the walls. Three dumbwaiters gaped open on the left, stretching up through the ceiling to the dining room. Several stoves stood in a row, scrubbed by cooks in dark suits and white aprons. Five other men huddled at one of several square worktables in the middle of the room, one of them motioning to a hand-written white paper in his hand.

Captain Barrett spoke up ahead. "Here we have the map and navigations room. We need charts of every kind to make sure we're on course or as close as we can fly. They let us identify landmarks and know how much farther we have to travel. Some of our maps show the basics, and others are highly detailed. It's those maps of precision that helped us fly out of Albany and will help us land safely in Bordeaux."

A man's nervous, boastful guffaws burst out from the front of the crowd. "Don't tempt bad luck, captain. It's a long way to the water."

Celia spoke up with cool assurance. "He isn't. We can trust Captain Barrett's abilities and his familiarity with the ship. I know."

Captain Barrett cleared his throat. "Right. Thank you, ma'am." He strengthened his speech for the whole audience. "You may step foot in the map room if you like. It won't disturb anything. We're going to keep making our way to the front of the airship. Like the top deck, this floor goes all the way to the bow."

A woman murmured, "I haven't seen the top deck."

Rudolf Greisman answered in his thick Polish accent. "You aren't missing much. Just the view. The murderess is up there half the time. Do you really want to join her?"

Amelia tensed on Elizabeth's behalf, sorry for how much the jury's decision impacted her life year after year. How much would Elizabeth suffer to know the sole living witness of her husband's murder selfishly chose to remain silent?

Alvin muttered to her. "There's no wondering why Mrs. Cole is sailing the breezes to France. I bet she can't wait to get away where fewer people know who she is."

Amelia tried to relieve her conscience in a whisper. "I don't think she did it."

Alvin's eyebrows shot up. "Really? Why not?"

"Why would she? She had everything she wanted. Money and a husband to earn it for her. A young lover to give her what her husband couldn't."

Alvin tilted his head. "I didn't realize you knew so much about Mrs. Cole."

"I've had occasion to speak with her. She's a far cry from the monster everyone believes her to be."

He blinked at her. "You seem to have dealings with the most questionable characters on the ship. Perhaps I should worry even more about you?"

"Not at all." Amelia hugged his arm closer to her. "They won't harm me."

They stepped through the doorway of the map room. Several crewmen sat at tables and desks in the center, consulting charts and compasses. They tapped printed figures and recorded new notations. One of them clutched a half-eaten sandwich in one hand, brushing fallen crumbs off his pant leg onto the floor. Gigantic maps covered two walls, magnifying the east coast of the United States, the west coast of France, and the long stretch of ocean in between. The right-hand wall held shelving and cubbyholes storing maps and small pieces of equipment.

Alvin led Amelia back to the hallway, the opposite wall lined with doors a cabin's width apart. The Coateses and Bankses stepped into the map room.

"Are you bored, Priscilla?" one of the two men asked her. "Cheer up. Perhaps someone on the crew can entertain you with his harmonica."

A man volleyed from inside the room, his enunciation muffled by food. "Sorry. I can only play the bass."

Captain Barrett's baritone rang out from deeper in the hallway. "That's it. Keep following me. You might've been wondering who's steering the ship if I'm giving a tour. Not to worry. I have carefully trained crewmembers who are able to take over the helm whenever I'm away from it. We all had plenty of practice before any of you fine folks came on board."

The group shuffled forward one half step at a time. The undertones of an expressive conversation sounded from the other side of the wall on the left. A toilet flushed somewhere nearby.

One of the women, snuggled in a fur wrap, stumbled as far from the rush of water as she could. Her mouth drooped in disapproval. "Oh, my."

Captain Barrett raised his hat in a genteel gesture. "My apologies, ladies and gentlemen. Life as a crewmember is a little more savage than the refinements you're used to upstairs."

"And at home," the woman grumbled.

"Quite right," the captain agreed. "Step in, all of you. We've ample room but little time. We don't want to interrupt the running of the ship and miss our docking time."

Amelia and Alvin followed the others to a connecting hallway. They filed into the room straight ahead. For a moment, Amelia could not glimpse much of it. Small tables with chairs sat to her left along the inner wall. In the other direction, she found tall windows twenty feet away, curved to fit the shape of the ship's bow. Beyond their panes floated only blue sky and white clouds. She slunk closer to Alvin.

He gave a start. "What's wrong?"

"I try to avoid reminders of the ship's elevation when I can."

He glanced at the windows. "You've been on deck."

"I'd prefer the deck to this. I can either ignore the endless horizon or peer down and remember there's still a world below us."

"Let's move closer to the windows, then."

Amelia nearly dragged Alvin along with her. A sturdy counter prevented her from setting the tips of her boots and nose against the glass. Beyond the spotless wooden surface, the navy-blue Bay of Biscay and the rolling green mountains of Spain reassured her.

"Don't be shy," Captain Barrett invited. "Come all the way in and see what I do when I work every day. Don't let the switches, knobs, and meters overwhelm you. We know what they mean."

With the sturdy earth below grounding her a little, Amelia surveyed the room. The counter wrapped around the inside of the ship's bow. It widened into a complex control panel at the tip of the room. Several crewmen, calm in demeanor and easy in their motions, attended to the numerous dials, gauges, and control sticks.

Yetta Greisman gestured at the dials and switches. "What do they all do, Captain?"

Captain Barrett turned to the controls. "In short, these gauges tell us everything we need to know to maneuver the *Duchess*. How the engines are doing. How high we're flying. Even how fast we're traveling and what time it is. We don't like to miss meals any more than you do."

He beamed. "These levers and buttons let us control the ship based on the information from our maps and gauges. They're how we keep the *Duchess* steady and on course."

Yetta suspended her shoulders in a shrug. "I'm afraid I don't understand."

"Have you been on a steamliner, ma'am?"

"Yes, but the captain never invited us into his private work rooms."

"You understand how a boat floats." Captain Barrett flattened his hand in the air, bouncing it in slight up and down movements. "A craft floats on water because the men who designed it ensured its pounds are not more than the water can buoy."

Yetta splayed her hands in front of her. "There's no water here, sir."

"There's some in the air, but I'll touch on that in a minute. You see, air works on a similar principle. When Samuel Langley invented the *Duchess*, he had to make it light enough to float." Captain Barrett held his finger up to postpone any objections. "Beneath us and filling out the majority of the ship's structure is a carefully orchestrated system of bags containing hydrogen gas. It's lighter than the air we breathe and keeps us afloat."

"Then what are the engines for?"

"Moving forward, mostly. This might be a good time to show you the engines. Follow me."

Captain Barrett cut through the crowd. Some of the passengers inspected the meters and controls with thoughtful purses of their lips. Others scrunched their eyebrows low, blinking in confusion.

Alvin nudged Amelia. "How many of these aristocrats do you think have seen an engine before?"

She noted the other passengers' pristine clothes and flawless hands. "None outside of any factories they own. How much experience do you have with engines?"

"At least I know what they're for."

"Have you done much traveling back home?"

"A few train trips."

"Did you ride with your father for business?"

Alvin gave a low hum. "Never. It was nice when he went away for a week or two, though." He rocked back on his heels. "I guess my experience with engines is letting them pull my train car and drive my dad out of the station."

They trailed after the rest of the group down a second identical hallway, even the Coateses and Bankses walking ahead of them.

Amelia skirted around the obvious personal aversion Alvin harbored for his father. "You have no interest in joining your father's business?"

Alvin relaxed a little. "No offense to handkerchiefs, shirts, and pants, but I'd like something a bit more exciting for my life than cotton."

For the first time since Luther's pocket watch went missing, Amelia understood Alvin. "You want to travel more."

"Yes, of course. I'm twenty-two. Unchained by the demands of wife and family. Yet. But even as big as the United States is growing, I want more. I want culture and alcohol and dance and excitement. Am I wrong to seek those things?"

"No. That's how I got my start in traveling. Well, aside from the drinking. It wasn't my intent, just something that naturally happens in France."

"You've been to France already?" Alvin could hardly contain his enthusiasm, almost skipping in place. He swung his free arm in front of him. "I can't believe it! What are the chances of that?"

"I don't know. I never thought I'd go to France again."

"Then why are you?"

"Because I wanted to ride on the first airship, and that's where it happens to be steering."

"What was France like? Have you been to Bordeaux?"

"Paris," Amelia forced herself to say.

A frown burdened Alvin's mouth. "Were you in Paris with Mr. Shank?"

Amelia raised an eyebrow. "Have I become transparent?"

"I made a well-informed guess. They both have the same effect on you. Like nausea's keeping you from speaking freely."

She let out a breath. "It doesn't matter. I'll leave Bordeaux shortly for other parts of the world."

"You really don't like France, do you?"

"I have nothing against the country. It's beautiful, and it has more to offer than you'd assume."

"You only hate it because of him?" Alvin stopped walking. The rest of the passengers moved away, leaving them behind in the corridor. "Do you want me to speak to him? If you're afraid to tell him—"

Amelia's chest puffed up. "I'm not afraid."

"He obviously doesn't know how you feel. I could approach him for you."

Amelia knew what the real trouble was. Darius himself could feel nothing. "That's unspeakably generous of you, but I don't think it'd be effective. Even if it was, there's less than a day left on the ship. It wouldn't make much difference to the rest of my journey."

"Are you concerned I'd only make his behavior worse?"

Amelia leveled with him. "I'm afraid it could end badly for you. Mr. Shank doesn't approve of anyone trying to come between him and me."

"Do you think he'd throw me over the rail of the top deck?"

Lewis' hat had soared beyond the rail and disappeared on the wind. Would Alvin's body be next, lost to the oblivion of the air? Amelia took the more hopeful approach. "Nothing so dramatic as that. But he could hurt you, Alvin. I don't want that on my conscience. It's not worth it, and I might not be near him much longer."

Alvin's worried eyes fixed on her for a long time. "I don't understand your connection to him, but I understand your eagerness to get away." His shoulders pulled back as he bent toward her like a co-conspirator. "I want you to know I'm not dissuaded. You asked me not to interfere with him on the

Duchess. I'll honor that request. But if I see him one step beyond the exit, I'll tell him exactly what I think of him."

"I wish you wouldn't, but I can't stop you."

"I can't abide bullies. He has no business harassing you or anybody else."

A spark fired in Amelia's brain. Alvin's father had done little but rant and control since boarding the ship. She was about to ask Alvin if that was the reason he disliked and avoided his father when Captain Barrett's discourse carried the length of the hallway.

"You won't be able to hear me once we step inside." He chuckled. "Hard to believe, I know, but the engines run quite loudly. The *Duchess* contains six engines to give us all the power we could need. I'll also point out the special mechanisms that let us benefit from steam engines without packing any extra water on board. It's the advantage that keeps us as light as we are, relatively speaking."

Other passengers gasped in wonder. Alvin kept his serious eyes on Amelia's.

"They're called dehumidifiers," Captain Barrett explained. "A recent invention by the young Willis Carrier of New York. When Samuel Langley heard what Mr. Carrier was developing, he plucked the lad out of Cornell and worked him overtime to finish his plans. The result is a magnificent device that strains water out of the air, cools it into liquid form, and lets us generate the steam we need to power our propellers."

"Ingenious," someone breathed.

Alvin's crystalline blue irises conveyed only intent and intensity now. Amelia feared one day Darius would ring them in black and purple bruises. "We should catch up." She took a step toward the gathered crowd.

Alvin joined her with reluctant lagging.

Captain Barrett opened a door on the right, and the rhythmic churning and chugging of engines flooded the hallway. Amelia and Alvin caught up to the others, and the captain ushered them into the room.

Whirring and rushing filled Amelia's ears. She and Alvin joined the group crowded into the only empty space large enough to hold them in the long room. Six active metal engines occupied the center of it, towering at equal distances from each other. Stationary tanks stood idle while numerous arms fired back and forth. Wheels spun, and pipes extended upward to disappear into the ceiling. Captain Barrett strode past the onlookers and motioned for them to follow him. He hugged the right-hand wall, leading them along one row of three engines. Amelia and Alvin tailed the others, forced into silence by the roar and intensity of the unfailing machines.

A steel panel marked *Dehumidifier 1* listed against the wall, leaving the mechanism's inner workings exposed. Two sets of coils wound their way from the top to the bottom of the box. One of the spiraling metal tubes dripped water into a chute that carried it away. On both sides, fans circulated air through the box.

Alvin shrugged. Amelia grinned. She valued the effects of the process and the genius behind it, but she would warrant a more thorough explanation to fully understand it.

They filed into the corner of the room and changed direction to follow the back wall. Iris swayed closer to one of the engines, squinting in fascination. A man sporting short sideburns and a handlebar moustache jerked her away from it, probably her husband. A member of the crew squeezed through between the passengers and the machines, tipping his cap in repetition at the tourists. Amelia swept her eyes over the clean lines and continuous movements of the engines as she passed the last of them.

Stuck to the engine's tank clung a cottony patch of white fibers. A spider's nest, something she had not encountered amongst the tidy passengers' decks. Despite the organization of most of the lower deck, the nest seemed at home amongst the machinery and crumbs. Elwood's jovial disclosure of Dorothy's fears rang in Amelia's head. *"Spiders, and that's just for starts."*

Amelia peered over the tank and accompanying structure for the spider itself. The crewman stopped beside the machine and propped an arm on its casing in pride. He joined her in surveying it, and his jaw dropped. He grabbed the nest, wiping away any residual fibers with his fingers. He sauntered on his way. Amelia frowned but did not linger. With how long Dorothy's list of aversions ran, Amelia could certainly find another item from it. She returned to the doorway and preceded Alvin into the same corridor they had begun in.

Captain Barrett stood pleased face and broad shoulders above the crowd a few planks up the staircase. "So concludes the tour, my fellow adventurers in flight! I hope this voyage thrills you as much as it does me. I look forward to concluding our trip tomorrow and spending a few days relaxing in Bordeaux before setting off on our return to New York. Thank you for accompanying me on the lower deck. Have a pleasant dinner."

Captain Barrett remained on the step, beaming at everyone who ascended past him.

A door closed behind Amelia, drowning out the thundering of the engines. The crewman who had cleared away the spider's nest rubbed his hand on his pant leg. A second crewman approached him from the far end of the hall, the one Amelia had seen eating in the map room.

The man from the engine room pointed a loose finger at his companion. "Did you clean up after yourself?"

The crewman brushed at his suit. "I think so."

"I mean the floor." He jerked his thumb to his right. "You know Edgar will gnaw his way out of his box to eat those crumbs if he smells them."

The crewman bobbed his nose up. "What did you bring it for, anyway?"

"I had to. My wife would've let it go before I got back if I didn't."

Amelia's cheeks tensed in thought. Cat? Dog? She had not heard meowing or barking at any time on the ship.

The crewman tilted his grey eyes askance. "A rat, though? Not my first choice of a pet."

"Can't afford a dog. Company's company just the same. And, hey, I've known that rodent longer than I've known my wife."

They wandered off snickering in the other direction.

Amelia could hardly maintain her composure at Alvin's side. Dorothy's reply snapped in her head. *"I hate rats and mice and all those. Doesn't everybody?"*

The passengers around Amelia started up the stairs past Captain Barrett, and she climbed up after them. Her mind churned as effectively as the engines. A bold rat superseded a well-hidden spider any day. The familiar couches of the first deck's parlor sank into view. The pet rat stuck in her brain, but Alvin guided her aside from the other guests. She resolved to finish her conversation with him before she devoted herself to hatching a devious plot against Dorothy.

Alvin pulled his arm away from Amelia's grasp and slid his hands into his pockets. "I know we've barely met, but I'd be concerned for anybody in your shoes. Maybe you think I'm overprotective."

After Darius had broken her heart, stolen her clock, and left her for dead in a burning hotel? Amelia assured him of the truth. "No."

Alvin flared his elbows out. "I'm just enjoying the new friendships I've made on this trip, such as they are. I wouldn't want to see anything bad happen to any of you, and you're traveling alone. The only person on board you've known longer than a few days seems like a madman."

Amelia stretched the truth as far as it could go. "He's not as bad as he sounds."

"I still wouldn't mind giving him a piece of my mind. Or popping him in the face." Alvin took his fist out of his pocket and examined its white knuckles. "What do you think? Am I too old to get into my first real fight?"

"No. I appreciate your concern." Unable to dissuade him, Amelia made the one decision that would keep him out of harm's way when the time came. She pecked a dry kiss on his cheek. She swiveled her foot, crunching it down on top of Alvin's shoe.

He cried out and jerked his shoe away, hopping several times on his good foot. "I'm all right," he insisted through gritted teeth.

Amelia grimaced. "I told you I could be clumsy."

"You finally proved your point." Alvin set his foot down and tested his weight on it. "See? I'm good as new."

Amelia laid her hand on his arm and met him with solemn honesty. "I'm sorry, Alvin."

"Don't worry about it. It's only fair after all the times I smashed your toes in the ballroom."

"I'd like to rest in my room awhile before dinner. Thank you for the tour. It was quite the education."

Alvin made an amused sound in his throat. "Thank goodness there's fun, too, eh?"

Amelia nodded and walked away.

He called after her. "I hope I see you in Bordeaux before you leave."

Knowing she would never let it happen, Amelia met Alvin's earnest, shining eyes. "I hope so, too."

Chapter Twenty-Seven

Amelia sauntered through the first-deck lounge, analyzing the framed works decorating the airship's walls. The paintings represented the recent tonal style, capturing posed figures and a variety of landscapes in moody, contrasting hues of dark and light. Interspersed among them hung an array of maps displaying Europe, the Americas, and the United Kingdom.

Behind her, Elwood's impassioned confession burst out of him. "I didn't know."

Dorothy seethed. "Now we can hardly get a peek through our own spyglass." Her whining voice dropped so low it grated in her throat. "Everyone else is taking advantage of it, and we've been pushed out. Where's your mother in all this? The one we gave up the spyglass to spend more time with?"

Elwood grounded himself in insistence. "She's enjoying herself."

"Painting." Dorothy spat the word out. "As if she can't do that on sturdy, stable ground!"

Amelia immersed herself in a scene of blue, bare-branched trees against a shadowed blanket of even snowdrifts.

Elwood blew out an exasperated breath. "What would you suggest I do? Tell her not to? It's the last day for it, and you know I've always been fascinated by art. It gives me something to talk about with her."

Dorothy groaned. She plunged her body into a chair across the room from Amelia. "Don't remind me. I've lost both of you now."

"Art isn't so hard to understand. Is it, Miss Harlow?"

Amelia swept her eyes over the scowl contorting Dorothy's face to Elwood's expectant blinking. "I try only to enjoy it."

Elwood pressed his lips together in mild appreciation.

Amelia pointed to the ceiling. "Is there more art upstairs? I've been so busy with other things these last few days, I haven't fully realized what's here."

Dorothy slid her shoe over and knocked it against Elwood's, her frown a warning to them both.

He stepped away from her toward Amelia. "There is. My mother's up there now making more of it."

"Not these depressing tonals, I hope. They don't seem your mother's type."

"No, the last attempt I saw was a floral affair. A still life."

Amelia strolled toward the far set of doors. "I'm trying to make the most of my time left on board. Would you like me to say hello to your mother for you?"

"Please."

Amelia moseyed out of the lounge, grateful to rid herself of Dorothy's acerbic disposition. She did not know much about the spiritualists' beliefs, but if they were interested in clearing anything or anyone of bad vibrations, Amelia would gladly recommend Dorothy for a demonstration. She took the staircase up to the second deck and crossed its tidy parlor to the lounge she had possessed no reason to visit before.

The long yellow room stretched out before her, separated into different areas of activity. In the front portion of the room, a circle of women stationed at easels ringed a table topped with a vase of flowers. Tulips, lilacs, and azaleas lent a light scent to the air. The white, wide-mouthed vessel tapered into a slender middle, flaring into a fluted base with gold accents. Amelia spotted Claudia, dark eyebrows furrowed and the tip of her tongue parting her lips as she scrutinized the vase eight feet away. She ducked behind her easel, dipping her brush and dotting it to the canvas.

Amelia moved around behind her, hugging the wall of windows forming the outer wall of the ship. From here, she gleaned what she could of the shape of Claudia's painting, pretty close to that of the flower arrangement in the vase. Amelia cut across the center of the room, noting the groupings of chairs and desks in the deeper half of the space.

The painting instructor, a slight man sporting a narrow moustache, hovered over the ladies as they worked. "Vary your strokes like we talked about. That's right. Dots for spots, smudges for shadows. Very good."

Amelia approached the inner wall and its variety of framed pieces. More landscapes, more models. More maps. Australia, the Orient, Africa.

A woman's thin voice rose in a preoccupied hush. "I may continue painting when I return home."

"Oh, yes," others chimed in.

Claudia's full-bodied timbre called out. "Amelia."

She met Claudia's delighted expression peeking out from beside the white canvas. "I didn't want to disturb you."

"Nonsense. Any mistakes bestowed upon this artwork are my own entirely." She swirled her brush in the air, indicating the circle of women. "You should join us. We can still make some room for you." She lowered her arm and wiped at her sleeve. "Thank goodness that was only water and I already rinsed my brush."

Amelia motioned with her hand in disinterest. "Painting's not for me."

"This is your last chance before we land."

"Thank you, but I lack the dexterity for it."

The instructor lifted his bearded chin at Amelia. "We begin each session with the proper hand and wrist exercises. I could give you better results than you've ever achieved."

Amelia kept an eye on him in case he ran off to fetch her an easel and chair. "I have all the hobbies I need. Thank you."

Claudia rested her brush in the easel tray. "Will you come see what I've done and tell me what you think? Be honest. It could be better."

Amelia moved toward her, trying to ignore the efforts of the women she passed. One provided a morose interpretation in a heavy-handed style of navy and hunter green. The next proved light and fanciful, more like a sketch in thin brush strokes and pastels. Another captured the realism in color but posed in all the wrong dimensions, the flower petals distorted and stems rising in odd degrees from too wide a vase.

Amelia braced herself for Claudia's version of the details. "I saw your son and his wife before I walked up here. They send their hellos."

Claudia set her jaw. "Don't kid me. Only Elwood would do that."

"How well you know them both."

Amelia faced Claudia's painting. Her eyes took in every decision, every nuance of shape and hue. No museum or gallery might ever celebrate Claudia Molt's name, but Amelia found more promise than she expected. Where Claudia was garrulous and unrestrained in life, her artwork was careful and perceptive. Patient brush strokes formed every petal, captured every stem, and recreated the curves of the vase below. The colors brightening the picture to life were well mixed and applied, vibrant and natural.

Amelia's heart picked up a faster pace, and she praised Claudia for being an above-average student. "Very good."

Claudia gleamed with pride but fought it back until her mood was demure and somber. "Tell the truth now, like I asked you to."

"You have real talent, or you take good direction." Amelia pointed out the purple and yellow tulips near the top of the canvas. "See how you spaced these flowers here? Note the real ones. To the right. Left of center. All the way left. Just as you painted. It's marvelous work."

Claudia beamed and bit her lip. She fluttered her fingers along the bottom of the canvas. "My shadows are off, I think. They're too low."

"But you could make them higher. Do you still have your dark paints?"

Claudia picked up her brush and dipped it in a charcoal-colored spot on her palette. She applied a thin line at the top of her existing shadow, returning to smudge it into a thicker application.

"See?" Amelia asked. "It's perfect."

Other ladies nearby set their brushes down, craning their necks to glimpse Claudia's work.

Claudia rinsed her brush in a cup of murky water. "How do I fix the color of the flowers, then? It's a bit darker than the real thing."

"You don't fix it."

"No?"

"Any lighter would make the flowers in your painting less commanding. They're kind of like you. Cheerful and in charge."

The other women laughed, stretching closer for a better angle.

Amelia waved them over. "Come see."

Claudia wagged her finger at the puffs of star-like lilacs. "It's too simple."

"That's what makes it so elegant. It's not bogged down, and I can still tell what flower it is."

The women stood up, surrounding Amelia behind Claudia's chair.

"Neat lines." Amelia swept her hand up past the tulips' stems. Even the instructor inched closer. "You can almost smell the lilacs, light and intoxicating."

The women muttered to each other in agreement.

"Isn't this more uplifting than the tonal paintings on these walls?" Amelia gestured to the framed artwork she had inspected earlier. "Sad colors. Morose subjects. Claudia did just as well if not better representing these flowers."

Yetta Greisman tapped a finger against her broad chin. "I think..."

"Yes?" Amelia prompted her.

"The walls should be decorated in paintings like hers."

The other women made approving sounds, judging the row of hung paintings.

Amelia laid a hand on her chest. "Mrs. Greisman, are you suggesting we redecorate the lounge? You're not afraid to challenge the status quo. Your husband better be careful. You'll come up with your own ideas while he's running his sausage business."

Yetta held her palms up, smudges of dried paint discoloring them. "I don't get that many ideas. That's Rudy's department. I wouldn't dream of disturbing the airship the way it's decorated now."

"But you did." Amelia set her hands on the upper corners of Claudia's canvas. "May I?"

Claudia leaned out of the way. "Do you really believe it's elegant?"

"Would I do this if I didn't?" Amelia lifted the canvas off the easel and carried it over to the map of Africa. She unhooked the map's frame from the nail behind it and secured Claudia's canvas between the round metal head and the wall. She stepped aside, toting the map with her. "What do you think? An improvement?"

The ladies applauded.

Claudia stood up, offering shallow curtsies. "Improvement indeed."

Amelia waved her free hand at the other easels. "You should all display your paintings." She eyed the sickly colors and jerky brush strokes. She pressed on. "They all deserve to be up on these walls. Who decided on these countless maps and articles, anyway?"

The women rushed to collect their canvases. Behind them, the instructor's mouth popped open, his hand reaching up but failing to divert their mission.

Amelia raised her eyebrows at him, astonishment buoying her voice. "I'm sorry. I've completely taken over your class."

He bowed his head. "Not a problem. We were almost finished. Just applying the finishing touches."

Half a dozen women breezed up to the wall by Amelia, replacing the appointed decorations with their own. They cooed and gushed amongst themselves.

Amelia brushed her palms against each other. "It's a fine way to commemorate the *Duchess'* first flight, ladies. Well done."

Cora Burgess approached, her painting in her small, white hands. She scanned the wall, and disappointment crushed her shoulders. Her eyes fell, and her painting drooped. "There's no more room."

Amelia stepped toward her. "There's the whole rest of the ship."

Claudia's voice rang out. "Of course there is. Let's straighten these paintings and find room for the others."

Amelia took in Cora's depiction, her white, five-petaled azaleas delicate and precise. "You do nice work, Mrs. Burgess." She moved toward the French doors to avoid being pulled into any more bustle and decision making. She raised the framed map in her hand as she passed the instructor. "I'll drop this off at the purser's office."

The women's chattering followed Amelia to the door, the glass and wood muffling their excitement as it closed behind her. She tightened her grip on the map's frame on her way to the stairs. Of all the conversation she had woven in the lounge, her promise to the painting instructor counted among the lies.

Chapter Twenty-Eight

Darius stayed close against her this time instead of retreating to the bedside chair or his own cabin. Amelia's breath came back to her slowly, sweat tickling the backs of her knees where she couldn't wipe it away without disturbing him. His balmy chest rested on her arm, one hand cradling hers, his lips leaving slow kisses over her shoulder.

Captain Barrett's appearance in the dining room during dinner played through Amelia's whirring mind.

He had paraded in just past the French doors and clasped his hands together, happiness swelling his chest. "How's the food this evening?"

Exclamations of "Excellent!" drowned out murmurs of "Delicious."

"It's your last dinner aboard the *Duchess*, I'm sad to remind you." Captain Barrett's twinkling eyes landed on every face in the room stretched out before him. "Happily, our trip remains a safe success. We'll be landing late tomorrow afternoon."

Applause struck up around Amelia, and she joined in it with a racing but reluctant heart.

Captain Barrett raised his hands, gloved in pure white cotton. "Right on schedule!"

Darius' hand slid across Amelia's belly under the bunched sheet. No doubt the captain's announcement had driven them together and kept them in this bed, their last certain night together before the uncertain unfolded tomorrow. It was often their way, making the most of their adventures together before parting for distant destinations.

Darius edged closer, sliding his leg against hers. His words rumbled low in his register. "You remember my generosity in allowing you to safeguard the map for us once we acquire it."

Amelia caught up to Darius' line of thought. "Yes."

He kissed her arm. "We don't have it yet."

"I haven't forgotten."

"We'll be in France tomorrow."

"I plan to take the map while Elizabeth and Lewis are at breakfast."

Darius brushed against her side, tucking his head into the dip of her neck and kissing it. His renewed proximity surprised her, but in a way, she understood it. It was the same force gluing her to him now, despite everything else.

Not knowing what the next day would bring. Where the first week off the *Duchess* would propel them. How many years until they met again.

Darius moved his open kisses to the hard ridge at the back of her jaw. As his romancing wore on, she came to prefer his sarcasm to his silence. He never acted without thinking, and she could not always guess his motives.

She freed her hand from his grasp and wrapped her arm around his back. Could he possibly be so naïve as to believe she would not try to flee with the map? That this voyage was the start of a longer, more intimate relationship? Amelia almost sniggered and stopped herself. She patted Darius' strong, languid muscles. She would call herself worse than naïve to mistake this wild creature for a harmless cub.

So what, then, the usual? He prepared for the chance she did disappear with the map and the strange loneliness that crept into them when they lived apart for too long.

Or he aimed to pluck her heartstrings, those jaded phantoms that rarely showed themselves anymore. If he could win her loyalty now the way he had that first time in Paris, he could control her. His silver tongue could persuade her to share the map as she promised and split the profits with him.

Amelia slunk lower on her pillow, her eyebrows tensing. That would never happen.

Darius nestled his hand in the curve of Amelia's side. He settled his head on her shoulder, unmoving at last.

Realization struck Amelia so fast, she almost jerked away to stare at him. *He thinks he's going to win!* She did not need to study his face to know it was true. He pictured himself strutting through the streets of Bordeaux, the map hidden amongst his belongings, leaving Amelia behind to board the earliest train. He'd vanish into the vast network of European transportation, lost to her amidst the mountains and farmlands. Over half a dozen countries claimed stake in Africa, and Darius could present the map's worth in any of them. Or, smartly, choose another location in the world and write to them from a place Amelia would never find him. The buggy, muggy Floridian swamps. The thick, tropical forests of Panama. Beijing's striking architecture and tumultuous political climate.

Darius' fingers pressed against her side, stroking her skin, holding her near. Could it be nostalgia driving him? Seven years apart, her life or death unknown, had changed him, if only a little.

Amelia, although she wondered what her life would be without Darius, had changed, too.

Seventeen years after their first meeting, she had to admit she was part of the problem between them. She had been since their second round in Paris. He wouldn't know who he was without her, but she was remembering who she could have been without him.

Amelia bent the elbow rested on Darius' back to ruffle her fingers through his hair. She had told so few lies during her childhood in Seneca Falls. No, she had not taken a slice of her mother's sponge cake, although her sugar-sticky fingers smelled of lemon. Neither did she neglect to return a book of love poems to the town library, the red volume she had hidden beneath her pillow.

She had told so many lies on board the *Duchess*, no one but herself knew what was true and what she fabricated. No one knew her truly except herself, a fact that comforted her with smugness.

But that meant Lewis and Alvin, too, and that needled her. Claudia thought she was a kind and generous person, which soured Amelia's mood. Even Luther would have regained ownership of his pocket watch by now if Amelia did not have use for it to remain missing.

The obfuscations and cover-ups began in Paris, even before Amelia knew her beau to be a fraud. What had sent her there except the most honest and understandable of hopes? A pure, true love. The excitement of the promise of forever. The lure of desire and delight in another person's arms.

For the first time, Amelia sidled away from Darius' body, a sliver of withdrawal he did not seem to notice. Only two nights before, it had been Lewis in her arms. Fervent, doting, and shy. More earnest and forthcoming than anyone she had ever known. She never needed to guess what Lewis was thinking.

And sweet, endearing Alvin. Amelia's lips curved in irony at her sympathy for him. Despite his thievery, he aimed to protect her, concerned and proactive. He threw himself into waltzing with her, never minding his lack of talent for dancing. His impetuous nature made him too immature for her romantic preferences, but she cherished his spirit.

Any woman could count herself lucky to have such friends or lovers. Yet what man occupied her final evening? Elizabeth's quiet, courteous boyfriend stolen away to a private place or the energetic thief trampling her toes in the ballroom?

No. Amelia sighed and slid her fingers deeper through Darius' hair. The man who spurned her, tricked her, stole from her, and left her unconscious on the Archduke Stephan's airless second floor.

She regarded him as well as she could from the shallow height of her pillow. He rested motionless and relaxed against her, either asleep or lost in his own thoughts. What of her other interested men? What would they do if positions were exchanged? Lewis would cradle her, caring and attentive. Alvin would chat, of course, boast or dodge her questions.

What of this silent man stealing half her bed? Why could he not be decent? Carefree and entertaining? Make himself vulnerable to her the way he'd ripped her open and bared her heart to the astonished oglers on the streets of Paris?

He could never be like them. Never offer her another steady hand in or out of a carriage. Never hold an umbrella for her. Never expose his thoughts or apologize for anything from the smallest misunderstanding to the greatest of crimes.

Amelia's upper lip curled at his audacity to snuggle up to her. He enjoyed making her who she was, sharp minded and seeking every possible angle with which to get ahead. He took her for granted, and she begrudged him for it. If he had not left her in the hotel fire that ruined the face her family knew, she could have called on them during her time in New York. Even a brief visit would have soothed her aching heart, but her first trip to the States in seven years had lasted mere months before it carried her onto the *Duchess*.

If Darius' conscience registered this and stirred in malcontent, he kept it secret. Could it make him guilty and uncomfortable enough to speak? He could still get close to her, enjoy her body and her warmth, revel in the knowledge of who she was under this constructed face.

Meanwhile, Amelia had no idea how her family fared. Were her parents alive? Her siblings married? She had avoided visiting any of them since her first trip to Paris. Her adventures had changed her too much on the inside to be content in Seneca Falls, to sit on her parents' long sofa and talk over tea. Their darling daughter was gone, and in her place, a restless vagabond fought to win illegal races against her own lover. She had hoped to avoid seeing her father's reluctance to send her abroad embittered into know-it-all brush offs. She had no wish to hear her mother prattle on about how she was right to want to keep her oldest daughter at home.

Now Amelia could never go home again. What was the use in trying? They would not recognize her voice, her face, or her mannerisms. Her siblings used to delight in torturing her for her ideas. Would her new experiences and demeanor fascinate or frighten them?

Darius nuzzled his face against her shoulder, pressing a lingering kiss against her neck.

Would Amelia ever say goodbye to him and mean it for good? Was she doing that now? Was that what pinned her here, to the man she hated more than she loved?

Darius twisted away from her, sitting up and sliding his palms over his face. He dropped a hand and patted her leg through the sheet.

Yes, he expected her by his side. Amelia pitied Darius. She had no intention of rubbing her affair with Lewis in his face, but he had clearly missed the changes occurring in her. He was the same old Darius by any name. Casual, self-indulgent, and indifferent.

His voice croaked to life, thick and low. "I admire you, my dear." He supported himself on one arm to kiss her mouth.

Her curiosity piqued. "For what?"

"Leaving the most important thing up to the last. We both know in a time crunch, you can pull off anything."

Amelia pushed herself up to join him. She kissed him, letting her lips stay against his for a long moment. "I know I can." She could not wait to prove it to him.

Chapter Twenty-Nine

In the haze of early morning, Darius long since returned to his own cabin, Amelia stole out of hers dressed and ready for the day. The light fit of her hat rested on her head. Her black-dotted, pink cotton dress swirled around her legs in a full skirt. She crept along the corridor to the stairs and tiptoed down to the crew's deck.

A weary voice grated from out of sight. "The overnight shift is so boring."

More chipper tones responded. "It's peaceful."

"Why does it take two of us to navigate in the dark? There's nothing to hit out here."

"If we drift even five miles off course, do you want to deal with Captain Barrett? I don't."

Amelia had little idea where the crewman's pet rat resided, which of the numerous cabins concealed it. From her pocket, she pulled the piece of almond cake she had saved from dinner the night before. She broke it apart, hoping walls and doors would not be enough to keep the rat from smelling what she offered. And wanting it.

Amelia inched toward the left-hand hallway of rooms she had traversed with the tour group the day before. Metal pans and ceramic dishes collided in the kitchen near the parallel corridor. Amelia's heart leapt into her throat, picking words out of the din.

"Use all of the eggs?"

"Get coffee going. No stronger than yesterday."

"Is there enough flour for muffins and popovers?"

She had nothing to fear, she told herself. Just a guest overrun with curiosity seeking another, albeit self-guided, tour of the bottom level. The almond cake? A coveted snack for herself, of course.

Once the kitchen fracas settled into a routine of clinks and taps and orders called above the cacophony, Amelia snuck forward. She listened, straining to hear what the crewman had described as his pet gnawing its way to freedom to acquire the sugary cake in her hands. She paused at the end of the hall, her eyes fixed on the doorway to the navigation room in front of her.

The disgruntled man groaned. "You're never tired."

The satisfied voice spiked. "Drink more coffee!"

A light scratching at the bottom of the door beside Amelia stopped her in her tracks. Keeping an eye on the open doorway and readying her explanations in case her plan went awry, Amelia gathered the bits of cake into one palm. She rested the other on the door's handle, revolving it by millimeters.

The dragging voice sounded louder and more agitated. "I can barely hear you with all that kitchen racket going on."

Amelia locked her hand where it held the handle, swinging her body flat against the wall. The door to the navigation room thudded shut, and she breathed again. She popped the cabin door open, and a brownish-grey rat bounded out into the light. Its tiny face elongated, sniffing the air in Amelia's direction. He scurried closer, and Amelia deposited half the almond cake in her pocket. She crouched and lowered her hand to the floor. The rat raced into her palm, seizing the cake in its pink front paws.

Amelia stood up, lifting the rat with her. A snore ripped out of the cabin, and she eased the door shut. With the feeding rat preoccupied in her hand, she retraced her steps to the staircase. She peered into its face, round black eyes excited at the sweet treat it devoured.

"Edgar, I presume," she murmured. "A relative of Mr. Shank's by any chance?"

Clangs and bangs continued in the kitchen.

"Butter!" interjected a call.

"Salt!" punctuated another.

Amelia climbed the stairs as she removed her hat, red swaths of fabric showcasing a black georgette chrysanthemum at the front. She flipped it over, the inverted crown producing a shallow bowl. She placed Edgar and his breakfast inside, keeping it close, away from any interested eyes she met along the way.

Just as she had left it, the first-floor deck remained quiet and still. She ascended to the second floor, also peaceful at this early hour. Amelia settled in for the long walk to the top, saving her stamina for the grueling day ahead. Cora's delicate painting of flowers in a vase hung with the newspaper articles framed on the wall, one tulip stem straining up into blank white canvas. Amelia's mouth perked up.

She attained the square room on the top deck and propped one of the doors open with Elwood's spyglass case. She let herself out into the open air, Edgar pausing his snack to sniff the breeze. Sweeping her focus across the large area, Amelia discovered the instrument set up along the right-hand railing. She carried Edgar over to it, wary to use the viewer for its intended purpose. It would be her last chance to see Europe from this height – on board the *Duchess*, anyway. She doubled over and checked the view.

A coastline spread out below her, followed by green hills and brown mountains further inland. Amelia shared her suspicions with Edgar. "Spain, I think."

She pulled away from the spyglass and lifted the contraption by its tripod. She lugged the sturdy metal frame into the square room. Her foot slid the case in with her, letting the door swing closed.

Amelia sank to her haunches and set her upside-down hat on the floor. She unfastened the spyglass from its stand and set the viewer aside. Collapsing the bottom piece, she stood up enough to set the bottom of it against one of the hinges on the back of the case. She stove it down hard. The hinge loosened but did not break. She jostled the other clasp as well.

Lowering herself, she flipped the case open, exposing two hollow spaces encased in velvet-covered wood. She nestled the spyglass into its cubby, only too glad to see it packed away. Into the other empty space she dropped the other half of the almond cake from her pocket.

She picked up her hat. "Here we go, Edgar." She lifted him with gentle fingers circled around his belly. He splayed his hind legs, eyes popping with uncertainty, and she set him amidst the velvet.

Edgar sniffed the fresh piece of cake and sank his teeth into it.

Amelia brushed crumbs from her hand into the case beside Edgar. "You'll have plenty to eat. Don't get too thirsty." She paused over him for a moment, finding an unexpected cuteness in his expressive face and white patches ringing his ankles. She made sure his tail was in the clear as she closed the case around him. She clenched the two metal buckles on the front of the case and flipped one of the rattling hinges on the back of the box with her finger. "Sorry, Mr. Molt. Not even a rat should have to suffer pulling a prank on your wife."

Amelia stood up with the compacted stand in one hand, using her other hand to set the case upright. The bottom of the case parted between the loose hinges, letting in air. The feasting rodent gave a short, high squeak. Amelia measured the width of the crack with the pad of her index finger, satisfied it would be all right. "Good luck, Edgar. Don't let the screaming scare you. I'll rid myself of my own rat soon enough, I hope."

She jarred crumbs loose from the bowl of her hat before returning it to her head. Leaving Edgar behind with some chagrin – he had been her most silent, agreeable traveling partner, after all – Amelia headed down the tall staircase, concealing the metal spyglass stand in the deep creases of her skirt.

At the second deck, she heard the bustle of newly awakened passengers shuffling along the cabin corridors. Descending to the familiar first floor, Amelia made sure the metal contraption sank deep within the extra fabric of her dress.

A yawn stretched Yetta Greisman's compact accent. "I'll miss the painting lessons."

Claudia sounded much more energetic and optimistic. "We can take some in the States. Are you going straight back or staying in Europe?"

"We go straight back."

Amelia peered down the corridor ahead on her right.

Yetta threw her hands up. "We've got to oversee them making sausage. What for? They know how to do it. Rudy hires good managers."

Claudia tossed her hands up in solidarity and opened the bathroom door.

Yetta ambled inside. *"Dziękuję."*

Claudia disappeared behind her.

The few men in the hallway, Rudolf and Elwood included, did not converse. They filed into their own lavatory and left the corridor a much more deserted place.

Amelia strolled forward, her heart hammering as she sat down on the bench beside the women's restroom. She laid the metal stand on the carpet behind her feet and used her shoe to slide it back against the wall.

She stood up and opened the door to the women's lavatory. Claudia washed her hands at one of the sinks.

Amelia remained in the entrance, propping the door ajar. "I just came down from the upper deck. I see the painters' efforts extended halfway up the climb."

Claudia radiated with pride, drying her hands on a towel slung through a ring on the wall. "I promised Mrs. Burgess the highest place of honor we could find."

"Thank you. I hope that cheered her up."

The door across the hall swung in, Spencer Burgess emerging from the men's lavatory. He afforded Amelia a scant tip of his head on his way toward the dining room.

"All the other paintings?" Amelia pressed, passing more time.

The closest door on her right jerked in, and Darius strode into the hallway. He eyed her with a knowing glint, watching her more than the key he used to lock his cabin door.

Claudia approached Amelia in the doorway. "We found room for them all."

Amelia tilted her head. "That's wonderful."

Darius smirked with encouragement as he walked past Amelia.

Claudia raised her dark eyebrows. "Are you coming to breakfast now?"

"In a minute."

The door across the hall from her opened, and Elwood wandered into view. Amelia let Claudia squeeze past her and veer toward the dining room.

Amelia fluttered her hand at Elwood. "Mr. Molt."

He stopped, his long features picking up into a pleasant expression.

Amelia stepped closer. "I wanted you to know I've already packed up your spyglass and stand for you."

He ducked his chin. "You didn't have to do that."

"I wanted to. It's a small favor to help repay you for all the joy your spyglass gave to your fellow passengers."

"Thank you for saying so."

Amelia inched closer. "I'm afraid the case suffered some damage, though. Someone's rough handling, no doubt. It's quite fixable."

Elwood's mouth formed an even line, but he digested the news with patience.

"If I were you, I'd open the case as soon as I settled into my hotel room. Just to make sure everything's all right with the spyglass."

His forehead creased in two wavy lines. "It's not broken, is it?"

"No. I used it one last time. I'd treat the case with care to keep it that way." Amelia hummed. "I bet after carrying it around so much, it'll seem several pounds lighter today."

"It might at that." Elwood withered with a weary sigh. "Some trip abroad, eh?"

"Yes."

"May I escort you to breakfast? Dorothy should only be a moment."

Dorothy skirted around Amelia's left side, her eyes piercing Amelia with contempt. Dorothy swooped her arm around Elwood's and speared her nose up, leading him away.

Amelia kept herself from rolling her eyes. *As if I'd steal him. He wouldn't know what to do with me.* She caught Darius observing her from the end of the corridor. Rudolf Greisman vacated the men's room, his wife right on cue from behind Amelia. They fell into step together, Rudolf guiding Yetta with a hand on the back of her arm. They passed Darius before he tucked his hands behind his back and followed them.

Amelia ducked into the silent restroom, holding the door open a crack and listening at it.

Lewis' placid voice spoke up first. "There's nobody waiting for you. They've forgotten everything if they even knew we had an argument."

Elizabeth regained her old suspicion. "How thick do you think these walls are, Lewis? They know. They're just too scared to say anything about it. They think I'll murder them."

"It'll keep them from bothering you until we land."

Amelia could barely hear Elizabeth's low reply, but Lewis chuckled. Their intonations faded, and Amelia opened the restroom door. She peeked out into the empty hallway. The only conversation and clatter issued from the dining room behind the cabins across from her.

Amelia sank to her knees in front of the bench, straining her fingers all the way under it to grab the stand beneath it. She scrambled up, smoothing her skirt, and pulled Elizabeth's extra key from her pocket. She let herself into the room catty-corner from her before anyone could see her. No more time remained to waste.

Elizabeth's luggage had changed positions since Amelia last intruded, but it stayed on the right-hand side of the cabin. Amelia opened the trunk she remembered concealing the bronze statuette, setting aside Elizabeth's other belongings to reveal it. Amelia lifted the metal woman out, fresh and statuesque for spending a week trapped in a traveling case. Amelia replaced her size and poundage with the spyglass stand, covering it over with Elizabeth's things.

Rising from the range of luggage, Amelia wiped her sweat-slick palms against each other. She licked her lips as she crossed the room past the bed, her eyes pinpointing the framed husband and wife. Her hands quaked as she retrieved it from the wall. Was Darius playing her? Had he snatched it? Had Elizabeth moved it somewhere else?

Amelia turned the picture over. The tear she had eased into the map's border gaped at her, the tiny crevice that meant so much. She exhaled in disbelief and gratitude, steadying herself. Darius had not gotten to it, and she slipped it with care from its hiding place. Setting both on the bed beneath which she had once stored herself in shadow, Amelia rustled up the bottom hem of her dress. Secured underneath it by a safety pin stuck through her pocket's inner fabric hung the map of Africa swindled from the second-deck lounge. Amelia folded it to the same size as Elizabeth's, hoping the widow would not investigate it too closely. From arm's length, a failure to read details could have fooled Amelia herself.

She inserted the replacement map into the back of the picture frame, squaring the artwork in place on the wall. She pinned the real map beneath her dress, poking holes in such a treasure making her wince. She lowered her skirt and swept the wrinkles out. *Two tiny pricks won't devalue what this map shows.*

Amelia hoisted the bronze lady off the floor, obscuring her in the valleys of fabric at her side. She stepped to the door, her free hand fumbling for the key. Her eyes languished on Elizabeth's jewelry box on the dresser beside her, resting beside a green-feathered hat and yellow gloves.

Amelia forgot the key in her pocket for a moment. She flipped the box lid open, fingers digging through, vision hunting only for a flash of cherry red and silver white. The earrings that had caused so much trouble manifested, and Amelia slipped them into her pocket. She arranged the remaining jewels to fit neatly inside the box and lowered the lid over them, never to be disturbed by her again.

Taking both keys out of her pocket, Amelia let herself out of Elizabeth and Lewis' room. She secured the door and hurried away from the common area. She used the slim passageway at the front of the ship to revisit her cabin in the smallest number of steps. Employing the other key, she slipped inside her room and closed the door behind her.

Her stomach gurgled at so much activity prior to breakfast. Amelia opened the top dresser drawer and stashed the statuette beneath an arrangement of handkerchiefs, stockings, and gloves.

Amelia's stomach rumbled in a louder, groaning ripple, but she had one last stop to make before retiring to the dining room. She followed the corridor from her room to the open space by the stairs, passing the small parlor to arrive at the purser's station. The door to the ship that had provided her entrance six days before stood closed in front of her, the portal that would soon allow her exit. She pried her eyes off it as she stopped at the counter.

The man behind it ticked his bushy dark-and-grey eyebrows in acknowledgement beneath his stiff hat brim. "How may I serve you, ma'am?"

Despite the clinking of silverware on plates and lively conversation floating out of the dining hall behind her, Amelia kept her voice low. "I have information about a matter of security – or insecurity – on the ship."

"Oh?" The gentleman tented his hands on the counter between them. "What information is that?"

"The person who stole Mr. Luther Wallace's new pocket watch."

The man withdrew into his former, formal posture. "Should I fetch a guard?"

Amelia set her hand out above the counter. "I wouldn't want them to interrupt everyone's breakfast. Just pass his name along." She procrastinated over a labored exhale. *Why did you steal it, Alvin? Why did you constantly insert yourself into my life?*

The man blinked at her, his glassy eyes flicking over her face and clothes.

She betrayed her new friend in a breath. "It's Mr. Alvin Burgess."

"Burgess?" The purser confined his surprise to a hissing whisper. "It was one of the other spiritualists, surely. Or the murderess or her friend."

Amelia remained grim. "I'm afraid not."

"This accusation is serious, ma'am."

"I understand. If you'd only have security seek the missing timepiece in Mr. Burgess' room, I'm sure they'd find it. I believe Mr. Wallace would be eternally grateful to have it recovered and back in his possession."

The man bobbed his head, agreeable but unconvinced.

Amelia swayed toward him. "I'd hate for such a theft, especially left unsolved, to leave a black mark on the *Duchess'* reputation. Things like that can take years to correct, and she's just getting started."

His head dipped in deep, decisive motions. "Certainly, ma'am. I'll notify security of your findings immediately."

"Perfect. Thank you for your help."

He gestured an upturned palm to her. "Your name?"

Amelia backed up several inches. "What for?"

"To be lauded as a hero, of course, in the solving of this crime."

Amelia perked up her lips and took another step back. "I wish to remain anonymous." She spun away, mere feet from the open doors of the dining room. The medley of buttery eggs, tangy grapefruit, and earthy coffee filled her nostrils stronger than ever before.

"Ma'am?" the purser called.

Against her growling stomach and tired mind, Amelia faced him. "Yes?"

"Don't worry." The purser dabbed a finger at her in the air. "We won't bother anyone's breakfast. It's a promise."

Amelia hummed in gratitude and swept on through the doors of the dining room. More than two dozen people remained in line at the buffet, but at least Amelia had finally joined it. Another gurgle complained from her stomach, making her cringe. The passengers in front of her chatted and pointed up ahead. Of the various activities they had partaken in that morning, Amelia was willing to bet hers made her delayed breakfast the most well deserved of them all.

Chapter Thirty

A round of knocks sounded on Amelia's door.

She rose from her perch on the bed, reading the last lines of the first chapter in Kate Chopin's *At Fault*. She closed the book and carried it with her. Rousing the painting class had broadened her list of acquaintances to such an extent she could no longer whittle the list of suspected visitors to a manageable handful. "Yes?"

A man's voice came through the door, throaty and quiet. "It's me."

For once, Darius' appearance delighted her. Amelia unlocked the door, pulling it open.

He raised his forearm and leaned it on the doorjamb. "How was your breakfast?"

"Filling." Amelia had devoured two omelets, an entire grapefruit, and half a muffin before her stomach threatened to rebel.

"Your lunch?"

"Delicious."

"Have you ever eaten so many oysters in a week?"

Amelia could not guess at his reasons for toying with her, but she obliged him. "Sometimes."

"Did you find the caramel custard a refreshing sweetness after the saltiness of the steak?"

Amelia narrowed her eyes at him in a warning. "Naturally." She stepped back to let him into her cabin.

He moseyed in and closed the door.

"Please tell me you have a better reason for talking to me than to share notes on the chef's buffet selections." Amelia discarded the book onto the bed.

"Naturally." Darius sank his hands into the pockets of his charcoal-grey trousers. "I hope you're doing more than brushing up on your reading." He tossed his head at the book.

"Of course." Amelia walked around the side of the bed and opened the drawer in the nightstand. "I haven't finished packing. We'll be on the ground within a few hours. We were still sailing over the Bay of Biscay when I used the spyglass earlier."

"Sightseeing?" Darius hissed. "Is that all you've been–"

Amelia lifted the map of Africa out of the drawer.

Darius took a step toward her, his wide eyes locked on it. "Is that it? Did you get it?"

"I got it." Amelia pushed the drawer closed and carried the map over to her open flat-top trunk.

Darius bent toward the map, mesmerized. "Such a small thing. Yet worth so much."

"It's worth everything we've spent to get this far." Amelia crouched down, sandwiching the map between her copies of *A Bride from the Bush* and *The Sign of Four*. "The tickets, the lies, the sneaking around."

"You really trust me enough to put it away when I'll know where it is?"

Amelia stood up. "Are you saying I shouldn't trust you?" She tilted her forehead at him. "Are you saying you don't think I'll move it someplace else before we leave?"

"Darling." Darius produced his hands and wrapped them around Amelia's upper arms. His smile gleamed as brilliant as Amelia thought it phony. "There's no reason for us not to trust each other. We have our agreement, yes?"

Amelia dipped her head.

"Just because we're journeying to France doesn't mean you should be nervous or flighty."

Amelia raised her eyes to the ceiling, shuffling through her memories. "I haven't been flighty since a bee stung me on my eighth birthday. As for nervous..." She met Darius' eyes. "Not since the hotel fire almost killed me."

Darius dimmed his enthusiasm to serious. He inched closer, still holding her arms. "It'll be different this time."

"It will be." Amelia's agreement glossed over the condescension lying beneath it.

He pressed his lips against her forehead, a token any casual witness would have proclaimed tender and endearing.

Amelia knew it was nothing more than another snare in his charming trap. "You really want that map, don't you?"

"Not as much as I want you."

"Do you think you fool me?"

Darius pulled her toward him, kissing her with clear passion despite his restraint. Amelia set her hands on his waist. She had once stabbed him from this close, the resulting scar resting between her thumbs. After everything they had lived through – and before everything left to commit – Amelia kissed him back and wrested as much enjoyment out of it as she could. This could be their final goodbye in private, and she did not want to waste it.

A baritone puff of air sounded through the brass speaker in the wall. "May I have a moment of your time, brave passengers?" The good will in Captain Barrett's voice lost itself on Amelia. "I have one last speech I'd like to impart to you before we part ways. Would you make a stop by the ballroom, please? I'll join you shortly with some updates about our impending landing."

Amelia pressed closer to Darius, the familiar heat he sparked in her spreading through her core.

Captain Barrett broke his silence. "I hope to see you all there. Thank you."

Amelia pulled away from Darius and cleared her throat to center herself.

He planted his hands on either side of her waist. "Are you going up?"

"I don't see why not. I'd like to hear what Captain Barrett has to say, and it'd be a nice farewell to the others."

"You've grown fond of them." His realization glided with surprise, but his eyes flashed with jealousy.

Amelia corrected him. "Accustomed."

"You've far surpassed me. I label most of them nuisances." He ran his hand down her arm.

"You're not going?"

Darius pecked her on the lips. "I might. I need to make sure everything's covered over with the staff member I've been bribing." He backed up toward the door. "I need to return Elizabeth's copy to him so it's not missed."

Amelia fished the silver key out of her pocket.

Darius dropped it into his. "I'd like to finish packing. I don't know how soon we'll land."

Amelia lifted her chin. "You're not thinking of packing the map amongst your belongings, are you? While I'm upstairs and you're down here?"

Darius cocked one ear toward her. "You think I'd break our bargain?"

"I know you would."

"Won't you lock your door?"

"Indeed."

"Then you have nothing to fear."

Amelia reached for the door handle. Darius kissed her cheek, then alighted his fingers under her chin to tilt her face toward him. He kissed her in a more tender way than he ever had, even while plotting against her in Paris.

"I never wanted you to die," he said, his nose an inch from hers.

Thrown off guard, Amelia fought to keep them in the present, away from the worst years of her life. "Prague is in the past. Paris, too."

"Vienna. London." With extra gravity, he added, "Berlin."

"Past. We have nowhere to go but forward."

"And up to the second deck."

Amelia grasped the handle, and Darius stepped aside for her to open the door. They filed into the hallway, where Amelia secured her door with her key.

Darius splayed his fingers in a gesture at the handle. "See? All is safe."

"Will I see you upstairs?"

"I'll be up before the end of his speech."

Amelia touched his arm and walked away, striding the length of the hallway toward the stairs. From behind closed doors, couples called to each other.

The gruff accented bark of Rudolf Greisman. "Where's my other hat?"

The lyrical, cultured song of the Frenchwoman. *"Où sont mes gants?"*

The barely contained hostility of Spencer Burgess blew through the lounge's open doors. "No, Cora, there isn't time to write another letter."

A staff member flew down the stairs twelve feet in front of Amelia, doffing his hat to her. "Pardon me. Have you seen the senior Mr. Burgess?"

Amelia pointed into the lounge.

The man steered his racing legs into the large room. "Mr. Burgess? You should come with me. There's been an incident."

Spencer exploded. "What incident?"

Amelia stepped aside, keeping close to the wall at the outer rim of the common space. Spencer shot out of the lounge, arms pumping as he stomped to the stairs and bounded up. Moments later, Cora and the uniformed man emerged, following at a swift but sensible pace.

Amelia gave them a minute to achieve their probable destination, several couples passing her to climb to the deck above. At last, she moved to the staircase, a timid sound choked by tears emitting from the parlor on her left.

Priscilla crumpled a pale pink handkerchief halfway to her face, peering up into Edwin's conflicted eyes. "I'm not *supposed* to talk to you anymore. I still want to."

Edwin ducked his head down, bridging part of the gap between their heights. His large hands covered her small ones. "Then you can."

"There isn't much time left on the ship. Then we'll be in France, officially."

Amelia propped each heavy foot on the step ahead, Spencer's boisterous outrage filling her ears before she arrived at the next floor.

"I paid for your ticket! How could you embarrass me like this? Me and your mother. The family name I raised up from rags!"

The other passengers' hustle and conversation lulled for a moment.

Spencer shouted again. "I won't lower my voice! Stealing? Whatever for! It makes no sense."

Amelia made herself step off at the second deck. She peeked down the right-hand corridor. In front of the nearest door on the left, two security guards stood with the three members of the Burgess family.

Spencer's nostrils flared in his red, sweating face. Cora hovered at his side, wondering at her son, her thin lips agape.

Alvin rested his hands on the back of his head. His words snapped with aggravation. "I saved you the cost of a return ticket, didn't I?"

Spencer threw his hands in the air. "So you embarrassed me for the low price of four hundred instead of eight hundred!"

Alvin snarled at him, his jaw quivering. "I offered to work in Europe to pay my way back. Doesn't that mean anything to you?"

"Yes," Spencer growled. "You've avoided your duties in Fall River for years. Now you're abandoning the factory before I even have a chance to train you in it."

The crewman closest to Alvin lifted Luther's pocket watch in his hand. "If you'll excuse me, sir, we still have some questions..."

Spencer waved the timepiece away. "To hell with your questions. You found it in his room, and he hasn't given you one word of explanation that I've heard."

Alvin lunged at his father. "To hell with you!"

Cora jumped back. The skirt of her baby-blue dress swung around her, its repeated pattern of decorative taupe emblems bouncing on it. Her startled eyes welled with tears.

Alvin grimaced into his father's blotched face. "Yes, I was disowning you and the business you built and everything else in Massachusetts. I never intended to go back there! Or to the United States at all."

Cora drew a spring-green handkerchief from her pocket. "Alvin." She could barely say his name as she sobbed and raised the fabric to her mouth.

"I'm sorry, Mother." Alvin's creased brow softened. "I have to escape this tyrant. Yes, I stole the watch. I meant to sell it to start my life abroad." He scrutinized Spencer's face and crisp, black suit. "Sorry I've embarrassed you, Father. You've always embarrassed me."

Amelia's heart crinkled to a painful degree, and she slipped away. *It wasn't your fault,* she told herself. *You know that. What Alvin did would've hurt them all. Sooner or later. With or without your intervention.*

She pattered past the other corridor of cabins into the ballroom. The last time she had seen it three days before, two to three dozen people enjoyed it. This afternoon, passengers crowded it like almost all seventy-three of them converged within its golden walls. No music played except the excited, eager sounds of dueling accents in conversation.

Some of the others waited in the rear of the room with Amelia. Taking up one sofa sat the other three-quarters of Priscilla's traveling group. Her husband lifted his pocket watch and consulted it with a discontented sigh. Iris and her husband exchanged quick murmurs, their critical squints dissecting the crowd before them.

Near the opposite wall, Elizabeth and Lewis stood calm and still. They looked her way, and Amelia raised her hand in recognition. She swiveled to face the thick of the crowd, determined not to dwell on Lewis.

A woman's tenor drawled. "I can't wait to take a bath."

A man countered. "You're staying in Bordeaux? Not me. I'm straight off to Paris on the next train."

Amelia snuck a peek at Lewis and Elizabeth. He stood with one arm stretched behind her, his bare hand resting in the crook of her violet dress. When her lips moved with words Amelia could not hear, Lewis' curved up in response.

But when Elizabeth's attention roamed to the people around them or the grandeur of the room's decorations, Lewis peered back at Amelia. The distance between them pulled at her heart. His proximity to Elizabeth made it harder to bear. *Someday,* Amelia thought, for better or more bitter.

It was a fool's thought. Had she not been through enough to shine the glaring light of the world's harsh truths on the dark corner of such innocence? She chose to hope for it anyway, just to believe in something good, something more than she had right now.

Applause rose up on Amelia's other side. Captain Barrett strode in, his hands held high and waving. He picked a path through the crowd as passengers parted for him.

"I'm here." At the front of the crowd, the captain's hat and head rose above those surrounding him. "Is this high enough? Can everyone see me?"

The trio behind Amelia stood up as Priscilla scurried in the door. Lewis and Elizabeth made no move to answer the captain.

Iris propped her hands on her hips. "Where were you?"

Captain Barrett addressed his audience. "Let's proceed, then. I apologize for the delay. I wasn't privy to everything happening on the ship. But not to worry."

Behind Amelia, Priscilla's halting answer trembled. "I was taking care of delicate female matters I'd rather not discuss in present company."

The two men coughed in discomfort.

Captain Barrett lowered his hat. "As you know, we've made it safely through our journey thus far. It's been a great pleasure steering you toward the coasts of Europe. We'll be tethered in the outskirts of Bordeaux within the hour."

The passengers clapped in uproarious unison, and Amelia joined them.

The captain waved his hat in the air, and the crowd quieted. "Some of you may have travel plans ironed out, and some of you may not. I've made arrangements with all of you in mind. A few of my crewmen will come in – there they are, right on cue – and hand out maps showing you the most important parts of the city. This is to help you find hotels, restaurants, and transportation."

Four crewmen in neat, black suits arranged themselves just inside the doors. Brochures rested in their grasps.

"You needn't worry about securing transportation upon arrival. Numerous carriages should await you outside the station." He held up a finger. "In case there are more of you than there are carriages, please share." He propped his hat on his head and clasped his hands together with a clap. "Dear friends, do you have any idea how momentous an occasion this is?"

Amelia blew out a breath of understatement. *Do you?*

"The world's first transatlantic flight!" Captain Barrett threw his hands up over his head.

Applause erupted around him.

He raised his voice to thunder over it, pointing at the crowd. "I tell you, in a matter of years, Samuel Langley's successes will multiply manifold. Airships will dot every horizon. Every man, woman, and child from the frailest grandparent to the tiniest infant will clamor and plead to ride on them. The Wright brothers..."

Captain Barrett pursed his lips. He tipped his head back in guffaws. "I've forgotten their names already! So will the rest of America and the world." He mulled over the walls and splendor of the ballroom over the heads in the crowd. "This is the future, ladies and gentlemen. This fantastic flying machine that's carried you farther than most dared to dream. And I leave you with this."

The captain licked his lips, his face falling solemn. He raised his eyebrows in excitement and held his upturned palms out. "Tell your friends. Your family. Strangers and acquaintances you meet in the street. It's important because you should be proud. You're fortunate to hold the ticket stubs of the first flight of passengers on board the airship *Duchess*. They should know how safe, how accommodating, how wonderful air travel is. This voyage, though there may be thousands of them just like it, should not be forgotten. And all of us on board right now are a true part of making history."

The crowd slumbered on their feet in a daze before breaking out in cheers.

Captain Barrett stepped down from his orator's height.

Amelia sought out Darius but did not see him. She spotted Claudia moving back from the crowd. Amelia settled her hand in her pocket, motioning the older woman toward her with the other. Claudia brightened despite a weariness clouding her round, pink cheeks. She walked over, and Amelia swept her arms around Claudia in a hug.

The older woman jumped. "Oh." She recovered into languid muscles, her arms wrapping around Amelia's back. "It was so sudden. I didn't expect it."

Amelia pulled back. "I know you didn't. I wanted you to know how much I've valued your friendship these past six days."

"It was nothing, dear. A tremendous pleasure to meet you. It's as easy befriending you as it is to sip a mint julep on a hot August day."

Amelia shared a genuine smile. "I don't think everyone would agree with you."

"Nonsense. Point them out to me, and I'll talk some brains into them yet."

"Speaking of talking, I have great news to share with you."

Claudia's eyes widened. "What happened?"

Amelia guided Claudia away from the passengers seeking maps from the crewmen. "Have you made acquaintance with Mr. Darius Shank on board?"

"I don't think I've had the pleasure."

Amelia stilled her tongue against making any sarcastic remarks at his expense. "Perhaps you've seen him. Slightly on the tall side. Cool blond hair. Grey eyes. Immaculate suits."

"I think I've seen him talking to you."

"Very likely. We're old friends."

Claudia cracked a grin. "How funny to find each other here on the *Duchess*!"

Indigestion from breakfast, lunch, or Darius soured Amelia's stomach. "Quite. He praised some of the paintings you ladies did in your class a short while ago. He showed me which one was his favorite, and it was yours in the lounge that impressed him the most."

Claudia set her hand on her chest. "Mine? A child could have done better in some places."

"Absolutely not. The best part is, he wants it."

"As a gift or a souvenir?"

"He wants to buy it, Claudia." Amelia laid her hands on the woman's arms. "Your first art sale. Am I right?"

"A purchase." Claudia's eyes lost their focus as her fingers fumbled with the ruffled lace on her bodice. "Of something I painted."

"Exactly. He wasn't sure you'd sell directly to him, but I told him I'd approach you about it."

Claudia patted Amelia's hand. "Not to worry. Of course, I'll sell it to him."

"Set a fair price for yourself. Don't let him talk you down. And don't let him convince you he doesn't want to buy it."

"I won't. I'll find my ground and stick to it."

"Just between us, though." Amelia lowered her voice. "Don't approach him about it now. Let him stew a little longer. Then dig into his wallet for all he's worth."

"I will." Claudia hugged Amelia. "I can't believe it's almost goodbye. Whatever will I do without your support and sympathetic ear?"

"Elwood's better at listening to you now than he was a week ago."

"But he has Dorothy, and you're not married."

A crewman tipped his hat to them and passed them each a brochure.

Claudia rested hers at her side. "Do you have plans in Bordeaux, Amelia?"

"No."

"If you're staying, I'd like to visit with you. We'll be at the Hôtel de Garonne for a week."

"I'll see if I can stop by." Misleading Claudia's hopes sabotaged Amelia's good mood.

"If you'll be too busy, perhaps I can write down an address for you back home. It'd be awfully nice to write to you."

Amelia considered it for a moment. But the enormity of the heist she stood in the middle of could never be tracked to her. Could she keep her identity – and her whereabouts – secret enough from Claudia to evade the police? "I'll try to get you an address before we leave."

"There's so much to do with leaving an airship, isn't there? How could we have known?"

Elwood led Dorothy over, his wife clutching his arm with both of hers.

Amelia squeezed Claudia's hand. "Goodbye. Thanks for everything, all of you."

Dorothy averted her eyes, her mouth pulled down in a frown. Claudia and Elwood waved to her.

Amelia strolled out of the ballroom, opening her brochure. *The streets of Bordeaux. Sleeping arrangements. Places to eat. Attractions and entertainment.*

The top of the brochure bumped into a solid grey suit. Darius' voice greeted Amelia before she could fear who else it might be. "Reading while you walk? You're lucky you ran into me before you got to the staircase."

Amelia closed the brochure. "You missed the captain's speech."

"That's all right. I'm sure you can fill me in some day."

"All packed?"

Darius bowed his head. "What do you have there?"

Amelia held up the brochure. "A map of Bordeaux with places to stay. You should get one from the crewmen in the ballroom."

"I don't need one." He swayed closer to her ear. "Meet me outside in the docking area after we land."

Amelia dropped her head. "I have a message for you, too."

"What?"

"Be kind to Mrs. Molt."

He rocked back from her, eyebrows bunched in confusion.

"Generous, too." Amelia tapped the pamphlet's long edge against his arm. "You'll know what I mean." Partly in jest at Darius' flippant concern for her safety, Amelia held the page at a safe waist level as she walked away and descended the stairs.

Chapter Thirty-One

Two stewards entered Amelia's room, touching their white-gloved fingers to their black hat brims. She waved a hand at her packed and locked luggage.

The taller steward knelt by her trunks. "Let me verify your tags, ma'am."

The other, a teenager in brown spectacles, elbowed his shoulder. "Miss."

"Miss," the first steward hastened to echo.

The standing one tipped his hat to Amelia. "I escorted you to your room the day we took off in Albany."

Amelia gave a little more thought to him. Low, shallow cheekbones. Long, thin nose. Weak, angular chin. "Yes, I remember." Had so much really happened in the past few days to smudge her memory without needing to prompt it for clarity?

"I served you in the dining room, too, if I'm correct."

"I'm sure you are."

The older steward rose to his feet, housed in black, shiny shoes. "Everything appears in order. I've prepared your receipt." He produced a small paper from his pocket.

Amelia took it.

"We'll carry your things to the door for you now. When you leave the *Duchess*, you can retrieve them at the station. There are attendants there to help you."

Amelia tucked the receipt in her pocket. "I'm in an awful hurry to get going." She motioned at the teenaged steward. "Would you mind seeing after my luggage yourself? There are only three pieces. I don't really need to go through the station, do I?"

The older steward answered. "We have many other duties and passengers to see to, ma'—miss. I'm sure going through the station won't take long."

Amelia frowned.

The teenager extended his gloved hand out to her. "I'd be delighted to."

She responded with a fresh smile. "Wonderful. You'd save me so much trouble."

The older steward positioned himself at one end of the forty-inch steamer trunk. He reached down and grabbed the leather handle. "Let's get moving. There's plenty more to carry."

The teenager leapt to the opposite end of the trunk, and they lifted it together. The young steward maintained as professional a posture as possible hoisting the heavy trunk into the hallway.

Amelia swept her eyes over her room, the cozy, lovely space she had occupied these last six days. Despite how widespread her travels had become, a sense of nostalgia always plagued her moving from one place to another. She had fled the grand architecture of London's sweeping palaces and numerous bridges. She tore herself from the palm trees and huts on the sands of Cuba. She missed its weather, the perfect warm temperatures in between hurricane seasons. The enormous paintings, full orchestras, and gold-trimmed rooms of Vienna still visited her dreams. In the sweetest ones, she tasted Esterházy tortes again, smooth chocolate and rich cream rendering every bite delectable. Sometimes, whether she wanted to or not, she longed for the two-story house she grew up in in Seneca Falls. It once seemed to contain an infinite number of rooms, but over time, in her mind, its space and decorations had become much more simple.

Just as small and understandable as her accommodations on board the *Duchess*. Categorizing them that way made them no less memorable. The flowered, refined wallpaper. Sturdy furniture. Plush carpeting. Tesla's lighting system, which Amelia believed would gain popularity and use much like Captain Barrett assumed of the airship.

The teenaged steward raced back in, doffing his hat. "It's just me this time, miss. For your other bags." He lifted the remaining flat-top trunk.

Amelia's lungs seized with apprehension.

He hoisted the leather bag with ease. He hefted the trunk up and down several times. "I could be mistaken, but this seems heavier than it did bringing it on."

Amelia grimaced, trying to hide her anxiety. "I must've packed my things differently this time."

"Not to worry. I can carry it for you."

"Be careful with it." Her palms sweated. "I have keepsakes in there that are breakable."

The steward adopted his customary solemn mood and stiff stance. "Leave it to me. I'll see it through this landing safe as houses."

"If you could bring a carriage closer to the station for me, I'd more than double your tip for it."

His tanned cheeks deepened to rose. The corners of his mouth perked up as he ducked his head. "Of course. It'd be my pleasure."

"Thank you."

He trudged out of the room, and Amelia swept her gaze around one more time. Nothing remained on the dresser, the nightstands, or the chairs. The borrowed *Delineator* from the parlor reclined on the bed, but it was all that marked her presence here. She picked it up and stepped out into the hallway. She locked her door out of habit, drawing a fingertip down the golden 2 and the rightmost curve in the 0 on its brass plate.

Amelia carried the magazine down the hall. A dozen passengers talked by the stairs. The scene more than repeated the chaos of the day the *Duchess* had elevated into the air. Luggage towered in piles around the parlor, a white string and paper tag dangling from a handle on each case. Stewards carted more trunks and bags down the stairs. It bustled more like a packed zoo exhibit than a high-class airship landing.

She set the *Delineator* on the parlor table. The sofa cushions offered enough vacant space to fit her, but Amelia chose to remain on her feet. She clasped one hand around her opposite wrist, fingers fidgeting as time crawled forward.

The Frenchwoman clamped her hands against her cheek. *"Ce serait bien de retourner en France."*

Her husband widened his eyes in tired agreement. *"Oui."*

Rudolf Greisman clenched the tip of a cigar in his teeth. He removed it to remark to his wife. "The *kiełbasa czosnkowa* doesn't have enough garlic in it."

Yetta deflated with a sigh. "You want to change the recipe? Why? We have enough success with my grandmother's directions."

He shrugged. "People like garlic. If we add more, maybe they'll like our sausage more."

A happy baritone echoed through the brass speakers in the common area. "Ahoy, passengers! This is your captain speaking. We've encountered land – France, to be precise – and we'll begin our descent to the Bordeaux docking station."

A woman swiveled her head toward the dining room doors. "Can we see France from the windows?"

She led the charge into the dining hall, attracting the French couple and the Greismans.

Amelia gravitated toward its doors, where she could see the purser's counter and the exit portal. She left room for the stewards to pass by her to access the luggage stacked in the short corridor before her.

A flurry of rustling clothes rushed up to Amelia's side. She found Lewis beside her and Elizabeth next to him. Elizabeth personified Amelia's emotions, ready to disembark at half a second's notice. A hat topped her head, white-and-black-striped ribbon looping and cascading about the crown. Silk flowers in cream and blush resided on the brim, ready to shade her eyes from the French sun. Her spine stacked in a rigid line beneath the purple cotton of her dress.

She spoke in quiet urgency. "I want to be the first ones off this ship. As soon as they allow it."

Amelia half expected one of them to notice her and make a joking apology about how eager they must be for the same victory. But Elizabeth and Lewis stared straight ahead. Amelia hung her hand at her side, half a foot from Lewis'.

Trunks and cases thumped on the floor behind them. A reminiscent and unpleasant force inserted itself into Amelia's ears. Elizabeth winced and pressed her far hand against her head.

"Not again," a man protested from the dining room.

A Southern drawl insisted. "You have to yawn. That's what helped me."

Amelia worked her jaw until a pop of air in her hearing released the stuffed, plugged pressure.

Lorena's high, British-tinged timbre approached. "I can't believe they found his watch."

Celia exhaled as the two stopped behind Amelia. "I wish Harold would stop pointing out the fact the three of us didn't divine its whereabouts."

"I tried channeling spirits last night. I honestly can't find any up here. Why would they be here amongst the clouds? The people they left behind are down there."

Celia said nothing.

Lorena hummed with pleasure. "Even with the pocket watch returned, I think the first thing we should do in France is a good séance."

Amelia checked over her shoulder. More and more passengers accumulated behind her.

Spencer Burgess spread his fingers wide as he passed a hand over his pale head of hair. His anger rumbled. "He's the one who's embarrassed me." He arranged his black top hat on his head.

Cora stood like a petite statue at his elbow, shadows swirling across her eyes.

"Do you think we can keep it from the press?" Spencer gave a sharp snort. "No. Not any more than that murderous woman could keep her ticket secret."

Elizabeth's jaw slid forward in contempt, her shoulders squaring inside her fitted sleeves.

Spencer grunted. "Just wait until my foremen find out about this. Do you think they'll want to take my orders from their managers once they know my son – my oldest son – is a coward and a thief?"

He huffed. "I can't fire them, not with them organizing. It's not enough I put the union label on everything we make. They want to strike over the damndest things."

Cora spoke up, barely audible to Amelia's ears. "Spencer?"

"Don't defend Alvin. Or the workers. I couldn't take it right now."

"When we get home, I want a divorce."

A thick silence crept over the crowd.

Some sliding sensation lured Amelia's insides to the left. She braced her hand on the wall, her silver reticule dangling from her wrist. Elizabeth and Lewis found support against each other.

He murmured to her. "I've got you."

Amelia's vision traced the curves and flourishes of the red-on-burgundy wallpaper. They collected in bursts like fountains of flowers and leaves, joined to other bunches with swoops like swags of lace.

The boom of Captain Barrett's voice through the speakers almost relieved her. "Thank you for your patience. The Bordeaux ground crew is reeling the *Duchess* in now to the docking station."

Amelia tried to even her breathing, but her heart hammered like its muscles installed a new track of railroad. How much more pleasant her definitive triumphs over Darius made her feel. Stabbing the knife into his abdomen in Berlin, his concern over his pain and bleeding superseding his greed for the rubies. He had made one half-hearted attempt to grab at her, but she slipped off in a clean getaway from their hotel. He must have calculated the risks and gains involved. What were the rubies worth if he suffered permanent damage or worse – his untimely death?

The floor stopped reeling under Amelia's feet. She relaxed her hands at her sides.

Men's undertones sounded behind her. "Excuse me. Excuse me."

The black-suited stewards pressed through the crowd, parting Lewis from Amelia's side. The first one strode up to the door, the others assessing the luggage surrounding them.

Lorena piped up. "You never answered me about a séance."

"Let's decide after we meet up with Luther and Harold. I hope we'll get out of here without too much trouble. I'm dying to see the hotel."

Lewis regained his place next to Amelia, perhaps a little closer. Bare skin brushed her smallest finger as Lewis wrapped his pinky around hers. They faced the door together as it opened, the stewards blocking all of the view except a band of blue sky near the top.

Amelia muttered under her breath. "All I've been able to see is sky for the past six days."

Lewis squeezed his finger around hers.

The lead steward stepped away from the door, sidling between the others to address the crowd. "Good afternoon. We have successfully landed in Bordeaux. The stewards will take down the luggage that blocks your path. You may then proceed down the ramp to the station to retrieve it along with any valuables you entrusted to the purser. Thank you for flying with the airship *Duchess*, and I wish you a lovely holiday in France."

The crowd applauded behind Amelia. She wanted to join them in celebrating, but she did not want to part from Lewis' touch. Elizabeth's clapping hands signaled the end of it before Lewis pulled himself away. Amelia applauded beside him, not daring to look at him, at least not yet.

One by one, the stewards disappeared from the doorway, working alone or in tandem. As the men and trunks lessened, Amelia inched forward. In her peripheral, Elizabeth did the same. Amelia hung back to let Elizabeth and Lewis shoot past her once they were able. Elizabeth was a wrongfully convicted murderess fleeing rumors and persecution in her home country. Amelia was merely avoiding Darius and stealing from that same woman. It was the smallest favor Amelia could do for Elizabeth.

Lorena squealed with delight. "I'm so glad we mended our differences, Cee. There's no one I'd rather experience this with than you."

The older woman tested her with a wry lilt. "Even Harold?"

Elizabeth moved forward.

Lorena's voice sharpened in thought. "His doubts keep him from being one of us yet, but give me six months to work on him, and I might prefer his company to yours."

Some chuckles went up around them.

The stewards returned for a second trip. They loaded up their hands for the descent.

The last one to leave gestured the passengers toward him. "Start down once we've cleared the ramp. The press will want good pictures of you." He lifted small trunks in each hand and stepped out through the doorway.

Elizabeth's features contorted in frustration.

Lewis murmured to her. "It's okay."

Elizabeth waited another five seconds. Even as she surged him forward, Lewis reached his hand back for Amelia's. In the fumble, their fingers slid off each other, and Lewis extending his hand behind him for several beats reassured Amelia's heart. It was as if her earlier thought of a future reunion had been a question and Lewis answered it now. *Yes, someday.*

The figures of Elizabeth and Lewis shortened as they left the doorway. Amelia gave them a little room to walk ahead of her. Someday was not today, and the teenaged steward needed time to collect her luggage off to one side. For now, the crowd pressing in behind her blocked Darius from catching up to her. If only they had reversed this scene for the departure from Albany, she might have eluded him altogether.

A man grumbled in the thick of the crowd. "What's taking so long?"

Amelia strode forward, passing the purser's counter, and stepped out onto the long, wooden ramp. No matter what she expected, unlike her first arrival in France years before, little seemed to have changed since she sailed out of the States. Fading sunshine presided over a mild spring day. Reporters and photographers waited, flanking the bottom of the ramp. Elizabeth and Lewis cut off to the left toward the white station building. The reporters swayed after them but let them go, remaining where they were.

They lobbed questions at Amelia.

"Comment s'est passé le voyage?"

Her brain tickled where her knowledge of her second language came back to life. How had the voyage been? She answered with the French version of the quick American quip *good. "C'était bien."*

The photographers motioned to her, and she stopped six feet from the end of the ramp. She posed for them with one hand on her hip, happy to hold up the line of impatient travelers behind her for a moment.

"C'était effrayant? C'était passionnant?"

Amelia waved off the particular questions of how the journey had been for her. She was glad to oblige them for a few moments but could envision this escalating into a half-hour interview. She moved toward the bottom of the ramp.

Two more reporters approached her with thick, constricted French accents.

"How are you?"

"What will you do now?"

Amelia stepped off the ramp. "I'm good." She left the second question hanging in the air.

Behind her, the reporters flared up anew.

"What are your thoughts?"

"C'était passionnant?"

Lorena laughed. "It was marvelous. I don't know much French now, but I'm raring to learn more."

Off to Amelia's right, the teenaged steward beckoned to her. Amelia put an extra spring in her step, counting all three pieces of her luggage at his side as she approached him.

She clasped her hands together. "Wonderful. Did you hire a carriage?"

The steward gasped and shot his back up straight. "No, miss. I'll find one right away." He raced off across the field.

At the end of the green lawn looped a cobblestone road. Horse-drawn carriages packed the circle, each manned with a suited driver. Amelia turned to survey the massive form of the airship looming behind her, passengers trickling down the ramp.

Lorena and Celia sauntered past the reporters. The photographers crowded around Spencer and Cora Burgess, but he led her in squeezing through the bunch.

He sneered at them. "I have nothing to say."

Lorena pulled Celia aside by her sleeve, letting the Burgesses dash off to the station. "I have something to confess."

Celia raised an eyebrow. "What?"

Lorena cupped a muffling hand around her mouth. "I did the naughty with Harold."

Celia swiped at Lorena, but the redhead dodged her. "When?"

Lorena sprinted across the grass to escape her. "Before I forgave you for doing it with Luther, of course!"

Amelia patted her hand against her skirt in a nervous pattern. Neither Claudia nor Darius appeared on the ramp, and she aimed to keep it that way.

"Pardon us. Coming through." The man's voice from the top of the ramp sped Amelia's heart up.

The two security guards led Alvin down the ramp, Luther and Harold following them. Spencer Burgess, loitering alone outside the station, disappeared inside.

One of the guards held a palm up to the photographers. "No pictures, please. Let us through."

The group of five ambled through the ranks of reporters.

Luther lifted his timepiece, treasuring its details. "I don't know if I want to press charges. I got my watch back."

Harold scanned Alvin, shoving his hands in his pockets. "He did pretend to be your friend so he could nick it from you. No offense to you, Alvin. Otherwise, you're an all right mate." He added with restrained well wishing, "Long may your lum reek."

Alvin hung his head.

Harold freed a hand and gestured to the guards. "What laws would you charge him by, anyway? This is something someone's got to work out if air travel's going to get popular."

Luther attached his watch chain to a buttonhole on his vest and situated the timepiece in its pocket. "Don't worry about it, gentlemen. Honestly. It's more trouble to prosecute Alvin than he caused me in stealing it."

"I, for one, am relieved to be off board." Harold caught sight of Celia chasing Lorena through the grass and slanted his hat backwards, baffled.

Lorena waved to him and circled back around. She arrived breathless at Harold's side and looped her arm around his. She wiped beads of exertion off her forehead. "Did we ever find out who it was that solved it?"

Celia stopped next to her, settling her fists on her hips, fuming and gasping.

One of the guards doffed his hat. "No, miss. I was told the tipster asked to remain anonymous."

Lorena tapped Celia's arm. "You hear that? Like there was a spirit on board after all, friendly and helpful."

Celia glowered. "I've heard enough from you for one day, thank you."

Alvin's head sank lower.

Amelia sighed with sympathy for him. *I'm sorry, Alvin, but it's better this way. You're safer at Luther's mercy than Darius' fury.*

A man's French-tinted English called out from the waiting crowd beyond the white, waist-high fence. "Welcome back!" A couple waved to the passengers walking to the station.

The French couple rushed over, loping with enthusiasm.

The ethereal woman beamed as she stopped at the fence. "Thank you."

The greeting man hugged her over the white wooden barrier, kissing her cheeks. "How was America?"

"Fine. Something new every minute, revolutions excluded. It's good to be back, though."

Amelia blinked off her shock at the Frenchwoman's perfect English.

A shout caught her off guard. "Miss."

She jerked her head to the right, her chest filling with hope.

The teenaged steward touched his hat. "My apologies. I haggled the price down and paid for your fare myself. He'll take you anywhere you want to go."

His thoughtfulness surprised her even more than Luther's generosity with Alvin. "Thank you."

"No need to tip me, miss. I forgot. It's my fault." The steward hoisted her flat-top trunk off the grass and lifted her leather bag. "Are you ready?"

Amelia ran her eyes across the grand curves of the *Duchess*, a mighty, headstrong female in her own right. Claudia stood at the top of the ramp, Elwood and Dorothy stopped at the bottom by reporters. "Lead the way."

Amelia strode off at the steward's side, grateful for his haste. They arrived at the carriage in half a minute, a gleaming black design with a bench in back across from a flat area for storage.

The steward boosted her luggage into the carriage. "If you'll wait here, I'll find some help to carry your steamer over."

"There isn't time. I'll come back for it."

The teenager slanted his eyebrows. "I can't be responsible for it. What if something goes missing?"

"Don't worry about it." Amelia held out the keys for her room and her trunk along with her receipt. "If I don't show up to claim it by the time you leave the station, you're free to keep it."

"That's an interesting tip." He hesitated but accepted her offerings.

"I have one more favor to ask." Amelia scanned the disembarking passengers. "Do you know Mrs. Claudia Molt? Grey hair. Vivacious and outgoing."

"I believe so. I moved her luggage before I came to your room earlier."

Amelia pulled a small piece of white paper from her pocket. "Would you give her this before she leaves? She asked for my address, and this was the best I could do."

The teenager took the neatly printed page. "I'll deliver it immediately."

It would not be the address Claudia hoped for, one where her words of enthusiasm and kindness would contact Amelia directly. Whether Amelia's parents still resided at their old address in Seneca Falls, she did not know. If they did, Claudia's letters, addressed to their long-lost daughter by her middle name, might jar them at first. In the end, it might comfort them to know she was still alive and traveling the globe.

"Thank you for all your help," she said.

He raised his hat brim. "I hope to see you on the return flight."

"I won't be flying back." She eased closer. "You might want to protect your new steamer trunk. It has a very valuable tip in it." Her stationery envelope rested inside with the five hundred dollars Darius had once promised her. Amelia would have given it to any steward stuck disposing of her valise, but it pleased her it was the staff member she knew best.

His eyes widened, and he ran off, holding his hat on with one hand. His words flew back to her on the wind. "Thank you!"

She raised her voice in return. "Thank you for calling me *miss." Somebody left me in a hotel fire, and I sound much older than I look.*

Amelia walked up to the front of the carriage beside the driver.

His gloved hands gripped the horse's reins. "Where to, miss?"

Amelia produced the brochure from her reticule and held it up, pointing to a plaza marked on the map. "La Place de la Comédie. I need a hotel. Take my luggage there, and I'll meet you."

He cocked his head. "You're not riding with me?"

"I'm walking." *Easier to lose myself in a crowd that way.*

He opened his mouth.

She held her hand up. "I don't have time to explain. Were you paid or not?"

He reeled the horse's reins closer. *"Oui, Mademoiselle.* I'll see you there."

"Wait for me," Amelia impressed on him.

"I will." He jerked on the reins.

With a few hoof strikes underway on the street, Amelia sped off with the brochure in her hand. The driver steered his carriage around the circle, down the straight lane leading from it, and veered right onto the street ahead. Amelia jogged toward the street, a double-wide boulevard teeming with strolling pedestrians and rolling carriages.

Amelia timed her momentum, waiting for a carriage to pass before she could dart across. As she lifted her foot, something soft and heavy threatened to knock her off balance. She regained her footing on the sidewalk.

Two voices, one high and one low, cried out. "We're sorry!"

Amelia squinted at the couple sprinting away across the street. Edwin's wide-shouldered form towered over Priscilla's. They lurched side to side as they ran, keeping a perfect, musical rhythm Edwin would have appreciated as a spectator. They held hands in a tight grasp between them. Edwin lugged a golden-leather satchel in his other hand, and Priscilla clenched a small trunk half a foot from her side.

Amelia gawked at them, amused. She lauded their gusto but hoped they were not making the worst mistake of their lives. With traffic stopped for their getaway, Amelia bolted forward. A horse started up on her right, and Amelia barely dodged out of the way. Her heart trotted faster, and she had blocks to go before she could let herself slow down. She ducked down the first side street she saw, a slim lane packed with houses on either side. Some of them hovered low in a single story, but most of them harbored two. Their façades read like a patchwork of colors, tan, grey, and creamy yellow. The occasional arch of a doorway or window frame stood in contrast to the sharper edges of the more common squares and rectangles.

Windows open to the spring air let out the sounds of babies crying, women singing, and phonographs churning out accordion music. The smells of potatoes frying in animal fat, toasted bread, and fresh mint competed in Amelia's nose. She pressed on, sweeping around a chattering group of old men in worn hats. A carriage passing down the middle of the road sent Amelia back to the sidewalk to avoid it. The row of houses on her right never ceased, the row on her left parted by intersecting streets from time to time.

The road strayed to the left and meandered back. Amelia followed it without concern. As long as she kept the sun behind her and the brochure's map with her, she could find her way to the carriage. Her feet ached in her low-heeled shoes. She had not walked this much during the six days she floated above the Atlantic.

A continuous row of houses met Amelia in a dead end, and she gauged both her options. The left-hand road curved until she lost sight of it, offering no clues about its destination. She cut off to the right, another restrictive street of narrow houses attached to one another. She took the next left, walking deeper into the city. A second T in the road forced Amelia to make another choice with little new information. She veered right, crossing a block to its intersection with a wider, busier boulevard. The thicker crowds and stream of carriages made her nervous. Darius could hide in any group or vehicle, especially this close to the airship. An open cemetery spread out across the street, and Amelia decided against exposing herself by staying near it. She hugged the buildings close on her left side as she walked the boulevard's curves and jogs until a buzzing plaza opened up on her right.

Jogging past a corner café and its enticing arrangement of outdoor tables, Amelia made up for lost time. Up ahead, a tall golden trolley rolled into sight above the hats of the surrounding crowd. Amelia hustled to gain on it, whirring past chirruping schoolgirls and women guiding babies in strollers. She climbed up onto the step at the rear of the horse-drawn vehicle.

Two children spun in their seats to gape at her. A sunhat crowned the curly-haired girl. The boy resembled a painting's charmed timelessness in a striped scarf and brown cap. Amelia held a finger up to her lips and winked at them. Although they continued to ogle her, they said nothing.

After several long blocks Amelia was grateful to avoid walking, the trolley curved with the widening road into an open area between structures. Leaning out from the side, she took in the stone buildings around her, all of them three stories or taller. She consulted the size and shape of the public square marked on the brochure's map. "La Place de la Comédie?"

The children, mouths still ajar, nodded.

"*Merci.*" Amelia dropped off the back of the trolley to the street and dashed out of the way of impending carriages. She paused by a tall, black iron lamppost, searching all around for the hired vehicle.

"I told him to wait," she mumbled, scouring the area. People milled about talking or passed by carrying pastries and loaves of bread. To her right, past the path the trolley cut through the street, an ornate three-story building asserted itself. A short series of steps led up to a row of a dozen two-story pillars forming its façade. Twelve carved statues topped them on the balustrade above. Her brochure identified it for her as the Grand Théâtre, Bordeaux's famous opera house. She perused the other side of the street.

In front of a substantial four-story building with a modest, flat front, the driver of her carriage signaled to her with an arm above his head. Amelia bustled over, almost limping from the pain in her feet.

"This was the best place I could park," he explained.

"You did fine. I'm glad for your services."

He gestured to the building towering behind the carriage. "Are you staying here?"

From up close, without the Grand Théâtre to compare it to, the architecture was simple but beautiful. Tall, thin windows covered its façade, decorative carvings adorning the top of each one. A long, dark awning spread over the sidewalk in front of the right-hand side of the first floor, advertising *Café de Bordeaux* and *restaurant*. "What is this place?"

"The Grand Hôtel de Bordeaux. One of the finest in the city."

Amelia weighed the reticule on her wrist. She had planned on spending a week in modest accommodations. With Darius potentially on her trail, she only wanted to stay a night to clear her head before traveling on. "I'll take it."

A doorman stepped forward from the entrance, his muscled torso filling out his uniform jacket. The driver flagged him over and climbed down from his seat at the front of the carriage.

Amelia walked around to the sidewalk to meet the doorman. "There should be a trunk and a bag."

The driver pointed to them in the back. "I safeguarded them, miss."

"Thank you."

The doorman pulled the two pieces down.

The driver climbed back up into his seat. "Is there anything else?"

"No."

He flicked the reins. *"Bonne journée. Au revoir! Bienvenue en France."*

Amelia faced the doorman with a deep, steadying inhale. *I'll breathe a lot better where Darius can't trace me.*

The long-legged man bowed his head. *"Mademoiselle."*

She preceded him into the hotel lobby, a long rectangular space with a high, recessed ceiling. Three gold, ornate chandeliers hung suspended over the marble floor, diamond shapes alternating in peach and white. A patterned red-and-blue carpet covered one third of the room by the elongated front windows. Couches and chairs sat arranged in groupings around every window, offering natural light and views of the square. Coffee tables and lamps supplied every possible accommodation.

The doorman carried Amelia's luggage to the inner third of the room. Several staff members stood at the ready behind an extensive wooden counter engraved with wreaths and flourishes of leaves. A young bellhop rushed over and combed his short yellow hair flat beneath his hat. His dark brown eyes sat far apart above his broad nose. The doorman set Amelia's valises down and reclaimed his post outside the front door.

The woman in the striped brown jacket greeted Amelia with a smile. *"Avez-vous une reservation?"*

Amelia stepped up to the counter, sweating despite the cool weather. *There's no way they have an empty room.* Her old tricks bubbled up. She crumpled her upper body against the counter as if exhausted. *"Non, excusez-moi."* One of the first phrases she learned before her trip to Paris surfaced on her lips, explaining her country of origin. *"Je suis Américain."*

The woman bobbed her head of dark hair. "I speak English."

"Good." Amelia pushed out a sigh. "My mother is sick here in France."

The woman's eyebrows drew up in sympathy.

Amelia wiped her forehead. "I came as fast as I could, so I have no reservations anywhere. I've been to three hotels already. They have no rooms for me."

"I can consult the ledger for you." The woman motioned to her fellow staff.

The three of them pored over a thick record book.

Amelia inspected its full page of handwriting. "Just one night. *S'il-vous-plaît.*"

The woman pointed to a slender, blank space. "*La petite salle.*"

One of the men clasped his hands behind him. "*Oui.*"

The woman picked up a pen but held it low against the counter. "We have one room open tonight. It's small. It needs work."

Amelia folded her arms on the counter. "I'll take it."

"I wouldn't have said anything about it, but your mother." She wrote something in the book. "It's very sad."

"Thank you."

"Your name?"

"Sophrona Albertson."

The woman quoted the price of the room, and Amelia paid it.

"René will take you to your room." She lifted a tagged key from behind the counter. "*Au rez-de-chaussée.*"

First floor. Amelia's aching feet took some comfort in that. She grabbed the key, and the bellman picked up her bags.

She turned back to the counter. "Could I please have a hairdresser sent to my room?" She pantomimed her first two fingers cutting her hair. "I don't want Mother to see me like this."

The woman pursed her lips in pity and understanding. "Of course."

"And the train schedule for tomorrow."

"Right away."

René led her beneath a high arch to the great curving staircase to the upper floors. The steps and landings formed an oval shape ringed with cast iron railings. Amelia followed him up and caught up to his side, seeking the same door number as her key. In front of the door, René lowered her bags to the floor.

"*No*. I do." He took the key with gentle fingers and unlocked the door, swinging it into the room. "For you."

Amelia lengthened her jaw, impressed. "*Merci*. They've trained you well." *Or I'm finally able to afford what I got accustomed to years ago.*

René carried her bags in, and Amelia sauntered in behind him. An ivory coverlet made up a wide bed spanning the middle of the right-hand wall. A wooden wardrobe stood in the far corner. To the left, René set her luggage down on the carpet patterned with swirls of red flowers. Beyond him, a desk and chair offered a place to write correspondence. An armchair sat beside it for resting and reading. At the far end of the room, dusky-blue drapery accented with pink zinnias hung from a high rod to dress the window. Sunlight streamed in between the panels, secured back from the panes to hang two feet above the floor.

Amelia stepped forward to peek through a doorway to her immediate right. "*Qu'est-ce que c'est?*"

"Bathroom," René supplied with slow uncertainty in his choice of word.

A carved wooden dressing table the color of honey provided a marble top for her makeup and an incorporated mirror for styling her hair. A sink and toilet rounded out the room's necessities, but the white bathtub propped up by four sturdy feet stole Amelia's imagination.

A cold drop of water on her head redirected her, and she took a brisk step aside. A thin crack in the ceiling let another drip loose to the carpet.

René ran over, sliding a bucket beneath the leak. "This works here."

Amelia accompanied René to the door. "Your English is good." She fished a healthy tip for him from her reticule, sure she could earn any funds she needed to ride out by train before leaving Bordeaux.

He counted it in his hand, eyes sparkling. "What you need... now?"

"Rest. *Je voudrais me reposer.*"

René backed up into the doorway. "Need anything." He patted the chest of his suit. "Call René."

"*Oui.* I will."

René laid the room key on the desk. He bowed and closed the door with his steps out into the hall.

Amelia took her time walking over, grasping the key, and locking her door. No amount of speed would change whatever had happened since she last stood alone with her luggage. She replaced the key on the desk, crouching to unlock her trunk. She flipped the lid up and sought out her two books.

Sandwiched between them waited a map, one untorn corner ringed with the silver bracelet she had entrusted to Darius. Amelia pulled them out and ran her eyes over the details in the map.

She sighed in disappointment of his substitution. "It's not even Africa. It's Australia. But I took the one of Africa, didn't I?" She ran her finger along the paper's blade. "It doesn't have my torn mark, not that you'd know."

Amelia sat down on the floor and secured the bracelet around her wrist. A piece of paper slipped out of the map, and she scanned its lines of pointed handwriting. She smirked. "A letter from Darius. How sweet."

Kate, my pet –

Amelia lowered her eyebrows at the use of her given name.

Sorry I won't be meeting up with you when we land. I'm sure with all the acquaintances you've made, I won't have much trouble convincing one of them to keep you busy enough to let me slip by. That is, if you even bother waiting for me.

I'm sure you realize by now you're carrying a completely worthless trinket, unless your future plans include visiting the land down under. I warned you I might've learned to pick locks, and indeed I did. I never needed your key to get in – just to do it as quickly as possible.

Find with this the bracelet I held for you. As always, you have immaculate taste. It belongs with you, as I have no use for it. With the proceeds of the map, I could buy thousands of them if I chose. It will suit you far better.

Your description of the statuette you guarded for me intrigues me, and I regret missing the chance to see it. But as you know, I always prefer a real woman to a carved one any day. If you retain it, I may find the opportunity to see it yet.

Yours in life, near-death, and world travel –

Darius Shank

Amelia set the letter and map aside on the carpet. She dug deeper into the contents of her trunk, pulling out the bronze statue. Standing up, she arranged it on the desk at a pleasing angle to the rest of the room.

"I don't know, Darius," she drawled. Her hand lingered against the circular base. "I think she's exactly your type. She's frozen in place and can't run away."

Amelia stepped over to the bed and sat down. She peeled up the skirt of her dress, exposing the map she had never removed from its hiding place since that morning. She undid the safety pin and lifted the map away, her fingertip running over the authenticating tear in its paper.

She nearly sympathized with Darius. She almost could not believe he fell for the bait and switch of the fake African map.

Did he honestly think I'd put the real treasure any place he could get to it, anywhere away from my person?

He must have saved his new lock-picking skill until he needed it most. If he would have plied it the night before, after leaving her room, he might have caught her slicing the map stolen from the lounge wall into two pieces with a steak knife borrowed from the dining room. She had only tucked half the page behind the frame in Elizabeth's room, saving the other to pack away in her trunk. Amelia had deliberately sat reading a book in her room, waiting for him to step in before pulling out the map and stowing it away. Only his greed and desperation must have blinded him to realizing that trick for himself.

Amelia slipped her shoes off and flung herself back onto the coverlet, her sore feet hovering in midair. She had warned Darius she always had a plan. Her performance – or his ego – must have convinced him her devious nature would work for him this time instead of against him.

Elizabeth's ruby-and-diamond earrings dangled in her mind's eye. Of all the things they stole, Amelia wished she would have ended up with those, too, but they had gone to a more deserving owner. She wondered how Claudia would react to find such expensive objects of beauty in her pocket, dropped there during Amelia's unexpected hug.

Elizabeth might blame Lewis for the jewelry's disappearance, which sobered Amelia. It could mean another argument, more anguish, more separation. Another night apart or more. But to repay Claudia for her genuine friendship and unknowing helpfulness in Amelia's scheme was a tradeoff Amelia was glad to make.

Amelia rolled onto her side, stretching her arm up across the coverlet and resting her head on it. The bronze woman on the desk pondered the upper portion of the wall where it met the ceiling above the bathroom door. Amelia could hardly call herself surprised to find Darius' substitute map in her trunk, that he planned to trick her as she double-crossed him. His letter was likely right. If Amelia traveled with the statuette long enough, his two disappeared women circling the globe, the three of them might unite again.

Amelia would also return one day to France, to find Lewis whether holed up in a crowded city's anonymity or lost amongst the sprawling landscape of vineyards and farms. Just as clearly, the scenarios played out when Amelia would see Darius. In the streets of an Australian city, British flags adorning it like the postcards she had seen. At the foot of an Alaskan mountain, braving frostbite following the most recent claims of discovered gold. Cheering the running of the bulls through the streets of Pamplona. Gliding across the dance floor in a lavish Roman ballroom.

The game would continue, but that did not bother her. Amelia would be ready. She settled onto her back, sinking into the still silence of the room and comfort of the covers. Until she and Darius met again, the statuette and the bracelet around her wrist would serve as two reminders of just her latest in a long string of heart-pounding adventures.

About the Author

Cassandra Leuthold's hilarious fantasy adventure, *The Corundum Conundrum*, won recognition as a New Apple Book Awards official selection. Writing hooked her at age seven, and she never really stopped.

She loves playing with ideas most people think of as opposites: the magical and the everyday, the modern and the vintage, the darkest nights and brightest lights. Even while delving into fictional worlds, she remains a tea aficionado, DIY crafter, and unapologetic music junkie.

Cassandra stretches out in front of the TV with her writer husband and their cats. She wields a Bachelor's in Liberal Studies and a Master's in English.

Find freebies and more book fun at her website, cassandraleuthold.com.